PAYDIRT

A Jake Lydon Mystery

I0635758

JOHN OWENS

Author of *Copycat*

OTTAWA PRESS
AND PUBLISHING

MYSTERY

ottawapressandpublishing.com
Copyright © John Owens Communications 2023

ISBN (print) 978-1-990896-14-9
ISBN (epub) 978-1-990896-13-2

Cover design: Glenn Torresan
Page design: Glenn Torresan
Cover photograph: Patric Fore

No part of this book may be reproduced, stored in a retrieval system, or transmitted in any form or by any means without the prior written permission of the publisher or, in case of photocopying or other reprographic copying, a licence from Access Copyright (The Canadian Copyright Licencing Agency)
320 – 56 Wellesley Street West, Toronto, Ontario, www.accesscopyright.ca.
This is a work of fiction. All of the characters, names, incidents, organizations, and dialogue in this novel are either products of the author's imagination or are used fictitiously.

*To my new grandson, John Brady Owens,
who, I've been led to believe, can't read yet.*

We think we know what we're doing
    We don't know a thing
    It's all in the past now
    Money changes everything.

— CYNDI LAUPER (WRITTEN BY THOMAS
GRAY)

I've been a miner for a heart of gold.

— NEIL YOUNG

PAYDIRT

A Jake Lyon Mystery

JOHN OWENS

PROLOGUE

W hat a perfect morning, he thought, as he finished his daily ritual and sat down in his nylon fold-up director's chair.

The sun was starting to rise, barely a cloud in the sky, a slight breeze. As he sipped the last of his black coffee, he surveyed his set-up and ran through his checklist. Three other chairs flanked him in a semi-circle facing the courts, the public park and lake in the background. Water cooler resting on the fold-up table. Beside it, fresh orange slices, newly cleaned sweat towels folded neatly and a Bun coffee urn and an assortment of doughnuts from Dunkin. As usual, he had timed the unplugging of the coffee urn so that it would keep the coffee warm until nine o'clock when Irv would turn up with trays of more coffee.

His pre-game preparations were elaborate and time-consuming, but the players in their unofficial "league" were always appreciative. So much so that word had spread and other pickleballers were eager to join up, for the sport, for the camaraderie and, he suspected, for the coffee and pastry.

He checked his new Rolex. They would start arriving soon. In about fifteen minutes, all three courts would be filled by foursomes, laughing, chattering, and thocking away at the hard plastic balls. He knew that then he could erase the recent troubles at work and immerse himself in one of the pleasures he'd found in his move to Florida.

This being Wednesday, he heard the garbage truck coming down the street bordering Crescent Lake. He checked his watch.

Sure enough, dead-on 7:15, as it had been last week and the week before that. Even though it was across the lake, the grating sound of its engine's loud revving and its banging and crashing as it emptied dumpsters carried over the water and disrupted his brief contemplation.

May as well get a few practice serves in before the gang shows up, he thought. A minute or so of stretching out his old age kinks. He stood at the service line, his paddle poised, as he eyed the spot for his hoped-for ball placement.

What he heard next, above the racket of the garbage truck, sounded like a loud zip.

Then his head was gone in a wet explosion of red mist, grey matter, and white bone fragments.

CHAPTER ONE

I pulled into Framingham, was feelin' bout half-past dead. The Google-promised an 8½-hour drive. Had been over 11. To be fair, Google couldn't have known—I don't think anyway—about the usual hassle my long-haired, dishevelled old beach bum look attracts at the Canadian-US border. Nor could its Maps have reacted in time to tell me about the frequent and inexplicable clotting of cars and trucks on every goddamned highway I travelled.

It was November 1 and the great annual southern migration of northern snowbirds had begun. It's a magnificent spectacle as flocks of senior birds, bumper to bumper in overpacked vehicles, move ever southward in their search for nesting places surrounded by palm trees and nearby medical facilities. If you listen closely, you can hear their shrill sounds of arguing over which highway off-ramp to take for their frequent pee breaks.

Random trip observations:

- Upper New York state features pretty countryside dotted with lakes and a surprising number of single mobile homes, many of them with their skirting draped in red, white, and blue bunting.

- American gas stations don't trust you. If you're paying cash, it's upfront, buddy.
- A lot of New Jersey drivers are tailgating assholes.
- I am befuddled by the simplest goddamn things. In this case: all the toll booths along the Mass Turnpike as I fumbled for coinage with growing line-ups behind me.
- But in general, the American highway system is a wonderful thing.

I am not what you'd ever consider a relaxed driver. So, eleven hours of pretty well white-knuckling all the way along strange highways with traffic blowing by me on either side (even though I was going ten miles over the goddamned limit!) took a toll of its own. These sixty-five-year-old bones seized up, such that, should I die behind the wheel, they'd have a job prying me from my sitting position and then straightening me up enough to fit in a box with the lid closed.

I would've been in a hell of lot worse shape if I had attempted the drive in in my beloved 16-year-old Pontiac Vibe. Carl, my neighbour at the lake, was now the proud owner of this soon-to-be classic car. Instead, I was driving a new and very comfortable Hyundai Tucson hybrid, secretly bought and "gifted" to me by my lady.

Once inside the door of Alexandra's tastefully restored Colonial, I let out a huge sigh of relief, at holding her in my arms again and at being off the road.

As I expected, Alex was packed and ready to go, her extensive, colour-coordinated luggage lined up in the foyer.

"Moving to Italy?" I asked.

"Six months," she reminded me about the planned length of our stay in Florida at the Hovel-by-the-Sea I'd inherited from my recently discovered and deceased father.

After partially renovating much of the joint last winter, this was to be the first in a tradition of spending six months together, avoiding the shitty Canadian and almost as shitty New England winters. That's why Alex had opted to secretly buy the Tucson when her inclination had been to go all-electric. Plus, it was roomier than her Prius so we hybrid-ed it down to Florida in the Tucson.

Thank Christ, Alex hadn't yet succumbed to her original vow to buy a fully electric vehicle. It would've been way too suspenseful trying to determine if we had enough juice between charging stations, along the I-95, never mind the wilds of northern Florida after we left Jacksonville on the Atlantic side and cut over to get down to Indian Rocks Beach on the Gulf Coast below Clearwater, travelling on slow-poke two-lane roads. And then there's the time spent charging that would've made me nuts.

One measly beer and a couple of smokes in the freezing comfort of her back porch was all the decompression time I got in before I started doing that head-snap thing as I nodded off.

Roused up at 5 AM, I almost elected to skip the hot water and just spoon the ground coffee beans into me to launch me into the land of the living. We loaded her luggage into the Tucson in chilly darkness.

Thankfully, Alex took the first driving shift, sparing me the agony of New York and the confusing spaghetti of Washington where, I understand, there are still out-of-gas cars that have been endlessly marooned on the Beltway since the first Bush administration.

We struck a deal before we left. I wouldn't smoke in the new car, and she wouldn't talk on her phone while she was driving. I don't know who had a harder time with the forced abstinence from their favoured addiction. During our bargained-for frequent stops, I paced feverishly and nicotine-loaded while she paced and yakked endlessly into the palm of her hand. Bonus for me: I got to stare at her while she walked in circles. Goddamn, she was beautiful. There was something in the way she looked with her longish, blondish hair threaded in a ponytail through the back of her Greenpeace ball cap that made me crazy. I decided that a) she could pass for Erin Andrews' older sister, and b) I was ridiculously lucky.

Trip observations (Part Deux):

- Quebeckers love giant RVs. Of the eighteen rolling apartments we passed on I-95 south of Richmond, seventeen had Quebec plates.
- The alleged trick I'd read about travelling on the weekend was not a secret anymore. While there were virtually no trucks on the road, every fucking snowbird bound for Florida was.
- Most memorable billboard (this in southern Virginia): An AR-15 in silhouette on a full-colour rippling stars and stripes with the caption: *Guns. Ammo. Freedom. Next Exit.* I was tempted to pull off to see just what freedom looked like.
- Virginia—minus a few billboards—was beautiful.
- Trees look a whole lot better with leaves on them.

As planned, we stopped for the night in Fayetteville, North Carolina. Unplanned was Alex's first reaction to the hotel I'd booked. She tried to hide her disdain. And here I was, thinking I'd upped my game by going with the $89.99 room when the nearby thirty-nine-dollar Red Roof jobbie was beckoning to my cheapskate soul. The room seemed perfectly fine to me as it had everything I was looking for after thirteen fucking hours in the car: a bed.

Literally and figuratively, Alexandra and I almost see eye-to-eye on just about everything, her being five foot nine and all, so I was a little surprised by her reaction to my hotel choice, but I could understand it. She wasn't being snotty; she was just used to something different as she now spent most of her travelling time in New York, Chicago, Dallas, San Francisco, and Washington where she'd address conferences and trade associations, meet with companies or investment groups to advise them on ethical investing, all in much nicer settings than Room 308 of the Fayetteville Quality Inn.

Not so in the early (and struggling) years when she was devoted to finding obscure, often family-run businesses in remote places, mostly in developing nations in Central and South America (where most of the hotels she booked weren't exactly five-star, I must point out). And she was delighted when she was able to help them succeed by unearthing these gems to attract investment.

And with their success came hers. She had been one of a small band of plucky pioneers who loudly insisted that companies should behave themselves wherever they operated and, if they didn't, Alex, among a very few others, would warn investors of their failure to mend their evil ways. The media picked up on this nascent trend which led to appearances on business TV (where she was darn presentable), op-ed writing, and interviews. And that meant more clients, more stock trades, and more commissions.

Now, she and half her growing staff spent their time investigating the "greenwashing" claims that companies, many of them giant corporations, were making in an effort to convince would-be customers and investors that they existed—and had always existed —solely to protect Mother Earth, profits be damned.

Bonus was the Quality Inn's location, right next door to a Texas Roadhouse where their grilled dead cow was wonderful. Vegetarian Alex assured me the salmon was "more than passable." Next morning, that's what she also said to me about the night's shenanigans in bed.

Again, we got away early with her taking the first shift.

Trip Observations (the sequel to the sequel):

- Going by the billboards, there are a surprising number of wildly successful personal injury lawyers in Georgia and Florida which also signified a large and uncommonly clumsy and litigious population.
- And speaking of billboards, Jesus and the gang were pouring a lot of money into advertising campaigns.
- The worst fucking drivers in each state are residents of that state, except for New Jersey drivers. They're awful everywhere.
- I was absurdly happy to see my first palm trees, in central North Carolina—even if they were of the short, squat scrub variety.
- Goddamn, the land is flat.

- NPR is a national treasure, although changing the dial every time we entered a new state was annoying.

I had a lot of time to listen to public radio and read billboards because Alex had grown less and less conversational. She needlessly apologized for her lengthy silences, saying it was likely the result of physically leaving the ethical investment brokerage she'd founded fifteen years earlier. I almost understood that; her planned six-month escape to Florida with me, (of all people), was going to be the longest she'd ever been away from the business that meant the world to her.

Alex's separation anxiety from her business deepened as we ploughed deeper into the Deep South. She hardly took or made any phone calls during our scheduled stops at the Welcome Centers for each state, those elaborate facilities seemingly designed to make you forget the state you just left. The few she did place—when she wasn't staring off or watching me smoke—seemed longer, quieter, and appeared more serious.

We made good time, as I happily slipped into the Florida way of driving like a fucking lunatic.

After the second day of driving in five-hour shifts, there was joint relief and a sudden happiness as soon as we got through Tampa and onto the long causeway crossing Tampa Bay. It was late afternoon and the calm waters of the giant bay had gone to full glitter. Already, the St. Petersburg-Clearwater-Beaches side of the bay had started to feel like one big Olly Olly Oxen Free.

But my joy was short-lived as we drove up Gulf Boulevard. To my horror, the Red Lion—The world's best dive beach bar ™—was gone. It hadn't been the victim of Florida's often-serious weather, but rather it had fallen prey to beach gentrification, an insidious trend to upscale and up-price everything near the water. Its change to Hurricane Eddy's could only mean good decorating, better TVs, bathrooms that didn't make you want to retch, and the disappearance of the scruffier locals, along with high staff turnover and doubled food and beverage prices.

I was in for a second shock the moment we pulled into the

narrow driveway alongside the Hovel just off Gulf. The humid and hot summer weather had caused a green explosion in our small and now completely landscaped yard. I had planted like a madman last winter and everything was bigger and greener. The areca palms had shot up at least two feet and thickened with a girdle of new fronds, the bougainvillea against the house had also put on two feet of new branches now heavy with brilliant red flower.

Likewise, the four hibiscus bushes had doubled in size. Our lime tree—the only vegetation in the yard when I inherited the place less than a year earlier—sagged under the weight of softball-sized fruit. Welcome to the jungle, indeed.

As much as I badly wanted to claim full credit for the insta-garden we now owned, I knew that most of the kudos had to go to Michael, the guy I'd hired to look after the place while we were in absentia. Last winter, he had just wandered up to me as he was walking by, and I was in full sweat laying the red mulch around all the new planting. I took an instant shine to small, wiry man with the easy smile, mostly because he complimented me on the landscaping.

He told me he did a bunch of gardening for far bigger places in the 'hood. So, I tried to hire him on the spot to water, prune, and weed during the summer season. Not so fast, Jake. Michael, more or less, interviewed me to ensure I would take care of the gardens after he passed them back to me. Alexandra was surprised when I gave him a key to look in on the place every once in a while.

"You gotta trust a guy like that," I said. I added the "I hope" part under my breath.

I didn't know his last name or where he lived other than fairly close by, because I'd frequently seen him out walking. My only way to contact him was by phone. The number he jotted down on a scrap of paper was—I later found out—a Virginia area code for some reason.

Alex and I did a quick tour of our "estate"—the only kind of tour you could do on our tiny scrap of Florida real estate—and she pronounced herself pleased at the astonishing amount of green. But she was keen to get inside.

That's when my gob took another smacking. An entirely new

kitchen greeted us. Somebody had thrown out everything including the old kitchen sink, and replaced it with gleaming, white Shaker cabinets, new faux greyish granite counter tops and bright white appliances. It's not like I missed the dilapidated, chipped original cupboards or the scarred and cigarette-burned counter, or even the ancient round-shouldered harvest-gold fridge that constantly squealed and was complemented by the obsolete avocado stove where two of the four elements worked, and the oven didn't. But this was nothing short of an astonishing transformation.

"Beautiful, babe! But how did the kitchen elves get all this done?"

She patiently explained, as if to a Neanderthal (not too far off the mark), about the wonder of the Internet and phone system. Without leaving home, she contacted Michael to turn over the key to several companies she'd researched, got estimates from them, picked a winner, got and then revised the plans, chose finishes, agreed on a price and schedule, then rounded out the project with appliances, delivered and installed.

The overall effect was astonishing. The walls she'd painted white last winter, combined with the new, mostly white kitchen, appeared to have doubled the size of the joint. Except as a dismal memory, the tiny dark cave was gone forever.

"You can't call it a hovel anymore," Alex said. "It's officially a beach cottage."

"Can I call it a shack?"

"No."

"So, I suppose shithole's out too?"

She ignored me and turned her attention to the new bar-height island. Same Shaker cabinets and matching countertop. She tested the pot drawers and then effortlessly rolled the six-foot structure across the kitchen and down the hallway.

"Just like I'd planned. Now we can move stuff in and out the door."

"Sweet. Mind me asking how much all this cost?"

"Yes."

"The deal was, my dear, that we'd split costs," I reminded her.

"You get to replace the windows and re-model the bathroom."

To no one's surprise, Alex didn't want to just relax after our road trip. Eager to start filling the new fridge and cupboards, we quickly unloaded the Tucson and went on a grocery expedition to the nearest Publix across the drawbridge in Largo. I preferred Winn-Dixie for their insane discounts, but Publix offered a lot of two-for-ones to start provisioning for the coming winter. I was happy to contribute to the shopping: gin, tequila, triple sec, beer, white wine, tonic, and a carton of smokes. You know, the staples.

Now usually, I make a hermit crab seem like a gregarious extravert. But there was something wonderful about seeing the people we'd met the previous winter, my first of what I hoped would be many for us in Indian Rocks.

Molly, my next-door neighbour, was first to show up as her second-floor apartment overlooked our backyard so she had a bird's eye view of the comings and goings. A year earlier, Molly had been my guide to all the survival tips needed to survive a winter in the beachy town. She arrived with a couple of cans of beer, and we took our positions at the patio table. That's when she delivered the sad news that she would be leaving our beach town, going to join her daughter and granddaughter in northern Ohio of all places. And before the hard Lake Erie winters of all times.

Laura and Stan, the former hippies and erstwhile Colorado legal pot growers, came by the next day to welcome us back. They had become my favourite margarita sluts, as they were—like me—big fans of Cazadores Reposada. I plucked a bunch of fresh limes and fired up the blender.

Whereas I depended on Molly to bring me up to date about the goings on around Indian Rocks, Laura and Stan supplied their take on American politics and the red-taped bureaucracy and onerous taxation that came with running a legit, regulated weed business in Colorado when, for years, their illegal operation had been a lot less complicated and a lot more profitable.

Coming from the kitchen with another round of slushy, light green fuck-you-up, I surveyed the scene: Laughing lover and friends chattering around the table against a lush background of palm fronds and brilliant red flowers under a blue, blue sky and warming sun. I smiled. How could I not think: Is this Florida or what? All that was missing was for me to blow out a flip-flop and step on a pop top.

A couple of days later, I made another buddy. I had noticed a hole on the ground with a bunch of sand piled up at the edge of our property bordering the condo building. I had no idea what lived in that hole but, as long as it didn't bother me, I wouldn't bother it. One morning, I'm sitting outside with my coffee and butts, just meditating and dreaming around when I spotted a new arrival to our small yard. A green turtle, maybe a foot long by ten inches wide. It was just sitting there staring at me from the edge of the mulch where it met the river rock. I stared back, quickly realizing I had found my spirit reptile to go along with my spirit mammal, the two-toed sloth.

I had an idea and went inside, opened the fridge door, and searched for an item I normally wouldn't.

"What are you doing?" Alex asked.

"I finally found a good use for goddamned Romaine lettuce!" I said, as I ripped off pieces of that loathsome bundle of green.

Mystified, Alex came out with me and watched as I scattered the shreds around the turtle. It recoiled at the veggie shower, but didn't run...well, slowly crawl away. Instead, it carefully explored the manna from heaven, craning its wrinkled neck out, to examine the closest pieces. Satisfied, it seized one and began chomping away, moving on to the other pieces as soon as it finished that. In no time, it had hoovered up every scrap. Its olive drab colour and boxy shape reminded me of a tank. The way it planted one arm and leg then swivelled 45 degrees only added to the armoured military allusion.

We didn't know its gender (or age or species), but Alexandra instantly named him Mitch after a certain politician.

"He was starving," I said.

"That's your fault. He might've been here for years. You told me your father didn't garden at all. So, it was always just an empty yard with lots of weeds and grass to graze on. You destroyed his big old dining hall with your landscaping, you heartless bastard of a developer!"

"I gotta make it up to him. It's my duty!"

I went inside for more lettuce because, rather than heading home, Mitch just sat there staring at me as if to say: "Please, sir. I want some more."

I spread out his second serving and took my chair to watch. Alex came up behind me, lightly touched my shoulder then slid her hand gently up my neck.

She said: "You really are just a big mushball, aren't you?"

"What are you talking about, woman? I'm fattening him up. At that size, we couldn't get a decent pot of soup out of him."

CHAPTER TWO

We settled into a most excellent routine: I'd work away at my second novel, *The Sixth String*, in the mornings and Alexandra would long-distance work away at making money in her business. Mitch would emerge every third or fourth day. I had no idea how he filled his time in between, but most of it seemed to be spent underground. He'd just plop his ass down and stare.

None of this "please, sir" business anymore. His attitude was more like: "Hey, dickwad! Where's my fucking lettuce?"

In the afternoons, I tackled the two big jobs left on the place: replacing the windows and re-doing the bathroom. I wasn't allowed to do the work myself as the projects demanded licensed plumbers and window guys as well as permits from the city. I wasn't tempted to do it on the sly because the building inspector's office was across the park looking at our house. Word had it the lad was real dick, and the fines were hefty. Besides, you don't want to fuck around with windows in Florida. They have to be hurricane-proof to withstand 170 mph winds and installed with a lot of lag bolts. Sure, I would have been able to do something, but the glass would've probably all blown out in a million pieces if someone sneezed anywhere near one of them.

So, my "work" entailed the endless hunt for tradespeople. As the Northeast cities empty of boomer-age gummers looking to get out, it's clear they ain't opting to spend their winters in South Dakota. None too surprising that Florida's construction and renovation biz was insanely busy. More out of pity than profit when they sensed the desperation in my voice, I actually found people to do the reno jobs.

While I was doing that, Alex would shop. But not for clothes or shit for herself. She had named herself Mistress and Grand Overseer of the Hovel Interior and she took her self-appointment very seriously. While she could easily afford to buy brand-new everything, she didn't. Instead, she'd roam the thrift shops and neighbourhood garage sales for all the things the place needed or looked better by having.

When we weren't busy renovating and accessorizing, we soon developed a comfy habit of walking. I've spent years, decades really, trying to avoid overextending myself. The trick, I discovered, is to not extend myself in the first place.

I'm not a complete couch potato; I still play a little tennis and I do walk more than the distance between the beer fridge and deck. I do so exclusively with Alex, and in a forest or on a beach. I gave up the very amateur boxing I had done for years, largely because there had been nothing enjoyable about it anymore. A three-minute sparring round had become excruciatingly exhausting and the thrill of getting the shit beaten out of me had lost its charm.

But generally, the idea of physical exertion did not sit well with me, which coincidentally was the position I usually yearned to be in.

And I had things to keep me busy on a long, boring walk: Stopping to watch a hovering pelican go into its power dive, dropping its wings back just before it smashes face-first into the water or staring at a trio of dolphins breaking that water's surface as they sleekly undulated just offshore. Or maybe a nifty shell catches my attention.

Alexandra usually seemed fine with this distracted stroll, but I could tell that she was sometimes itching to break into a run like a three-year old thoroughbred chomping at the bit just before the start of the Preakness. Friggin' Type-A's. Sometimes she would just take off, her long smooth strides disappearing her into the distance.

Other times, she would suggest/cajole/badger/hector me into joining her for a "nice, easy jog." Bullshit! There's no such thing as a nice, easy jog for anyone of my age, condition, and general disposition, unless my life's being threatened and I'm relying on an adrenaline injection to carry me.

But once—just once—I agreed (What the Christ was I thinking?) and off we trotted.

I'm almost sixty-five. I'm not on the verge of challenging anybody to a foot race—unless it's one of those bastard snails lurking under my hostas. Why the fuck would I train a couple of hours a day, every day, all the while risking knee injury and shin splints, getting hit by a car or a stroke or any kind of pain just for the unlikelihood of someday needing to use my legs, like a sucker? (Thank you, Homer). And I wasn't in the market for the natural high of an endorphin rush which you only get to hide the pain and stress that you created by running in the first place. Not when beer and/or tequila produce the same natural high, but, crucially, without the effort.

I wasn't thinking about this smug defense of inertia as I struggled mightily to keep up with Alexandra. Instead, I imagined what the footage from the mini-mini-camera inside my body would show as my lungs exploded. I made it, I'd say, a good eighteen, twenty feet (well, maybe a little farther) before falling to my knees and sucking air like an industrial vacuum cleaner to repay my oxygen debt.

Alexandra came back and jogged on the spot while she regarded my heaving corpse. I can't be sure, but I think she wanted to kick sand in my face.

"Maybe that's enough for you today," she said, before resuming her run.

Friggin,' friggin' Type-A's.

Three weeks passed pleasantly enough. Except for the note of sadness as we said goodbye to Molly and wished her good luck on her counterintuitive migration north to Ohio in November.

She would need it because, as far as I knew, she had never spent one winter of her sixty odd years north of the Mason-Dixon line.

But something wasn't quite right with my lady throughout November, almost as though she was forcing herself to be happy.

On the surface, you'd say any change was imperceptible, but I knew her to be effortlessly content and smiling.

"Want to come clean, kid?" I asked. "There's something more than separation anxiety from your biz. You were talking to the office almost constantly all on the way down here. But you started to really clam up, around, I'd say, the South Carolina border. What is it?"

"I...I've been getting nasty calls."

"I expect you would, what with your business and all."

None too surprisingly, Alex was picking up her share of corporate enemies as she was relentless in sniffing out the greenwashing bullshit. In recent years, her once lonely voice in the wilderness had been joined by a growing chorus of similarly concerned investors. But she was tiring in the face of massive overwhelming corporate ad campaigns and intense company PR efforts by these big companies to convince the public of their impeccable enviro-creds.

"Pissed-off investors or companies come with the turf, don't they?"

"Not those kinds of calls," she said. "Anonymous ones at work, at home. And texts."

"Saying....?"

"Saying I should back off, just abandon a report we were working on."

"What was the report about?"

"It was a detailed, very comprehensive look at sketchy mining practices of some American, Canadian, and European companies. But here's the scary part: they knew we were working on it!"

"Maybe it was common knowledge you guys were going to put something out."

"Not a chance!" she insisted. "Everything we do is confidential; it has to be. We can't ever tip off the markets if we're going to slam or praise a company."

"Any idea who's behind this?"

"Well, the police said—"

"The police?! They're involved?"

"I called them. Jake, you know I don't scare easily. I've been in tight places, in South America, Mexico. With miners, illegal loggers, corrupt cops."

"I know, babe. Tougher than a bull's bag."

"Thanks...I guess. But I'm afraid now. It got...personal. They know...things."

"What kind of things?"

I looked at her with my normal stunned and uncomprehending expression. In reply, she picked up her phone and started rifling through it. She played a stored message. The voice was deep, metallic, with a quasi-Darth Vadar vibe.

"Hello again, Alex," he began. "Is that green skirt/blouse set new? I must tell you, it's very flattering. Have you reconsidered that report? I truly hope so. Talk to you soon." Click.

"That was about three months ago," she added. "Then the calls and texts just stopped."

"Did the report come out the way you wanted it to?"

"Goddamn right it did!" she said defiantly. "Five weeks ago. And I didn't change a word."

"Anything happen?"

"Nothing. Until sometime during the night we spent in Fayetteville. I checked my messages the next morning when you were outside smoking. I got this," she said, briefly searching her phone.

The same electronically altered voice: "You've been very naughty, Alex. We will remember."

"Holy fuck, darlin'! Can I ask why you didn't tell me?"

"After all the shit I put you—us—through about the stuff you never told me?"

Alex had almost ended us last winter because of the dicey bit of gunplay in the southern hovel that I had failed to mention. It had been the proverbial last straw after a series of shitty events I'd been involved in since we got together three years ago. I'd kept her in the dark about most it for the simple reason that there was fuck- all she could have done about any of it except worry. Patronizing as hell, I

know. The secrecy and all the fucking drama were—understandably
—getting to be too much for her. Thank the living lord, sweet
bleeding Jesus, she relented. And now, and yet again proverbially,
the shoe was on the other foot, and she had been matronizing me.

"Go back to the part about the cops," I said.

"The local police said there wasn't much they could do.
Untraceable burner phones, heavily encrypted IP addresses. Voice
disguised. They sent what I gave them to the FBI cybercrimes unit
but told me that was a long shot. Washington's backlogged forever
with all the crazies threatening people these days."

"So that's it from law enforcement?"

"Framingham police told me to just be careful."

"Whatever the fuck that means. So now what?"

"I...I'm being careful, I guess."

"That's just bullshit. We gotta do something."

"Aw, Jake. It's gone away. Looks like they realized they had been
worried for nothing. Maybe they're going to drop the whole thing
and just issued this last warning so I wouldn't forget."

"Maybe. But what if there's a next time? They know they can
get to you. It didn't work this time. So maybe they lean a little
harder next time out."

"Jake, the report's out; why would they keep bothering me?"

"Are you ever going to look at mining again?"

"Probably. Yes."

"Do you think the worst offenders will clean up their act?"

"I can hope, but chances are they won't. All I can do is steer
investors who care away from those kinds of companies."

"Are you going to say or do anything differently?"

"No."

"Then you've answered your own question. They won't go
away."

Most people who whistle past graveyards know they're
pretending to be nonchalant while they pray for no harm. Alex was
thinking. I was betting that lady of mine was realizing the problem
with being docile about all this.

"You're right, goddamnit!" she announced. "Let's find a way to get after those bastards. Where do we start?"

"That's my girl! Now, how many companies did you shit on in the report?" I asked.

"Eighteen by name."

"Any common factors?"

"None that I remember, except they were all being sons of bitches wherever they worked. Some were big, some small outfits. Some public, some privately held. Mining for different things. In different places all over the world."

"Then we have to look at all of them. Who do we focus on?"

"The bigger ones?" Alex suggested. "Whoever's calling me is obviously sophisticated."

"I know we've been saying 'they' but the electronic shit that was pulled on you—and I know this to be true—could've been done by some guy in his mommy's basement."

"But they're watching me too!"

"Hate to break it to you, but, with the right techie smarts and gear, they or he or she could be doing that through your own phone camera."

"OK, then what about the companies that have the most to lose by being outed as irresponsible assholes?"

"Makes sense, but there's some relativity going on here. What you have to lose depends on what you got. Cost a billion-dollar corporation a couple of million in their stock price and it's a rounding error. Do the same thing to a small company and you wipe them out."

"True. So can we rule out any of big companies that are already public?"

"Drop 'em down the list, but don't cross them off. They could be real sensitive about their image, especially if they've got financial problems or regulators are looking at them. How many privately held ones?"

"Eight of the eighteen. I'll focus on them. One of the private ones could be looking to issue their first stock offering or trying to attract a private placement. I'll go back over the report, make some calls. What are you going to do?"

"Fair division of labour. While you're pruning the list, I'll do the same to those palms. There's watering and fertilizing to do too."

"And then what?"

"There's beer in the fridge that just won't drink itself."

CHAPTER THREE

I n the early 1980s when I was living in the Bahamas, my wife at the time and I would congregate around the TV at 6 o'clock throughout August and September to watch Miami TV. We'd indulge in what everyone else on the island did at the same time: track hurricanes. Even though there was fuck-all we could do about them, we had to see where the next one was heading to decide whether hatches needed battening down or not.

Back when dinosaurs ruled the world (even though those big ol' lizards displayed no administrative skills whatsoever), [Sidebar: not my joke but I really like it], you had to be stationed in front of your tiny TV at exactly 6 o'clock to see if the weather was serious enough to be the lead story. Our favourite weatherman recalled a young Orville Redenbacher, right down to the bowtie. "Uncle Walt" had a string of great descriptors for shitty weather. A heavy rain was a "real palmetto pounder" or a "toad-strangler." The wind could be as serious as "a sack full of flatulence," (although I knew he was aching to say 'farts').

On a dead-flat island often in the path, we soon learned a healthy respect for the relentless ferocity even of a non-hurricane-y gale force wind with its ungodly buckets of rain. I went down to the beach once and tried leaning into the wind of one of those babies. I came close to becoming a tubby tumbleweed spinning down the sand.

Of course, nowadays, there was no need to huddle around the TV at specific times. 24/7 we could get up-to-date weather reports, so I had instituted a long-distance variation of that Bahamas habit during the late summer by checking the Florida weather online every day.

Alex poo-pooed my continuing the weather-watching in just about sea-level Florida as the hurricane season had "officially" passed. It took just one tropical November downpour with its accompanying howling winds to get her attention. Three or four inches of rain in less than an hour flooded the streets around the Hovel—I mean beach cottage—and backed up the overwhelmed storm sewers. Worsening the situation was the wake of water washing up to our front door, caused by yahoos in giant, jacked-up pickups charging through the sidewalk-to-sidewalk lakes like kids gleefully stomping through puddles.

So, weather-watching was added to my morning routine (I've got more habits than a nunnery). I read/watch local news wherever I am. Figuring on a lengthy stay, I'd bought an online subscription to the *Tampa Bay Times*, winner of a slew of Pulitzers stretching back to its days as the *St. Petersburg Times*.

With a massive geography to cover on both sides of the Bay, they had sections by city and county. But often, big stories would transcend the local designation. Three weeks after we'd arrived in the Sunshine State, this headline grabbed my attention: *Pickleballer Shot to Death in St. Petersburg Park.*

The accompanying story wasn't much longer than the headline. Any early morning shooting had claimed of the life of a pickleballer playing at the courts in Crescent Lake Park. The police supplied few details as "the investigation was in its early stages."

No suspect, no motive, no name of the victim.

In that pointlessly complicated official police language: *The unidentified deceased had received injuries incompatible with life.*

I didn't mention it to Alexandra, just as I don't yak to her about every murder I come across in the media. If I did, that's all we'd ever talk about.

More details came the next day. Robert Hale, 71, CFO of Southern Cross Mining of St. Petersburg, was named as the victim. The shooting had taken place at about 7 AM. The cops still had no suspect and no eyewitnesses, but indicated there had been other shots that, as usual, had sounded like a car backfiring, according to other people using the park at the time. The police then theorized that "very possibly" the dead guy had been hit by a stray bullet as a result of gang activity.

I want to be clear here: I don't read every article I come across about an innocent bystander being killed in a street gang dust-up, but a couple of things got my attention. First off, the dead guy was playing pickleball, that increasingly popular game I had dubbed Gummer Tennis. Our town had built two courts right across the street from us, so we were incessantly tortured by the loud racket their rackets and balls made. Secondly, the guy was an exec with a mining company. A Florida mining company. You dig six feet down just about anywhere in the state and you strike only one thing. Water. That's why, when you're flying over central Florida, you see so many freakishly square lakes (crowded by cookie-cutter houses). Just break ground with a backhoe and, voila, instant water-front property and future home to poodle-chomping alligators.

So, I e-nosed around a bit. The National Mining Association had an online listing for them. Status: Private. Activity: Unknown, with a link to Southern Cross's website. Scant reading there as well. Pleasant, generic-looking landing page simply telling me, *Southern Cross Mining has been a leading mineral extraction company for forty years.*

'Contact' and 'Operations' were the only buttons with the former just listing their phone number and address in NW St. Petersburg and the names of John "Jack" Duffy, President and CEO and Robert C. Hale, Executive Vice President and CFO, while the latter announced that *Southern Cross has active operations with neodymium-producing mines in Brazil and Vietnam.*

So, they weren't operating improbable strip mines outside of

Orlando; one mystery cleared up. But hadn't Alex and I just been talking about mining? I meant to mention the dead guy's connection to Southern Cross to her but didn't. And I had a great reason for not doing so—an excuse I was using a lot more frequently of late: I forgot.

CHAPTER FOUR

L ife is full of serendipitous events. You could argue—and I do — that our whole fucking existence on the planet is a series of random events. Alexandra was out shopping one late afternoon; I had declined to accompany her on account of my permanent and likely terminal disease known as store-sickness.

There were scattered clouds in the sky (oh, for fuck's sake, Jake; where else would they be?) in the later afternoon so I figured it'd be another postcard sunset (not that anybody sends postcards anymore). I poured a beer into a red plastic solo cup and walked to the beach. The opaque cup was a clever disguise to avoid detection by the vigilant beach police for the heinous crime of drinking on sand. The fine was $176 for such a transgression. In Mexico, the DR, and most other places with beaches, you are—rightfully—fined for not drinking near the sea.

It was early in the tourist season but still a decent crowd had gathered for the nightly darkening. Sun's down around 5:30, more than an hour after it disappears at my home in the Kawarthas up north. It was hard not to feel like you're part of some silent, reverential pagan ritual as I watched the sun purple up the sky behind the line of clouds hovering near the horizon, shooting out yellow and orange shafts before it sank into the Gulf of Mexico.

I became aware of a man standing beside me, almost shoulder to shoulder, a guy who hadn't been there a few minutes earlier.

"Spectacular, huh?" he said. "Never get tired of watching the show."

"Me neither," I said, turning to face him. He was an older guy, slightly built, kinda stooped with thinning grey hair that even short, looked dishevelled.

"Say, aren't you Jake Lydon?" he asked.

"If you don't have a subpoena with you, then yes, I am," I said, surprised as hell.

"Matt Kilmer. A real pleasure," he said, extending his hand. "You had that nasty business up on 16th last winter."

I heard the tinkle of an alarm bell in my wee brain. Yeah, I lit up the local media for a bit back then. But unless he happened to see—and remember—my one brief, profanity-strewn uncooperative TV interview eight months ago, there wasn't much of a way he would know what I looked like. Failing that, he would've been riding Google for answers and a photo—which was another whole new brand of creepy. He sensed my doubt.

"Somebody pointed you out at the Lion," he hastily added, "Small town."

"If you'll excuse me," I said. "I need a butt."

"Mind if I join you?"

We followed the last of the sunset brigade on the ramp over the sand and sea oats. I'm not a speed-walker by any stretch, but I had to slow my pace to Kilmer's who moved as if he needed a walker.

As we shuffled along (not an easy thing to do in sand), I thought back years ago, to another lifetime when Beth, my wife back then, and I were exploring the Pacific coast of Mexico north of Puerta Vallarta. After the bustle of Bucerias and Sayulita, the towns became more 'Mexican.' Small villages in coves with cobblestone streets, whitewashed, red tile-roofed businesses, wide beaches, regular strong waves, a cluster of bobbing fishing boats in the bays and very few hotels or restaurants.

The height of tourist season was barely noticeable in Lo de Marcos. A smattering of tourists and locals spread out on the sand, with a few rickety wooden restaurant stalls to serve them. We stopped to eat at one, felt guilty bypassing two others with their staffs of smiling hopeful faces. The menu boards and service were Spanish only. We took our tacos de pescados and sat down on one of the few plastic loungers in front of the restaurant.

A man was passing by, middle-aged surfer-type, tall, with fair hair, his skin burnt brown. Obviously as gringo as we were, he stopped to compliment us on our food choice.

"Best fish on the beach," he noted.

I offered to buy him a beer, something I just about never do, but I figured he was an expat resident who could tell us about the town.

He accepted and we had a decent slice of the afternoon shooting the shit about Lo de Marcos where, he said, he'd been living for the last six years. The town was evidently popular with cheap Canadian—I know, I know, a redundancy—snowbirds who filled up two RV/camper parks on the lip of the sand. He told us the seafood anywhere around there was always fresh and inexpensive. And that there were a couple of good restaurants away from the beach.

We chatted easily, until I asked him where he was from.

He said "Arlington."

"Texas?" I asked.

"No." But he didn't fill in the blank.

He then got measured and real careful with his words when I wondered aloud about what he did.

He told me he had retired from 'government.' Just government. No department, no profession, which I found odd. Ask a Canadian public servant the same question and you get the department, the branch of that department, his position, schooling, and wasn't it fucked up that Kevin in the next cubicle had been awarded a higher job classification?

Odder still was this stranger's apparent young age when he had packed it in. I reckoned he'd have to have been about forty when he fucked off from 'government' for a remote village in Mexico.

Oddest was him chugging the rest of the beer he had previously been sipping, getting up quickly, and skedaddling down the beach, before I had a chance to ask him to explain his move from a Washington D.C. suburb to Lo de Marcos.

Beth and I then had fun demonstrating that we watched way too many thriller movies. We speculated that he was a spook of some kind, maybe a black ops assassin who'd lost his nerve and got retired. Or maybe he threatened to go all whistleblower and had to flee for his life. But from whom? Plenty to pick from. There's an alphabet soup of three-lettered federal security agencies—twenty-one at last public count (I, of course, looked it up), although for all I —or anybody else—knew, there were another two dozen even shadier outfits.

I had no idea what happened to him or the town for that matter which, I assumed, had grown with more boomer-age turistas, higher prices, and better restaurants, as happened, it seemed, to about every town with a beach and a decent climate.

But I thought of him years later, after I'd spent a few winters in the Dominican Republic where I discovered it was routine for European or American expats to shy away from discussing their pre-Caribbean lives. Whatever they might have been running from was none of my goddamned business. Period. End of story.

And I thought of him yet again as I chatted with Matt Kilmer post-IRB sunset, as we sat on a bench bolted to the top of the sea wall and lit up.

Unlike that unidentified stranger I serendipitously met on a Mexican beach many years ago, this guy was an erupting volcano of conversation.

"Yessir," he said, "That was nasty business you were involved in. The Mafia and all."

As if I somehow needed reminding. "Ex-Mafia," I pointed out.

He didn't acknowledge my correction and instead elected to go with a clumsy as fuck segue.

"Just like that nasty business down in St. Pete's a couple of weeks ago."

"You mean the guy who got shot playing pickleball?" I asked.

"I do. So, you heard about it."

"Kinda hard to miss."

"Do you know the details?" he asked.

"Not really. Police don't have the shooter, or the weapon or anything that looks like a motive. They said it was likely a stray bullet. Apparently, there had been a bunch of other gunshots at about the same time at the far end of the park. Other than that, they apparently don't know shit."

"Well, I know. I did some digging," he said.

That remark got my attention. And not because of whatever he was about to claim he'd discovered. I had employed my Aspergian-OCD methods to doing some digging of my own into that death only because of its strangeness (who shoots pickleballers first thing in the morning—even though that's when they arguably deserve it most?). When my curiosity is roused up and I go digging, I'd put my e-shovel up against anybody's. Yet, about details of this story, I had come up empty.

"That wasn't a stray bullet," he stated. "The deceased was deliberately killed with one shot. And that shot came from a helluva distance away. Maybe seven or eight hundred yards."

I imagined eight football fields stretched end to end. "Like a sniper?" I asked.

"Not like. Had to be a sniper. I'm betting he used something like a Barret M82 or McMillan Tac-50, maybe a Dragunov-SVD. The problem is those sumbitches are loud."

"Suppose you're right, wouldn't a silencer work?"

"That's Hollywood bullshit. There's no such thing as a silencer. They're called suppressors. They reduce the decibel level by maybe 30, 35 per cent."

Isn't that just fucking wonderful, I thought. A gun nut. "Now how the Christ would you know that?" I asked. Kilmer didn't take too kindly to my challenge.

"Because...because for thirty-eight years it was my job to know!" he snapped.

That small, tinkling alarm bell had turned into the giant, clanging bells of Notre-Dame Cathedral at Easter. This conversation had gotten way too weird way too fast. A guy I'd never seen before sidles up to me while I'm watching a sunset and starts yakking away about snipers with specific rifles murdering pickleballers in a St. Petersburg park.

"Can we get something out of the way right now?" I asked. "This—you meeting me—wasn't an accident, was it?"

He thought for a bit. While he was doing that, I was hoping he'd come clean and drop the bullshit.

"No," he said.

"Oh, do go on."

"Like I said, I did some digging. That's what I do these days." He stopped.

"Actually, that's what I've done all my life."

"Digging for what?" I asked.

"I spent almost four decades as a weapons research analyst for the ATF."

Well, that firmed up his shaky credibility.

"And where did you do this digging about the pickleballer?" I asked.

"I started down here. The St. Pete cops have a pretty good ballistics guy. I met him online a while ago. He was in a couple of the same forum groups."

That made sense to me. I had come across some of these webby groups last year when I was looking to buy a gun (long story). Simple rule: Experts gotta yak about their expertise. They love nothing more than trotting out their detailed, arcane knowledge that only their smaller group has, while being surrounded by a larger group who pretend to. They can argue online about such monumentally important things like the best 9-millimeter cartridge to lessen bullet drop or the relative loading times of a Glock 19 handgun versus a Sig Sauer P-228. All of this chatter is really just shop talk, the harmless kind that everybody does—only about deadly weapons.

I tend to tune out when I'm around all this esoteric bullshit if it's a subject that doesn't interest me or, in this case, if the discussion ignores the fact that a human being is dead and focuses only on how he got dead as everybody tries to outdo each other with their supe-rior understanding.

But then Kilmer told me something that made me sit up. "Head shot. There was a lot of damage, so much that they could barely figure out what direction the bullet came from. And there was pretty much nothing left of either the target or the round. Even with a supersonic suppressor, that bullet would take apart a bowling ball at 50 yards. Imagine what it'll do to a human head. Yet the sound it makes is more a zip than a boom. The loud crack would've happened after the guy was dead."

"So that gave you the idea about the rifles you mentioned?"

He looked at me the way a patient parent regards a clueless toddler trying to learn stuff.

"No. The few bullet fragments did. They ran them through a metal spectrometer."

"What'd that tell you?"

"This ballistic guy found steel."

"So?"

"The only place for steel is inside the lead that makes up most of the cartridge."

"I'll repeat: so?"

"It means it was an armour-piercing shell. A military-grade shell. Illegal in most states, Florida being one of them."

"So, where'd it come from?"

He vaguely waved his hand to the east.

"Well, sir, right across Tampa Bay over there is MacDill Airforce base."

"Why in the world would the air force have a hard-on for a mining exec from a small company?"

"MacDill is also HQ for USSOCOM," he said, rather dramati-cally I thought.

"I have absolutely no idea what you're talking about."

"Strategic Operations Command runs all the military's clandes-tine operations all over the world. The dirty stuff you never hear about."

"Wait, what? Are you really suggesting the US armed forces put out a hit on this guy?"

"I'm not suggesting anything. I'm telling you what I found out."

"How easily could someone get their hands on one of those sniper rifles?"

He snorted.

"There's no such thing as a sniper rifle. Sniper is a job description of someone with a very good weapon."

"Can we please drop all this special terminology bullshit?" I asked. "You knew what I meant."

"Sorry," he said, obviously not sorry at all. "I'll dumb it down for you."

"I have a better idea. Why don't you fuck off? I need this like I need another arsehole," I said, motioning to stand up.

"OK, OK!" he said. "Please stay and hear me out." I settled back down.

"Now where was I?" I said. "Oh, yeah. Can anyone buy those rifles?"

"If you've got the money, pretty easy for the American-made ones. The Dragonuv is banned here, but if you've been overseas, they're still very common. Been around since the Soviet days."

"But you could bring one into the country."

"Of course, you could smuggle one in. Or it could've come from a private collection, bought legally before it was outlawed. But all those are supposed to have been registered. We know where they are."

"Let's suppose you're right," I continued, "and it wasn't an accident. How many people could make that shot?"

He thought for a while.

"Under those conditions, from that distance, with that kind of rifle? Hundreds. Maybe thousands. A lot more if we're counting foreign-born snipers. Everybody's got them. The fuckin' Swiss Guard at the Vatican has sharpshooters. Christ, a Canadian holds the record for longest confirmed kill shot—over two miles."

"They keep records for that kinda shit?"

"They do."

"In my sixty-five years on the planet, I haven't ever heard about that."

"In my seventy-five years, I made it my business to follow that 'kinda shit,' as you put it."

We sat and stared at the post sunset twilight for a bit, as I managed to get my resentment for his prickly and prickish manner under control. An obvious thought occurred to me.

"Should you be telling me any of this stuff—secrecy oath and all that?"

"Ordinarily, no. But I've found a direct co-relation between violating that oath and having inoperable Stage-Four prostate cancer."

"Oh...sorry to hear that."

"No more than me, brother. But the result is I don't give a fuck anymore, and that killing that just happened down the road is serious business."

"Talk to the cops?"

"Yes, sir. This is way out of their wheelhouse. They brushed me off."

"What about the media?"

"Thought about it. The world doesn't need to watch another crackpot conspiracy theorist yammering away, getting lost in the noise. This requires some discretion."

"If you're looking for discretion, you came to the wrong place, buddy."

"I don't think so. I remembered your name, so I went digging. I called some friends in Washington. They have access to a pretty hefty file on you."

Now I knew there was a 'Jake' file somewhere; I'd had dealings with the FBI on at least two separate occasions over the last several years, once in Boston, once in Oklahoma. I was a little surprised that he'd described it as hefty. But I shouldn't have been. With thousands of researchers and unlimited disc storage, there might very well be a junior clerk happily filling their day and that file with all things Jake.

"Correct me if I'm wrong," he added. "In just a few years, you cracked an international hacking ring, took apart a country-wide scheme to defraud tribal casinos and uncovered a rare publishing scandal."

"Just call me the fuckin' Zelig of big-time crime. All of it was blind dumb luck," I said, modestly leaving out a deadly land development play near my hovel at the lake and a Dominican-based human smuggling operation, neither of which he would've heard about.

"Whatever it is, you seem to have a knack. And you've got a good pair of legs. I don't."

"I have no idea what you want me to do."

"Look around. See what you can see."

"And do what?"

"Let me know what you find out."

"So, the wily veteran can come out of retirement to kick some criminal ass?"

"Not exactly. But I do know some people who are pretty good at kicking ass."

"So how do I get in touch you?"

"You don't. I'll find you."

"What the fuck is with this Spy vs. Spy routine?"

"It feels like there's something big going on. I need to be—and I need you to be—careful."

"Fine, I'll play along but I gotta tell you: This will probably be the last time I'm down here watching a sunset. They all look pretty much the same and I've got a good memory."

"I know where you live. Remember?"

"At least tell me where you live?"

"That's not important."

"Must be difficult finding your way home."

"Near here," was as specific as he got.

He slowly, painfully got up to leave. I grabbed him by a skinny arm.

"This is crazy! The American intelligence network with hundreds of thousands of employees, trained experts, is pinning its hopes on a drunken Canadian retiree?"

"Are you fuckin' nuts?" he said with alarm. "They'd never do that. I'm pinning my hopes on you —a retired and dying low-level analyst. Something's going on and it stinks. Nobody seems to be taking this seriously. With the shape I'm in, I can't do shit, but you might be able to."

"Let's face it: With the powers-that-be obviously looking into it, I'm not sure I can contribute anything much more to the deal."

"You didn't let me finish. They looked into it—past tense. My connection in St. Petersburg told me, the case was closed. Then my buddy in Washington called me yesterday, said they'd dropped it."

"Why?"

"I don't know that either, but you might want to find out why."

"Why would I go anywhere near this?"

"A trained assassin—possibly military, possibly foreign—executes a private American citizen on American soil and you're not concerned?"

"Maybe a trained assassin," I pointed out. "You said yourself you might just be a crackpot conspiracy theorist."

"Fair enough. How about this? Your girlfriend may be in danger."

CHAPTER FIVE

"**W**hat?!"

"Your girlfriend may be in danger," he repeated.

"How is that possible?"

"My pal in Washington called back after I asked him to check you out a little more closely than I could. He came up with your connection to Alexandra Simpson, so he looked into it, and saw that she had had contact with the deceased."

"Contact? What does that mean? A phone call? What?"

"I don't know, and he wouldn't tell me. Way above my security clearance."

"A three-year affair?"

"I told you I don't know!" he insisted. "All he said was quote she's had contact unquote."

And with that, Kilmer got up and left. I watched him shuffle down Gulf Boulevard while I waited to cross the busy avenue. He didn't look back and he didn't change his painful gait. So, he lived south, not north of me.

I thought about doing that stalking thing that I apparently have a talent for and follow Kilmer home. Not my toughest assignment as he moved like an elderly snail who'd OD-ed on NyQuil.

On the other hand, although it was after sunset, it was still hot, the air thick and sticky with humidity. Which meant I was in for another self-drenching in sweat if I took off after him. Luckily, I spied a guy I knew who might be able to help about a block down under a streetlight.

Bus Bench Bob. I met the old Black vagrant last year, helluva man with I'm sure a helluva story that I'd never learn. I never even learned his real name, but he was fine with the nickname I'd given him. Bob was one of the many weird and wonderful characters that beach towns everywhere seem to attract. He presented as a foul-mouthed, inarticulate, and aggressive bum but, as I had discovered, was actually a well-spoken, polite, and gentle soul. Bob loathed both profanity and contractions and only used them in public because it was "expected" of him.

"Bob!" I said walking up to him as he lounged on the bench by the Clearwater to St. Pete's trolley sign. He'd spend hours a day on that bench, to the point where bus drivers didn't slow down because Bob never hailed them. Even though the humidex had to be in triple digits, he wore the same ratty, oversized sports coat he had on last year, the same ancient and shiny black trousers covering his skinny frame.

"You!" he said back. "I was not aware you had returned. I have not seen you cruising around in that extravagant vehicle of yours." Bob was referring to my sweet ride of a 1976 Cadillac Fleetwood convertible. I'd inherited that pimpmobile from my father along with the Hovel. The giant car was collecting dust in a Largo garage while the Hovel was now a beach cottage.

"Fooled ya, Bob. Got a new car," I said as I sat down. "Smoke?" I asked as I pulled out my pack.

"No, thank you. I quit that filthy habit."

"You what?"

"Fooled you," he answered, smiling. He took out a wadded-up paper towel bundle and slowly unwrapped the bunch of cigarette butts he had scrounged from public ashtrays, when he wasn't busy sitting on the bus bench, "observing," as he had put it. Normally, I'd push the offer of one of my unsmoked cigarettes, but last year he got some kind of upset when I did just that. The intended gift offended his sense of pride which I found admirable. He worked for his smokes.

"I'd ask you what you've been up to these days," I said, "but I assumed you were you still observing."

"Yes, sir," he said.

"Did you happen to observe that guy in the maroon golf shirt who just passed by?"

"Affirmative, again."

"Any idea what street he turned onto?"

"I did not have to ascertain that fact this evening as I have encountered him before. He leaves particularly appealing cigarette remainders in the receptacle adjacent to the Groupers dining establishment."

"So, what street have you observed him walking down?"

"If I furnish you with that detail, you must assure me you plan nothing nefarious."

"I do not."

"I will take you at your word. Eleventh. Now you must provide me with some information in return."

"If I can."

"Is this man ill? I have observed a steady decline in his mobility over these past several months."

"Yes. I understand he is quite sick, maybe even dying."

"As I thought."

"Thank you, Bob," I said, getting up. I extinguished my half-smoked cigarette and laid the butt on the bench seat. Bob smiled. I walked back home, pleased I had confirmed two likely small details: the rough location where Matt Kilmer lived and the fact that he hadn't been bullshitting me about being close to death.

But the real concerning detail was Alexandra's possible involvement with a murdered guy. I picked up my pace.

Trust but verify. I love that motto. At that moment, I was in no position, no matter how convincing or outlandish they sounded, to verify any of Kilmer's claims. Except one. Out of the blue, he had named Alexandra and connected her to the dead guy. That part of his tale could be proved or disproved easily. I just had to do it tact-fully. Not my long suit.

I even debated whether or not to keep her secret a secret. I figured that if she didn't want to tell me, she had a good reason. But I wanted to know what that reason was, largely because I was pretty sure that up until that point, I or anybody I knew had never hung around with anyone who had their head blown off in a Florida municipal park. Plus, I am, by nature and history, a nosy little fucker. And the biggest plus: Kilmer suggested that the woman I loved like crazy might be in danger.

Alexandra was home when I got back. She was emptying the dish rack. She apologized for being late; I did the same.

"Hey, babe," I said. "I was just thinking. You're a math geek, right?"

"I suppose. Why?"

"I'm hoping you can tell me the statistical odds of you knowing that pickleballer who got shot twenty minutes from here?

In utter surprise, Alex dropped a dessert dish. It shattered. "How do you know about that?" she asked when she had recovered.

"Oh, let's grab a drink, shall we?"

We took our positions at the patio table. It was a warm night; the solar lights I'd planted throughout the garden lit the backyard with a soft glow. We'd learned that now was the time for the no-see-ums, those bite-y bastard sand fleas. They didn't bother with me, just as most insects, germs, and viruses wisely tend to steer clear of me. Alexandra sprayed them long beautiful legs of hers with bug repellant until they glistened.

She was quiet, drinking and thinking. I decided to get the ol' ball rolling.

"So, Alex, you obviously heard about the shooting. What the fuck?"

"You first. Who told you and what'd they say?"

I filled her in about meeting the mysterious Mr. Kilmer. I left out some of his wilder innuendoes about a military-ordered assas-sination.

She didn't deny she'd had contact with the victim, but she was a lot more concerned with how Kilmer knew about it. "Dunno. Maybe the Feds tapping phones."

"His or mine?"

"Don't know that either. What's it matter? Unless you've done a whole bunch more illegal or even sketchy things than I think you have."

"That's not the damn point! They've got no right to surveil me."

"Look, how about we agree to postpone this discussion about privacy and individual rights 'til later? Right now, I want to know about your conversation with this guy—this dead guy. That's what's been bothering you since before we left, isn't it?"

"One of things."

"What did he tell you?"

"Nothing really."

"He dies for nothing?"

"How the hell do I know?" she snapped. As she should have. How the hell would she have known? I apologized for my dumber than usual question.

"He called me exactly once, a week before we left to come down here. Didn't even identify himself," she continued, a whole lot calmer. "He just said he knew about a mining company that was looking at maybe going public and was exploring the potential of an IPO. He told me there was some strange doings at neodymium mines in South America and Southeast Asia. And he claimed he had the numbers that proved it."

Alex and her gang routinely followed a lot of these companies who go into poorer countries, get permits from their governments then run roughshod over the local people whom they seem to always piss off. Terrible wages and working conditions, breaking up protests violently, creating real environmental disasters. In total, a great argument for Not In My Back Yard, even if your backyard is a tropical rainforest.

"So how did you make the connection between that call and the recently deceased Robert Hale late of Southern Cross Mining?" I asked.

"I swear I didn't know his name then, but I had to be sure the call wasn't bullshit. Didn't take me long to figure out who he worked for. Only three of the companies in my report are digging for neodymium. And only one is headquartered here. That unidentified guy who spoke to me, called from a 727-area code, the same exchange as St. Petersburg's. I guessed that he was involved in finance if he had 'the numbers,' as he claimed."

"Superior sleuthing," I commented.

"Jake, we talked for maybe three minutes. He sounded nervous. I tried to get him to open up, but he wouldn't. Like he'd lost his nerve at the last minute. He had my cell and I told him I would be reachable all winter. That's when he said that we might meet up. He left it at that."

"And did you see him?"

"No."

I asked the obvious question. "What the fuck is neodymium?"

"It's a little-known rare-earth mineral that's really important." Then I asked the second most obvious question.

"Why would he call you?"

"We get whistleblower calls all the time."

Alexandra explained that, while she was only guessing, she assumed it was the result of that same mining report from her firm we had just talked about. It was that overview of the current state of mining in the developing world that had resulted in those threatening calls she'd been getting. None too surprisingly, it wasn't exactly complimentary.

Companies were scouring the globe in the race to find the so-called rare metals that run pretty much all hi-tech devices. Outside of China, which is lucky enough have most of them, these rare minerals are buried in really remote corners of the world where there's bound to be conflict with the local inhabitants as companies rushed in to get their slice of what had turned into a multi-billion-dollar pie. The indigenous people's perfectly understandable opening position is usually: "Fuck off and go somewhere else." They couldn't give a shit that their governments got paid and issued permits to dig up their land, the land they had lived on for centuries, if not millennia.

"So, babe," I said. "Lemme guess: you named Southern Cross Mining in your report."

She nodded her head. In one paragraph, she said, she had described how even one of the 'good guys'—Southern Cross—had apparently switched over to the dark side after decades of respecting and co-operating with local populations wherever they worked.

"I had almost forgotten. It was just one paragraph," she protested. "Not much more than a footnote."

"I gather Hale didn't call you to dispute your description."

"Not all. He claimed he wanted to confirm it—anonymously—with facts."

"But, m'dear, I thought we'd reached some kind of a deal here."

"What kind of deal?"

"The one where you stop hiding shit from me."

"Like you've been doing for years?"

"Yeah, like that. Why didn't you mention Southern Cross earlier?"

She didn't say anything.

"I don't want to be harsh [which of course meant that I was about to be], Alex, but there's a lot of sand around here. Do you really want to stick your head in some and hope like hell it'll all go away? Seems to me that Hale's death and that report are linked."

Pretty evident that Alex didn't take to any form of chastisement particularly well. And I felt like shit reminding her that we had already agreed to get to the bottom of this morass.

So, what do you propose?" she demanded.

"Drop looking into all the other lads you named and focus on Southern. Is it possible for you to find out about their finances, their plans, who owns what, shit like that?"

"They're private, but I can try. And you? More cigarettes and beer?"

"Probably, smart ass. And while I'm doing that, I plan to get a much better understanding of Southern Cross, the people involved and the commodities they're supplying. Somewhere in all this is a motive and the names of some bad people. But first, I want to read that report. Any chance you packed a copy in one of your steamer trunks?"

"As a matter of fact…" she said and with that, went inside the house and came out with a very pro-looking report, glossy, graphic-y cover and all. She slapped it down on the patio table. I thumbed through it and tried to whistle as I hefted it.

"A hundred and thirty-two pages and that's not counting the addenda and footnotes. Looks goddamn impressive."

"It is goddamn impressive," she said. "Probably the most detailed look at those shitty practices ever done. And it's current. That's why a bunch of people and institutions paid $20,000 for the report I just gave you. For free, I might add."

"I'm good for it. Take IOUs?"

"Now if you'll excuse me, I have some homework to do."

I looked at the report. It was late, I was tired and in no condition to read. I needed sleep. I went inside expecting to find Alexandra knee-deep in unravelling corporate mysteries. But she had baled too.

The difference between her and me—among many other things —is that she can go to sleep instantly, regardless of how pre- occupied she may be. When I've got a headful of bees, I don't easily drift off until my wee brain shuts the fuck up. Her soft rhythmic breathing beside me just pissed me off, so I got up, dressed, grabbed a beer and my shitty laptop, and headed back outside, to think about the last four or five hours beginning with my meeting with Matt Kilmer at the sunset ceremony.

In a very short period of time, he had unpacked and presented me with a slew of improbable conspiracies. The biggest, juiciest one was, of course, that Robert Hale's death was the end result of dirty deeds done dearly by the American military courtesy of their USSOCOM outfit based right here in Tampa Bay.

What does Mr. Google say about them, I wondered. SOCOM's own website announces that they're involved in "clandestine activity" ("Hey, everybody! We do secret shit!"). This activity includes a laundry list of neutral-sounding duties: "direct action, counter-terrorism, special reconnaissance, foreign internal defense, unconventional warfare, psychological warfare, civil affairs, and counter-narcotics operations." While quite a few of these jobs could very well produce dead bodies, nowhere did it suggest that one of them was cruising St. Petersburg parks to kill septuagenarian American mining executives.

Yet Kilmer's tale of what really lay behind the simple news story grabbed my interest, mostly because my fallback position on just about every new piece of news and information is raging cynicism. There's always more to just about every story behind the often-misleading headlines.

Meeting Kilmer wasn't serendipity but the fact that I just happened to be twenty miles from the execution site surely was. So too was the fact that Kilmer just happened to remember my name and that he happened to have secret, file-searching pals in Washington who just happened to connect Alexandra to a mess.

A lot of serendipity-do going on, I thought. That made me uneasy. I couldn't shake the feeling that we were being suckered into this weirdness. But by whom and why? A little bit of deductive reasoning gave me an answer: Fuck knows. I gave my head a shake and had a chat with myself.

Who the hell would bother messing with you, Jake?

But on the other hand, Jake, paranoids are sometimes right. There are conspiracies which means there are theories about them. I knew what I meant. I have a few conspiracy theories of my own. For instance, I'm convinced there's a cabal of grocery store workers who deliberately compress those rolls of thin plastic bags in the produce section just so they can laugh like hell as they watch the video camera footage of customers spending ungodly amounts of time licking their fingers trying to open them up. I'm also sure that there's a secret club of white Buick owners whose membership criteria are possession of a goofy hat, a white Buick, and being old enough to have served in the Boer War. These bastards spend their considerable free time by synchronizing their road trips whose only purpose is to make me fucking nuts by driving ten miles an hour slower than the speed limit. But they're cunning sons of bitches. So as not arouse suspicion, one turns off in front of me, but another immediately takes his place.

As absolutely batshit crazy as most conspiracy theories are, you can see their attraction. If your exposure to the planet comes exclusively through the Internet, you can fall down any number of detailed, convincing rabbit holes, like Alice in Wonderland, finding herself in a completely weird new universe with no relation to the world she'd left. But only if you automatically buy the original premise. Religion's like that. If you can swallow Genesis whole or the fact of a loving, merciful God who, for shits and giggles, gives kids cancer and demands worship after creating and watching over an ant farm of a world filled with murderous insects—that he created and could control—then every absurd story and rule becomes unassailable and everything else flows from that.

So's our understanding of government. Somehow, that perception has moved from governments are just big, dumb, and slow to them being crammed with gangs of evil geniuses enlisting hundreds, thousands of mute minions to rig national elections, plot world domination, assassinate fellow citizens and pump micro- chips into vaccines to track us, (even though cell phones already do that). All without a single one of them spilling the beans. Asterix for Russia; they do all that shit—and if you talk about it you die. But we're supposed to thank Christ for the few super-intelligent lone wolves who know the 'truth,' howling from their darkened lairs in basement rec rooms.

I ploughed through Alex's report which was entitled: *Extracting Misery: A critical study of the environmental and societal impact of current mining practises on host countries by foreign entities.* The first page told me the primary authors were Sasha Brownlee and Derek McCutcheon and edited by Alexandra Simpson. Armed with a pad of post-it notes and an almost stunning lack of knowledge about the mining industry, I dug in.

I appreciated the introduction and its explanation that much of the earth-hurting was caused not by the mining itself but by the refining process. Ore of any type is just a big hunk of rock usually packed with a bunch of different minerals. It has to be "boiled down" (and discarded) using different combinations of chemicals and massive amounts of water to get at the itty-bitty bits of the pure mineral that mines were after. It was really expensive to build these refining facilities next to a mine but a hell of a lot cheaper than loading thousands and thousands of tons of raw rocks onto trucks, hauling them down to the nearest port then shipping them somewhere else for refining. Problem was, these makeshift pop-up refineries often weren't adhering to all those nasty environmental rules that look so good on paper. Add to that the increasing popularity of open-pit mining where you just ripped the tops off mountains in an ever-widening circle.

There was nothing really different about mining for rare earth minerals as opposed to other minerals. Except the hunt for rare earths had turned into a frenzy, a quiet frenzy limited to the companies, governments, and miners, but a frenzy, nonetheless. We've all seen this before in other sectors. The dot com bubble of the late 1990s when anybody who had a buck threw it into start-ups selling vapour that would, they assured us, transform them into the next Apple or Google. Or the housing market recently, when prices shot up and everybody ran pell-mell into buying, speculating, and selling. Nobody wants to be left out. With stuff like neodymium, it was the California Gold Rush all over again.

True to its title, the report dealt mainly with the way many of the companies were fucking up the ground, water, and air in their licensed territory—and beyond (because, it turns out, surprise, surprise, poisoned rivers keep on flowing somewhere else and air moves).

And how some of the biggest—and smallest names—in the business were fucking the people they sent into the pits. Death and injury, brutal 12 to 14 hours days. Kids as young as ten were trading their childhood for a pick and shovel, often sent into the narrowest cracks because they're small. All for a buck or two a day. But wait, the companies said, what about all the good we do?

Then comes the bullshit argument that we're creating jobs and wealth for the workers where none had existed previously. That argument failed to mention that they were also creating demand by bringing things to buy and then driving up prices so that nobody ever really got ahead and, instead, became little more than indentured servants.

I finally found the mention of Southern Cross on page 98 in the report. As Alex had said: it was a brief paragraph.

"To further illustrate the almost frantic nature of the high stakes search for rare earth elements, we note the case of Florida-headquartered Southern Cross Mining. For over forty years, the small firm had developed a reputation for respectful, dare we say progressive practices in the remote places they have operated. Over the last few years, they seemed to have abandoned this approach by cutting workers' wages and aggressively and sometimes violently repressing dissent from the indigenous people about their pay and working conditions as they expanded their neodymium mines in Brazil and Vietnam."

In comparison with the other named companies in the report, Southern Cross got off relatively easy. The big boys were making the big messes. Alex and company excoriated them.

A hopeful note was struck near the end of the report by the contention that a growing number of countries were demanding companies either clean up their act or fuck the fuck off.

The report had me considering mining in general, a topic most of us don't really think about all that much. Probably because most of the operations are remote and out of sight.

Mankind has been digging shit up for millennia. And we need them to keep doing that. Keep it in the ground may be a handy slogan but it's a dumb idea. Except for asbestos. That can stay. Even coal, as odious as it may be to most people, will be needed for decades. The arrogance of the west to have gassed the planet then turned around and told developing nations they can't have any of the benefits that fossil-fueled transportation and manufacturing brought to the West over the last 200 years is—or should be —embarrassing.

Mining is one of your tougher jobs, made slightly easier by a union card that brought such things as a decent wage and government safety standards. But you still get to die earlier than most people because of the crap you're inhaling all day and, of course, there's always the possibility of tons of earth landing on your head. As per usual, not driven by the need to report anything to anybody, China took the long view and began cornering the market by aggressively moving into the one place that has most of the rare elements it didn't—Africa. But these elements also exist in lots of other countries.

While the hunt for stuff in the ground is now focused on rare minerals, what it looks like to the local people is the same old- school exploitation, just for a new commodity. Long, unsafe days, shit wages and even shittier wages for the children they often employ, desperate for something, anything. And, golly, look over there; it's a river that will carry away all the nasty stuff we can't use. A universe away from the sanitized and wealthy enclaves of Wall Street or the Florida Gulf Coast. The business overlords never even had to see what their companies actually did. So, the orders get passed down the line, ending up at a pit manager's office.

"Make more money! Right the fuck now. And we really don't care how you do it. Just don't tell us."

And it's not like we can say: "Oh, fuck it. For all the grief this mining causes, we'll just live without." You could do that with diamonds. The world doesn't desperately need diamonds. But without those rare minerals, our cars can't run, our computers won't remember anything, cell phones won't work (and you're back to using tin cans with really, really long pieces of string because every-body junked their wall and desk phones). Everything that needs a magnet, or an LED light needs those minerals.

That's why the new gold had become that group of seventeen rare earth minerals. And every time you have a precious substance worth big money, you get bad things happening around it.

Bad things like pickleballers being gunned down in public parks.

CHAPTER SIX

I read what I could find about Southern Cross Mining. Which wasn't much. A corporate database told me it was established forty-three years earlier in Reading, Pennsylvania. Moved headquarters to Florida in 2021. Private company. Its number of employees and revenue were marked: 'N/A.' CEO John "Jack" Duffy and CFO Robert Hale were the only officers and shareholders listed. Their bios were similarly sketchy. Duffy had a BA in Metallurgy, from the University of Pittsburgh, Hale a degree in Accounting, also from Pitt. So, likely they met at university and remained friends—or, for sure, at least business associates—for about the last half-century.

I found out more about Southern Cross from online mining newsletters and magazines. But again, not a lot more.

Apparently Southern Cross was still a junior mining company after all these years, along with thousands of others. A lot—but not all—of these companies existed as hype machines, grandly crowing about the potential of their latest discovery or their most recent assay report that "uniquely qualified" them to strike it rich.[Sidebar: if every fucking company is 'uniquely qualified,' doesn't that make them all un-unique?].

These publicly traded juniors—so-called penny stocks—are,

were, and will always be favourites among the 'pump and dump' financial lizards who talk up a company's shares by selling the lure of massive payoffs from hitting paydirt. They then sell and fuck off with their winnings long before the stock plummets to the basement from whence it came. It's the white-collar version of old school prospectors, saving them the fuss and muss of grabbing a long-handled shovel, rolling up their sleeves and digging for the fucking stuff.

In contrast, Southern Cross Mining was privately-owned, and they actually mined stuff. They didn't seem to have a specialty, at various times mining for gold, tin, uranium, lithium, copper, and cobalt. Nor did they have a preferred locale, at various times opening mines in Malaysia, South Africa, Indonesia, Uzbekistan, and Peru. And now Brazil and Vietnam.

With that background, I quizzed Alexandra.

"Why did you even talk about Southern Cross in your report? They're not big or public."

"There's a lot of private equity money out there. It hunts for bargains, makes direct contact and, for a percentage of ownership, have made investments in companies like Southern in the past."

"How do you know this?"

"I get paid to know this. All my years in New York, the people I hire, the contacts we make. We hear things, we know things."

"But not 100% confirmed things."

"No, and I make that perfectly clear. It's the beauty of phrases like 'We understand that…' or 'We've heard that…' based on corroborated interviews. People come to trust us when what we understand or have heard turns out to be what actually happened. All we have to do is be right more often that we're wrong. And we are."

"That must be kinda easy with public companies with all the disclosures they have to make."

"You'd think so, but no. Sure, the quarterly statements and shareholder calls and company guidance are helpful but they're not the whole picture. There's a shadow market out there where every-body's looking for an edge, like the way horse bettors search for the inside scoop to find sure things at the track. Papers left behind in a bathroom, overheard conversations in a bar. Or company execs shooting the shit with buddies over golf. That's how business gets done in this business, ahead of when all the info is publicly available. The general population—the day traders, the amateurs—get to bet on the scraps."

"So, what did you hear about Southern Cross?"

"Their name would come up when you scan government records in Malaysia or wherever about who's getting permits and for what. Mining analysts can find that info. Ours came to me kinda surprised."

"Surprised why?"

"She said Southern Cross stood out because they had a habit of filing huge claims for massive areas even though they're small. The more land in your claim, the higher the price of the permits."

"How'd they even get on your radar?"

"I came across them when I was looking at the big, publicly traded players from North America, god, maybe five years ago. Southern were or had been mining near the big boys in Malaysia, Indonesia, and Africa. They're a funny little company. Sure, they were small, but they always had a good rep for dealing with the locals decently."

"Did it pay off for them?

"Not really. You don't fuck around with the royalty payments you owe to the governments that gave you the permits. According to Sasha, who can track those royalties, they're based on the amount of ore you pull out. Southern wasn't reporting huge amounts so they couldn't have been doing that well. For years. But that all changed about two years ago. All of a sudden, they applied to radically expand their mines in Brazil and Vietnam, the only two mines they're really working right now. That costs hundreds of millions. About the same time, they moved to Florida."

"Maybe they hit paydirt somewhere else to pay for their expansion?"

"That's what I thought. But their older mines looked like they were pretty well played out. Sasha told me that their royalty payments were actually going down everywhere which means they were mining less profitably."

"Maybe rising commodity prices made up for it?"

"Some, sure. But not that much."

"Maybe they got new loans?"

"I called Jack Duffy, the CEO, directly about that. He, of course, wouldn't tell me, so I started nosing around. We asked around at the banks. They all said the same thing. Southern Cross was tapped out. Lines of credit maxed. Nobody wanted to lend to them."

"So private investment?"

"Had to be."

Even I knew that private companies are, well, private. They have to report fuck-all. They don't release financial results or even have to have them audited. Until they want to become public by selling shares. Why would owners give up that privacy? They might be looking for more investors to grow their business or, just as likely, they want to enjoy some lifestyle changes after years spent starving and busting their onions.

But first, they usually sniff around before an IPO, get a picture if it's a good time to go after investors, to get maximum bucks for their shares. Same thing done by politicians who think they're hot shit; they'll test the waters when they want to run for higher office. Spoiler alert: they always do.

"So, who could've put up the cash?"

"Dunno. Somebody with deep pockets. Expanding mines is an expensive and time-consuming crapshoot. Governments want their slice because you have to pay bigger royalties. New environmental studies, new assays, new refining facilities to handle the expected increased yield. Bigger workforce. It takes years and hundreds of millions of dollars before a mine is really profitable. All with no guarantee of a bigger pay-out. So, anybody putting new money into Southern Cross had to know it was hugely speculative. With a real chance of losing everything."

"Who takes that risk?"

"Not many firms could, but there are some. Mostly big private equity partnerships or hedge funds like XTR, HDW or Schumberger Capital. They all could probably absorb the possible loss."

"All without the banks?"

"No, no. Once a fund or partnership puts cash into a project, the banks are only too happy to lend them the money for the rest of the project because they have collateral from other assets to put up for loans to the mines that could flame out."

"What's the difference between private equity partnerships and hedge funds?"

"Not much these days. The private guys try to buy big slices of a private company and get involved with running them. Most hedge funds are content to just own shares of public companies. There's no record I could find of any of them owning a slice of Southern Cross."

"Confusing. Why don't I just go have a chat with Jack Duffy, get this all sorted out?"

"He won't tell you anything."

"Oh, he will—once I turn on the Lydon charm."

"Do that and the only thing he'll tell you is to get the fuck out of his office."

CHAPTER SEVEN

I f Duffy wouldn't answer any questions from Alex, I reasoned, he sure the hell wouldn't agree to chat with a stranger off the street. Time for a cover story. I figured being a reporter for a trade magazine might work. I'd used this bullshit trick a few times without a problem. Turns out businesspeople, especially those with small companies like talking about themselves and their companies to journalists for the boost that comes with a little free publicity.

That's as long as you don't act like Mike Wallace chasing a story for *60 Minutes*.

I picked *Engineering & Mining Journal* which seemed to be the authoritative source for the industry. I even read a back issue online. Well, not the whole thing. OK, OK, I skimmed it. They didn't seem to ever get aggressive or confrontational with their subjects. And I invented Lawrence Palmer for the name of their erstwhile reporter because ol' Larry would be untraceable on the Internet.

I called and a pleasant woman told me she'd ask Jack. I offered her my phone number.

"Oh no, dear. He's here; hang on and I'll see."

I wasn't on hold for more than a minute when she returned and asked me if 10 o'clock the next day was acceptable.

After I agreed and hung up, I considered my good luck. No demand to see questions in advance, no pre-screening by a PR agency insisting on knowing what approach I was taking. As a fake reporter in the past, I'd get asked about my 'angle.' I'd answer 'obtuse' (a little geometric humour there) to this question.

The next morning, Alexandra was appalled at my definition of business casual dress. Pretty much the same thing I wore the day before and would again the day after. I pointed out that a) this was laid-back Florida, so my red, hibiscus-heavy Hawaiian shirt was not out of place, and b) smart interview subjects care what reporters write, not how they dress.

It took me a while to find Southern's office in Northwest St. Petersburg. It was in an anonymous four-story building in a business park where it was surrounded by other equally bland buildings amid a sea of massive parking lots. The sporadic palm trees were the only clue that would have distinguished that park from one in, say, Omaha.

I met Marjorie, the receptionist/admin assistant. She looked like her voice sounded. Round, middle-aged with that greying, helmet-like hairstyle and what I took to be a permanent pleasant smile. After I introduced myself, I went to sit down in the small waiting area.

"Oh, no, dear," Marjorie insisted. "Jack will see you right away." I gather there is a breed of old school mining types who could trace their American ancestry back to the Yukon Gold Rush. They just really, really liked digging holes in the ground in an effort to find shit they knew people wanted found. It wasn't a job to them, just as it isn't for aircraft test pilots, mountaineers, or most teachers in their fields. It's an avocation, a calling. In their case, a calling that compels them to look for stuff under the earth that nobody else had discovered.

That's the kind of person I took Jack Duffy to be from the moment I met him in his nondescript ground floor office, its walls covered with contour maps. As he rose from behind his messy desk to welcome me with a hearty handshake, it was hard not to notice he was significantly overweight, but you couldn't miss his thick muscled arms partially hidden under the sleeves of his golf shirt. He was older than me but how much older I couldn't say, over seventy for sure. With a deep, booming voice, he was chock full of loud gregariousness and energy. Topping his ruddy face, his military buzz cut hair was red-blonde flecked with grey. He had piercing grey-blue eyes, surrounded by deep laugh lines cut by years of being in the sun and, I was to discover, by the humour he saw in just about everything.

I thought: give him a white beard and a red cap and suit to match his face and you've got Santa Claus come to life. Or give him a furry vest and a battle-axe and you get a senior-age Viking back from a fresh round of pillaging.

"Nice to meet you, Lawrence!" he said during his bone-crushing handshake across the desk. "Can I call you Larry?"

"Sure," I answered. "Can I call you Johnny?"

"Touché, ya bastard!" he guffawed. "Lawrence, it is."

I liked him right away, even more so when he seemed genuinely embarrassed by the possibility that he was going to be the subject of a feature magazine piece.

"Who the hell wants to hear anything coming out of my goddamned piehole?" he asked in a gruff, rumbling voice, the kind of Kristoffersonian tone that usually comes along with smoking at least two packs a day.

"Well, I for one do," I said. "I came across the adjective 'colourful' used several times to describe you."

"That usually means the guy's a goddamned asshole."

"And that's what I'm here to find out."

He smiled and offered me a Jack and Coke, then smiled again at my acceptance of the early happy hour. You couldn't miss his stiff, deliberate way of moving to the makeshift bar by the window then back again.

Passed the first test, I thought. I understood that a no-bullshit guy like him would instantly see through me and determine that I knew fuck-all about mining. Just keep him talking, Jake. But first, my turn to test him as we sat back in our chairs swirling our generous drinks.

"Mind if I smoke?" I asked.

His eyes lit up. With one hand, he opened a desk drawer and produced a heavy glass ashtray. With the other, he dug out his pack of plain-end Camels from under a pile of papers.

"Goddamned crazy they tell us we can't smoke on our own goddamned property!" he declared, as he slid the ashtray between us.

"We're a dying breed," I said, and he laughed.

"But I'll goddamned well choose how I go!" he vowed.

"Cheers to that!" I agreed, reaching across to clink glasses. With the infallible smoking/drinking connection established,

I had to mention his recently and very permanently retired friend. "Just let me start off by saying I was sorry to hear about the passing of Robert Hale. That was terrible news."

Jack's smile disappeared, replaced by a sorrowful expression. "Bob and I went way back almost fifty years. Spent more goddamned time with him than any of my three wives. Christ, we even bickered like an old married couple, him always trying to slow me down, me working him for a little giddy up. Travelled the goddamn world together, bitching and shit-talking the whole way. And it worked, goddamnit; we worked. We made a good team. He used to say that, together, we were Hale and Foolhardy. He was a goddamned prince of a man. There was this time in Borneo, the first mine we had, when it looked like all hell was gonna break loose…"

Duffy was staring out the window, knee-deep in memories. "They said I was crazy," he continued. "Bob said I was crazy.

Said the goddamned place was crawling with goddamned canni-bals. All bullshit, but it kept you on your goddamned toes. The locals turned out to be great. After I agreed to not go certain places on their land. And it is their goddamned land, no matter what any goddamned government says. A fact that gets forgotten these days. Not just there, but everywhere in the goddamned world."

His reminisces of his friend touched off an apparently unlimited motherlode of great stories. See Jack run. Jack runs on. And on. Oh, god.

I was there for a reason, one that I was tempted to ignore while I got shit-faced listening to his extraordinary tales as he hopscotched around the world, always on the frontier of mineral extraction.

"We went to Chile and got fucked. That was twenty-five—hell, almost thirty years ago. Back then, Chile was producing almost 40% of the world's lithium but the total wasn't much. I figured it was going to be the next oil. We bought our extraction permit, headed out to these huge salt flats where the big boys and the god-damned government were pumping tons of water to produce this brine where the lithium is. They had bought out the surrounding landowners for peanuts after they had poisoned the drinking water with the brine run-off. Then they paid the locals shit money to work while they got rich from the soaring prices. Ever seen a pile of dead flamingos? Just a big pink heap with feathers rippling in the wind. I couldn't do business there, with the government and those big miners doing what they were doing to the land and the people. So, we packed up, sold our claim, took the loss, and got the hell out."

"But still, you were right about lithium taking off."

"I call it lucky. You think anybody really knows how much the demand will be ten, fifteen years from now? Or even what's going to be demanded? Nobody has a goddamned clue. But you have to guess. So, I guess. Want to hear about my smartest move?"

I nodded. I was expecting to be told about a big strike with a big mine.

"Ever hear of tanzanite?" he asked.

"It's a gemstone, isn't it?" I said, exhausting my knowledge of sparkly things.

"Yup, a rare blue stone found only in northern Tanzania at the foot of Mount Kilimanjaro. In an itty-bit strip that's only three miles long by two miles wide. I read somewhere that it could be what's called a one-generation gem, so rare that all of it might be found and dug up in thirty goddamned years."

"So, you thought: 'Why not me?'"

"I did and we did, and we made a goddamned fortune. Then I turned around and lost it right away because I thought I was hot-shit. I ignored the advice I got—for the first and last time—and went looking for bauxite in India. All I found was a shit-kicking," Jack said, laughing. "Haven't touched curry since!"

Listening to this kind of anecdotal shit always fascinates me. Especially about midway through my fourth Jack and Coke, while I was appreciating the hum Keith Richards had operated under for most of his adult life.

I asked him how many employees he had to accomplish this globetrotting.

"Five."

"What?!"

"Me, Bob, Borje Hallstrom, our geologist, Mick Rogers who's the operations guy, and an admin. Marjorie's been with me for about fifteen years; she's the youngster of the group. Before her, it's always been us four."

"How is that even possible?"

"We built a network of subcontractors over the years, people to do all the stuff in the field that needs doing. Hiring and payroll, collecting samples, building the facilities, getting the supplies and equipment, hiring the truckers and shippers. Fixers to see us through the government red tape and translate when I had to deal with the locals. They all work on fee for service plus percentage of the yield. We trust them to get the job done and they trust us to pay them. If things work smoothly and Bob has done the figuring right, we can make us some money."

Here was a true original of a man, I thought. Outsized frame, outsized character, outsized stories, and an outsized view of the world as his personal sandbox—just give him a shovel. All with nary a trace of boastfulness. He talked more about his fuckups than his strikes, where he'd guessed wrong, played bad hunches in wild places, and learned the hard lessons of cutting your losses. His only bitterness seemed reserved for the wilds of Wall Street and the bankers he continually had to satisfy while he was laying it all on the line out in "the real goddamned world."

"Buncha goddamned parasitic worms," he said. "Thank Christ, Bob had to deal with them. He'd just trot me out for an occasional dog and pony for bankers but otherwise, hide me away. Wise decision."

I thought I saw an opening to steer the conversation towards more recent events. When I've been talking to people like this— strangers who have some undetermined connection to a nasty occurrence—when I don't really have a fucking clue what's going on, I've discovered that I have to go with wild guesses and hunches to see what hits and what misses. Sorta like playing Battleship—only about real-life murders.

On the spot, I plucked a name out of the short list Alex had suggested might be a possible investor.

"So, Bob brought in that big investment from HDW? That must've been a great relief."

Ever been to a party when you were a teenager—usually at a friend's place with the parents gone—when things were getting real loud and lively and then someone yells "Cops!"? Well, that was the kind of screeching halt our two-man Jack Daniels party arrived at.

"How would you even know about that?" he more or less demanded. "That was a private deal."

I thought to myself: Well done, Jake. You just sank his battleship with your first shot.

"I know a bunch of people in New York, part of the job," I said. "These days, you don't toss around tens of millions in total secrecy. Just a fact, Jack. I picked up the same rumour from different folks so it looked like it could be true, and, well, you just confirmed it."

"Smart." He smiled. "Goddamnit."

"I'm not going to ask you how much because you won't tell me anyway, right?"

"Goddamned right I won't."

"And I won't mention HDW in the article because you're not going to officially confirm it anyway, right?"

"Goddamned right again," he said, a half-smile returning to his perpetually red face.

"I figured you thought life would be a little easier for you with that cushion. I assumed that was one of the reasons you moved the company from Pennsylvania to Florida. Hell, E&MJ—the ones that are going to publish this piece I'm working on—did the same thing. Went from New York to Jacksonville."

"That so? Probably did it for the same reasons we had. Slow down a bit, play a little golf, stop freezing my ass off in winter."

"All the while, you'd still be in control of Southern Cross' future with its expanded mines."

"That was the goddamned plan. Better weather, cheaper booze and smokes, lower taxes. Turns out, I hate goddamned golf."

"Hear! Hear!" I said, and we clinked glasses again.

"But Bob was happy, and I was good with that," he continued. "God knows, he earned it. I even bought a boat and got interested in deep sea fishing, so it was all OK with me. And then that freak shooting…." Here, his voice trailed off.

"How are things going now?" I asked.

"All my life, everything I've done has been a goddamned challenge. And I like it that way. Christ, I make it that way. But these days, it's a new kind of challenge."

"Which is?"

"Now I have to deal with goddamn experts who think they already know everything there is to know about mining from their office tower in Manhattan. Never spent a goddamn day in the field, never got their goddamn hands dirty, and they're telling me how to do things when I learned the hard way—years ago—it ain't? If that's the world today, they can goddamn well have it!"

"So, you're thinking about quitting the biz?"

"Why would you say that?"

"You sound bitter."

"I'm bitter because I'm goddamned old now. I can't get to the mines like I used to. Christ, I can't sit in a plane for more than an hour because of my goddamned knees. And I'm bitter because this old dog has to learn new tricks. But I'll learn 'em, goddamnit. Jack Duffy doesn't quit."

"I think I have my headline."

"Oh, right, the article. You'll clean up some of my French," he said, more of a demand than a question.

"I'll just say 'Jack Duffy appears to be a 'man of faith.' How's that?"

"Good man!"

There was no way I could ask him for any more detail about his financial dealings or if he knew about Bob being upset about something without blowing my flimsy cover, so there didn't seem to be much more to talk about. I thanked him, unsteadily got up, and was on the receiving end of another bone-crushing handshake.

"Thank you for your time, Jack. I enjoyed this," I said. "Here's my number in case you ever want to get together for another threesome."

He looked at me quizzically.

"Me, you, and the other Jack," I said. "Goddamnit, I just might!"

Even though the tail end of our chat had a somewhat sobering effect, there was no way I could have driven. But I did. Relax, people; it was all of two hundred yards, around the building to the empty far corner of the same parking lot, I lay down on a strip of grass under a palm tree and passed out. For two hours. Tack on another fifteen minutes that I spent smoking and shaking off the Jack Daniels-infused cobwebs and I was some kind of late when I made it back to the Hovel—sorry, beach cottage.

Crawling up Gulf Boulevard, my only regret from the interview (besides the whanging headache in my near future) is that Jack had talked so openly and so nastily about HDW but because I was there under a bullshit premise, I couldn't warn him that his phone—like Robert Hale's—was probably bugged. Unless whoever had gone to the effort of surveilling the office, I wasn't too concerned about them identifying me as the nosy little fucker asking the questions. Let 'em try and find Lawrence Palmer.

So, what had I learned? In addition to the truth of Robin

Williams' observation that "if alcohol is a crutch, then Jack Daniels is the wheelchair," Jack Duffy was a helluva character. He seemed genuine about his grief over the death of his friend and long-time partner and convinced it was a "freak" occurrence, like the cops had said. And equally genuine in his understanding that he had to treat indigenous lands and its people with respect.

Believe it or not, sometimes, I'm occasionally capable of popping my head out of my own ass. Jack's insistence on friendly and reasonable treatment of the peoples he came across in remote areas struck me as really decent. In the early years, Southern Cross wasn't pressured by protesters or compelled by governments to do the obviously right thing. He just did it.

And that was only fair. Around the world, Natives have always been friendly to the invariably white strangers who stumbled upon their shores. You might be tempted to add an asterisk for both Magellan and James Cook, but Magellan was the victim of a poison arrow crossfire between two scrapping tribes while Cook cashed in his circumnavigating chips after he tried to kidnap a Hawaiian chief. Instead, think generally about American Indians keeping the pilgrims alive, or the Inuit trading with, feeding, and trying to teach Arctic whalers from Europe how to survive in one of your shittier climates or the Aztecs welcoming Cortez (what a killer) just before they were wiped out. And in return, the European interlopers repaid them with mirrors, trinkets, devastating diseases, enslavement, and wholesale massacres.

All because humankind has this insatiable urge to discover stuff in the name of "progress." So, electricity gets discovered fifty or a hundred years later than it did, so what? Did you think Edison and Tesla were the only people ever on the planet capable of coming up with it? Or that until the end of time we would only use our fingers and toes to count things, or that we'd always just walk everywhere? And today, you wouldn't miss television streaming or fridges that talked to you because you wouldn't have known they existed.

Jack was real pissed at the "new" challenges he was facing in his sunset years of digging stuff up. It had to be as a result of the investment from HDW which he had confirmed. But why was that a new challenge? He'd been brawling with banks for decades. Except banks didn't normally interfere with how a business is run (unless it's in receivership); they just want their loans repaid and don't much care where the dough comes from. But HDW, that could be different. Who knew how a private hedge fund operated? I sure the fuck didn't.

Time to summon your OCD/Asbergian powers, Jake, and find out.

CHAPTER EIGHT

My initial research took me all the way out to our back patio. Over our customary evening drinks, I quizzed Alexandra about HDW and their field of endeavour.

"Tell me more about hedge funds," I said. "And please, talk baby talk to me."

Turns out, hedge funds had nothing to do with being a way to finance the trimming of cedars as I had previously believed. Alex explained they'd been around since before the crash of '29 (I was just a kid at the time) in some form or other, but they weren't consequential. Their insane growth was a recent phenomenon, something I never had to deal with when I was, laughably perhaps, appointed as Investor Relations Director in my old, old, job. HDW was part of a burgeoning industry. How burgeoning?

Rough estimates said that around five trillion dollars were being held in hedge funds, up from 300 billion only twenty years ago. For size comparison, the entire US economy is twenty trillion. Two-thirds of these companies are in US, but Europe and Asia getting in on the action.

What kind of action? Essentially, the hedge funds attract large pools—lakes really—of moola to invest in whatever. Most of the time it's buying (and reporting) publicly traded stocks available to anybody.

Hedge funds have membership rules, chief of which are: you have pony up at least 100 grand of all that spare money you have lying around, and you can't touch it or pull your money out for at least a year while they fuck around with it. A subsection of that is the SPACs or Special Purchase Acquisition Companies. Essentially, here's their pitch. "We don't own anything yet, but if you give us your money, I'm sure we'll figure out something to buy. Maybe."

All of it relies on a phenomenon, actually two very human traits: People like getting money for doing nothing that requires talent, time, and training (please see 400-billion-dollar annual lottery ticket purchases). There's a second, related human characteristic based on our innate tribalism: people want to join any group that looks like it's making money for doing nothing that requires talent, time, and training.

Call it the Sutter's Mill Principle. The discovery of gold at Sutter's Mill near San Francisco in 1849 led to a frenzy of prospecting. Same thing happened thirty years later near Deadwood when a couple of hundred settlers illegally squatting on native land in the Black Hills of South Dakota swelled to 25,000 almost overnight after the cry of "There's gold in them thar hills!" These gold rushes have happened pretty much everywhere in the world and as far back as ancient Egypt.

While precious few prospectors actually found enough of the equally precious shiny stuff to have made it worth their while, the people who really made money were the ones who outfitted them with all the accoutrements they'd need to feverishly hunt for El Dorado. Mark Twain may or may not have said: "When everybody's digging for gold, it's a good time to be in the pick and shovel business."

In today's world, the pick and shovel businesses have been replaced by hedge funds charging high management fees and big bonuses paid to their managers for using such esoteric "tools" as leverage, short-selling, special asset classes, and derivatives—whatever the fuck they are.

Most of the time, I have a problem with people stating that their chief occupation is investor. Always struck me that's about the same thing as a guy pumping quarters into a Vegas slot machine claiming that what he's really doing is investing in a casino. Same principle. Only the Wall-street types have a really big pile of quarters that they're trying to turn into a much bigger pile of quarters.

Let's make a bet that the Vegas guy doesn't report every penny of his cash winnings to the IRS. The billionaire investor does likewise, only through an army of accountants and lawyers and access to numbered offshore bank accounts and dummy corporations in an effort to protect his 'hard-earned' money from the government. Again, same principle. It's a true fact that companies (and people) who make a shit-ton of money will do everything in their power to resist any attempt to tax that money or limit their ability to make even more money.

High-wealth investors don't exactly strike it rich with hedge funds; ultimately, they perform only a little better as you would if, blindfolded, you threw a dart at a list of stock indexes.

But boy, can you make money producing these so-so returns for your clients. Of the list of top 25 US hedge fund managers—the ones that have to report such things—the lowest paid (poor bastard!) took home $200 million the previous year with the highest earner personally raking in 2 billion (and that's in real money, not Canadian dollars). This has, of course, touched off a mini-Sutter Mill Principle where, all sorts of people in and outside the financial biz have decided that they're now hedge fund managers, much the same way that Icelandic fishermen made the tricky career shift to investment banking right before the world's economy went for a shit in 2008. "Care for some toxic mortgage-backed securities with those herring?"

But, Jake, you cynical son of a bitch, we need investment, we need the stock market to help grow the economy. Sure, except that's like saying the world must have music. That's also true, but that doesn't mean we needed BTS or that Kids for Kars commercial.

Near as I could tell, hedge funds have only flourished because there are a whole lot more rich people than there used to be. Those rich people seek out exclusive ways to get richer, wanting a way to invest in something other than those common icky mutual funds or with stock brokerages that any Joe Schmoe could sign up for.

They simply do not see themselves as any Joe Schmoe. That's why they agree to the rules that automatically disqualify everybody who doesn't have 100K of loose change lying around to fuck around with.

But there is a discreet, hush-hush slice of the pie that's gobbled up by private hedge funds like HDW which pour money into likewise private companies. How big a slice? Fuck knows. And that's the point; they're required to reveal squat to any regulator or pesky reporter.

And that can get messy. How messy? Two words: Bernie Madoff.

"Tell me, Alex, do hedge funds—private ones—get involved in running the companies they invest in?"

"Depends."

"On what?"

"Sometimes it depends on how much they've got invested or what percentage they own."

"What about HDW?" Alex seemed startled.

"Why would you ask about them?"

"I think—no, I know—they've got money in Southern Cross."

"Really? They're the great white whale, more accurately, the great white shark, of hedge funds. Nobody seems to know anything about them, except that they're big."

"How big?"

"That's the idea. No idea. Rumour has it they're invested in all sorts of industries, all through private companies. Defense, communications, logistics, healthcare, pharmaceuticals. But mining. That's a new one. Guy named Harrison Wagner runs it. Used to be a hotshot with Lehman years ago, before they went bust. Quit in '06. Although I heard he got fired for playing fast and loose with clients' money."

"And since?"

"He fell off the radar for a couple of years and then came roaring back with HDW."

"Ever meet him?"

"Once. At a reception after a tech outfit, we were following went public. We chatted for a bit."

"And?"

"He gave me the creeps. Stared at me, complimented me on my dress. That kind of bullshit."

I could imagine Alexandra all gussied up, made up, in heels, hair done. Christ, she was stunning in jeans and a paint-splattered T-shirt.

"Doesn't make him a bad person," I said. "Just means he had eyes."

"Jake, do you not think, after all these years, that I've learned the difference between an innocent appreciation and the look of a pig?"

I thought back to when I first met her in my old, old job about twenty-five years ago. It was at an analyst conference in Boston at Copley Plaza, and she was a rising star with a big Wall Street firm. I distinctly remembered trying to either look away or focus solely on her face while wondering if my drool was apparent. I saw her a year later in Manhattan at a pitch my boss was making for another stock offering. Afterward, she escorted me, arm in arm, to my hotel. I left her at the elevators.

"Hey, babe, do you recall that time when I saw you in New York —what was that?—at least twenty-five years ago?"

"I do," she said, and she blushed.

"So, I gather by your red cheeks, you were intending more than just seeing me to my hotel safely."

"I was," she admitted.

"That's what I thought! I'm surprised you didn't hear me banging my head against the elevator wall all the way to the twelfth floor."

"Yeah, well, I didn't feel too good about it either."

"Sorry for leaving you standing there."

"That wasn't why I felt like hell."

"Huh?"

"I was disgusted with myself. I saw your wedding band and I ignored it. You didn't. Only a pretty good guy does that."

CHAPTER NINE

J ust in time for Christmas, I was pleasantly surprised to get a helluva gift in the mail. It was a cheque from Steve Golding, my writer buddy from Toronto. Well, the cheque was from Stephen Golding Enterprise Inc. for "editorial consulting" on his second best-seller, Beating the House: The Great Casino Heist. We had a deal; he'd give me whatever he thought was "fair" for giving him the inside scoop of my misadventures investigating a giant scheme to defraud tribal casinos. That was the second time he'd paid me for telling him about one of my clown jobs.

I knew the book had done well; I can read (most of) the *NY Times* Book section. But exactly how well was proved to me by the size of the cheque: $150,000.

Alexandra whistled when she saw the cheque. "Friendship has its privilege," she said.

"Even after the Canadian tax man takes his chomp, I can at least help support your extravagant lifestyle for a little while."

I wrote to profusely thank Steve, but stopped short of saying the always-unnecessary thing that his donation to the Jake Lydon Florida Relief Fund wasn't necessary.

He wrote back to tell me, *"Now we're square,"* and that he had quit his job as a crime reporter for the Toronto Sun. He had also decided to quit Toronto for sunnier climes to which I replied: *We're square, bud. Please remember me as one of the little people you stepped over on your ladder to fame and money.*

Who is this? How'd you get this address? was his reply.

I was happy for his success because he had earned it. He saw the potential in those books, did scores of interviews, a ton of research, and he actually wrote the goddamned things. Above all, they were both fine efforts, well-written, lively, and accurate accounts of two of my shitshows in which he had me play the role of a bumbling moron. Like I said: accurate.

Under tough deadlines, he had put in the work to produce a finished product—from endless rounds of revisions to brawling with editors to fact-checking and dealing with an ass-covering legal department. He'd also taken on a successful writer's life after publication, hitting the road for exhausting book tours and interviews plus time-consuming podcasts and Twitter activity. All of which had nothing to do with actually writing books.

Later that night, I got another e-mail from him.

Got anything going on that I could use for the next book?

I wrote back: *Fuck-all. All quiet on the southern front. You might have to actually work now.*

The cheque from Steve and all my wading around in hedge fund lore, got me thinking about money, specifically our desire to get our hands on some. And even more specifically, the reason why some people have a shit-ton more desire to get lots and lots more than the rest of us.

What's it get him or, mercifully to a lesser extent, her? Why, lots of money can buy lots of stuff.

"The guy who dies with the most toys wins." I always liked the justification for this greed because of its exquisite irony. It's a swell saying because that guy with all the toys doesn't know it; he's dead.

Jake, is it really that simple?

Fucking right it is. Why else are you willing to pay 195 million goddamned dollars for a Warhol, a billion smackeroos for a boat (that doesn't even have a basic surface-to-air missile system) or 18 million for a Bugatti La Voiture Noire that you're never going to take to a Wendy's Drive-Thru. You're tickled pink that you've got some one-of-a-kind thing nobody else has, which entitles you to say: "Nyah, nyah to you."

This is dick-flopping on a grand scale. And, for fuck's sake, we cheer them on. Who has the most money? Most expensive house? We keep score, as if it fucking mattered. [Side bar: to their gender's credit, you don't really hear much about women engaging in this juvenile attempt to create grand-scale envy].

Ah, envy, one of the Big Seven. I'm pretty clean as far as committing that Deadly Sin. I'm not jealous of most people, couldn't care less what they earn or have. Besides sunshine, oh, and beer, I'm not really greedy for anything. Looking down the list at the other five, I did all my lusting over my first wife and now Alexandra. Besides being my favourite 'wild' animal, Sloth is the member of the Big Seven that I spend most of my time embodying, although I am a beer and tequila glutton. I also admit to getting me some of that pride (often as a result of making the perfect margarita) and wrath (usually because the Raiders and/or the Maple Leafs fucked up yet another season).

You can't really create envy of material possessions without looking at the things we value. There are over five thousand minerals. That's a lot of different shit in the ground. Why is gold the gold standard for luxury and not, say, manganese? Because centuries ago, everybody nodded their collective heads and said it was. Same reason printed or minted money matters. Because we all agreed that slips of paper depicting dead presidents or living monarchs are worth something and because it's hard to lug around bushels of wheat whenever you want to trade for a goat. Gold is prized mostly because it's pretty, shiny, relatively rare, and because hundreds of thousands of people have died in the quest for it, so it must be valuable. Oh, and it's inert, meaning you won't get skin cancer from it and, bonus: it won't blow up in your face.

[Sidebar: I may very well be the human embodiment of the gold standard. Despite all the activity of recent years, my preference, my natural state, is inertia. Just how lazy am I? Put it this way: I pour the milk for my coffee from as great a height as possible, just so I'm spared the extra effort of stirring. That level of lazy.]

But there are different levels of effort to get valuable things. With some people, it's an obsession, a driving force. Why? Fuck knows. Why do some other people have to have an outstanding butterfly collection above everything, or willingly spend years of their young lives practising figure skating?

Short answer: just cuz.

"It's for you," Alexandra said handing me the phone.

"Hello, Unknown Caller," I said.

"You know me, goddamnit!" said the booming voice.

"Jack! What's up?"

"Still interested in a get-together?"

"Fuckin' right I am," I said. "Glad you called. I need to clear some things up for the article."

"Me too,"

"O-kaaay,"

"What are you doing right now?" he asked.

"Nuthin.'"

"Where are you?"

I gave him the address; he said he'd be there in half an hour and hung up.

I told Alex and, immediately, she started to fuss. But the place was already spotless, the outside manicured to hell, and I had enough beer to get me through the afternoon. I insisted on her sitting with us because she likely knew about the things we'd probably be discussing. But she would have none of it.

"Think, Jake. You want this to go well. I know he read my report; it wasn't exactly complimentary. He called me and yelled a lot, so I'd rather he wasn't pissed the whole time."

"Maybe he won't remember you or make the connection."

"Maybe."

I went back outside to watch for him. A cream-coloured Escalade pulled up and attempted to ease its bulk up our narrow driveway. It wasn't going too well, either for his monster SUV or the corner of my house so I waved him off. He backed out and pulled around to the side street of our corner lot. Jack fought his way through the thriving wall of eight-foot areca palms to join me on the patio.

"Worse than Borneo. Need a goddamned machete!" he roared, as he plunked a big bottle of Coke and his namesake square bottle on the glass tabletop.

I went inside to retrieve glasses and a bowl of ice, coaxed Alexandra out for at least an introduction and to see if he knew who she was. Reluctantly, she agreed.

Gentleman Jack hauled himself upright to shake her hand and invite her to join us. She declined. It was impossible not to notice the expression on his smiling face as he watched her walk away. It was the very definition of what Alex had described as an appreciation of beauty, not the look of a man who wanted to prey upon it. "You sure did alright for yourself, lad," he said to me "Sorta like a goddamned journeyman infielder playing double 'A' ball in Visalia suddenly finding himself in the bigs."

"Not 'sorta like,' Jack. Exactly like that," I said. "I know I hit paydirt."

His ruddy face clouded over at my show-off pandering to his profession.

"Is that about all you know about mining…a few expressions?"

"What do you mean?" I asked, feeling a well of dread about to bubble up and overflow.

"What I mean is: who the Christ are you?"

"Huh?"

"Because you sure as hell ain't a writer for the Engineering and Mining Journal. I called them. They never heard of Lawrence Palmer."

"You're right. They don't know about me yet. I'm writing this article on spec. I was going to send it to them because I was sure they'd publish it."

His expression darkened further. The cheerful, ruddy pie-face had turned into an angry red planet. Then it went sad. "Lawrence," he said. "Or whatever the fuck your name is—I place a lot of stock in getting drunk with a man just to see what there is to see. You goddamned well fooled me."

I felt like shit. Even though he was less than ten years older than me, his look—the penetrating eyes—made me feel the way I used to as a kid when my old man would tell me he was disappointed in me. It hurt.

At that moment, my only option was to find a petard to get hoisted upon.

"I'm the same way, Jack, believe me. I'm sorry about my bull-shit story. I didn't think you'd see me if I told you the real reason."

"Now would be a goddamned great time to tell me what that reason was. Otherwise, we're done here."

I took a deep breath, my mind racing ahead to what to tell him and what to leave out about the outlandish conspiracy theory that had brought me to his door.

"I'm not an American mining reporter," I began. "I'm not even American. My name is Jake Lydon and I'm looking into Robert Hale's death."

"Why?" he asked.

"Because I'm sure it wasn't an accident." That got his attention right quick.

"What? Cops closed the case as a freak stray bullet!" he thundered, angry perhaps at questioning that which he had already accepted as fact, angry at the potential U-turn as he was trying to move on. "What gives you the goddamned right to say different?"

"How about you pour yourself another drink, Jack? I'll get you some more ice and me another beer."

Inside, I asked Alex to look out once in a while to see if I hadn't become a bloody pulp spread out on the patio.

"Looks like he didn't make the connection between you in person and you as a nasty report editor," I pointed out.

I also took a step back to consider the possibility that Jack was in on whatever scheme that called for his friend's whacking. I immediately ruled it out. When I first met him, he had seemed a) genuinely distressed by his friend's death, and b) genuinely uninterested in money, which can be the great motivator that might even lead someone to sacrifice a good buddy.

Duffy had settled down by the time I returned.

Jack took a slug of the other Jack, looked at me, and asked: "You police?"

"No."

"One of those goddamned true crime nuts?"

"Nope."

"So, I'll ask again: who the fuck are you?"

"Jack, I'm going to need you to bear with me. I want to tell you the whole story, but I have to put it together first. I've never described it out loud."

"Then start talking."

I tucked into my gobsmacking tale, beginning with my not-so-random encounter on the beach with a dying ATF retiree who was convinced that a trained sniper had snuffed out Hale from a great distance. I left out Kilmer's name and his batshit suggestion that the US military might've pulled the trigger. I told Jack to google me to see my so-called credentials that had attracted Kilmer to me. A guy like Jack is pretty pragmatic; he would take nothing on faith, so I tossed in news of the forensics report from the fragments that "proved" the high-powered bullet probably came from a pro.

A bushy eyebrow shot up when I spoke of the connection between my Alexandra and his former CFO who was trying to blow a whistle of some kind at her just before he died. I took a side trip to lay out the anonymous intimidation visited upon Alex around the time she was putting together her mining report, and then finished up with the obvious conclusion (to me, anyway) that, with Southern Cross' finances somehow at issue, HDW, their new "white knight" investor, had to be involved.

What followed next couldn't be called a pause, more like an intermission. Near as I could tell, Jack was alternating between reacting to the sucker punch to the gut I'd just delivered and recreating the last twenty-four months since HDW's appearance on his scene for any clues.

"You sure of all this?" he finally and slowly asked.

"Jack, I'm not sure of any of this! Beyond the fact that Robert's dead, he called my lady before, and now someone's been leaning on her."

"So, what do we do?"

"Fuck knows."

"Police?" he suggested.

"Like you said, the St. Pete's cops shut it down; same with the feds, I understand."

"That's goddamn strange."

"A whole other question that needs answering." We sat there for a bit, thinking and drinking. "What do you know about HDW?" I asked.

"Not much. I know they got bags of money but beyond that... like I said before, Bob kept me out of all that. I met a couple of them when they first came in and they just appointed an acting CFO, a snot-nosed kid who I only know through goddamned Zoom calls."

"What's he do?"

"His main goddamned job is being a prick. On my fucking back all the time about expenses, progress reports, projections. He had every scrap of paper, every file Bob had sent to him in New York, and he goes through them like he's studying the Dead Sea scrolls."

"Other than typical bean-counter behaviour, how are things running?"

"Not good. Remember when I was telling you about the network of suppliers and subcontractors? It took us years to find subs we trusted and did good jobs. Well, one by one, goddamned HDW is replacing them. We've got a new international shipping broker, new operational security company, new refiner, and a new worker hiring outfit. We also got a PR company coming. Never had one of those."

"They probably wouldn't have let me walk in the door. The other four any good?"

"They're OK. But they're slower and more goddamned expensive and half the time I don't know what they're doing."

"That must make you crazy."

"Goddamned right it does! And that's not the worst. I got told I have to ask permission to visit either of the mines! Said I was a security risk. It doesn't matter that my goddamned knees don't let me fly; they're my goddamned mines!"

"Why did you even let HDW call those shots?"

"No goddamned choice," Jack growled.

"Maybe it's time you tell me what you got from them and what you had to give up in return."

"Three hundred and fifty million of their own cash," he said without hesitation. "With their pledge to put three hundred ten million of that into expanding the mines in Brazil and Vietnam. They were also going to take out loans, at their risk, for another $300 million. For that, they got forty percent of the company and three seats on what used to be our two-man board. Turns out that even I can figure out that three beats two, not most, but all the time. And with Bob gone, it's four to one."

"With that kinda dough on the table, why didn't you just take the money and run?"

"Can't. Robert and I got 750 thousand each up front, Borje, the geologist, and Mick, the operations guy, got 500K. The rest of it's locked up in trust and we're on salary under a goddamned personal services contract. A good steady salary, but if I leave within five years, I get nuthin' else. Same with the others. And I even had to sign a non-compete clause and an NDA, so I can't just go off and start another mining operation."

"What's 'the rest of it' that's locked up for the next three years?"

"Ten million each for Bob and me. Five million for Mick and Borje."

"What happens with Bob's slice?"

"I asked. Got a one-sentence answer from their goddamned lawyer. Same note they sent to his widow. 'Regretfully, Mr. Hale did not meet the requirements of his services contract with us.' Christ!"

He lapsed into silence again, just stared at his glass. It could've been the Jack Daniels, but more likely Duffy was contemplating how ultimately sad it was to be this far down the line only to find himself trapped by what amounted to a very tempting bribe. Lots of people make that trade every day and are content. But after an outsized lifetime of doing what he wanted where and whenever he wanted to, I didn't take Jack Duffy to be one of those people. And once you think it's an inescapable trap, you can't ever unthink it. So, you either suffer in silence or you do something about it.

"I don't know if I can spend the next three years under goddamned house arrest," Jack said, without taking his eyes of the glass of booze.

"You have any money?"

"Not much. Half that seven fifty went to Wife #3 as a parting gift on her way out the door last year. But I own the condo down on Treasure Island. Well, the goddamned bank owns it. That's about it."

He lapsed into another silence.

"Hey! Maybe I can get a job as a Walmart greeter," he said, ruefully.

"Oh sure, I can see that. "Hello, I'm Jack; welcome to Walmart. Now what the fuck do you want?""

At least, Jack laughed.

"Jack, we gotta do something. We gotta find out what's going on."

"Agreed, goddamnit."

"Do you have any idea what Bob had discovered that made him try to pick up a whistle and blow?"

"None."

"Then we have to start with your financial results. Do you have them?"

"Bob always sent me quarterly statements and loan details. I can read an assay report but not a spreadsheet. Goddamn hieroglyphics to me. But I got them."

"On your computer?"

"And on a memory stick thingy."

"I'd like to see them."

"Why?"

"Look, if HDW is involved, they're trying to hide something. They were worried about what Bob might say, worried about what

Alexandra might find. If it's in the financials, my lady is pretty good at reading stuff like that."

"You're just up the coast from me. I'll drop that memory stick off tomorrow after work."

"Not a good idea. I'm betting they're watching you."

"What!?"

"I think they're really worried. They knew that Bob was thinking about going public—specifically, to Alexandra. That means at the very least they were bugging his phone. So likely yours too."

"Jesus H. Christ!"

"It's gonna be hard for both of us but we have to be careful from here on. Like I keep saying: if HDW is involved, they play rough. They likely had a hand in Bob's death, they're tapping phones, trying to scare off Alexandra, and they probably know that Escalade is parked right here. We can't see each other for a while. And we both have to get burner phones. No calls otherwise."

"How do I get the financials to you?"

"Gimme a minute."

I went inside to my shitty laptop, pulled up a map of Treasure Island.

Back outside, I asked: "Do you know Caddy's down there?"

"Sure. Right around the corner from me. Go there a lot."

"Leave the stick and your new phone number in an envelope for me with the bartender."

"Deal," he said. "His name's Derek. Now, I'd like something from you."

"What?"

"That forensics report."

"Why?"

"Sounds like they did an analysis of the bullet. Depending on how detailed it was, I might be able to find out where it came from. Particularly the steel used in the cartridge, if I can remember my college metallurgy classes."

"They can tell you that? The bits must've been microscopic."

"Guess what they use to look at them."

I had to smile.

"Different locations leave different signatures," he continued.

"Basically, it's the percentage of different minerals in the ore taken out of the ground. Even after refining, there are traces that, in different combinations, tell you the area where it was mined."

"I'll get it; it'll be in the envelope."

"Anything else?" he asked.

"Yeah. That neodymium you're going after, that's all made-up shit like kryptonite, right?"

"You really don't know diddly about minerals, do you?"

Chemistry of any sort falls squarely into my Don't know/Don't care bucket. Other than a middlin' successful 1970s rock/R&B group, Rare Earth didn't mean much to me.

But get Jack talking about mining for them and he will just not shut the fuck up. I was treated to an interminable lecture about how important that obscure hunk of rock was to the world. It was one of seventeen rare earth minerals. It's used to make permanent magnets, stronger than electromagnets that need power to make them keep attracting. A neodymium-boron mix made the strongest magnets on the planet. So, what, you may ask, as I did. Well, depending on the size of the chunk of neodymium, you can light up your cellphone or run a giant wind turbine. They're the reason you can store data on a hard drive. It was a key reason why battery-run cars work, why anything with a battery works.

It's all in the chips. Somebody—with waaay too much time on their hands—estimated that on any given day something like eight trillion micro-processing chips are e-beavering away around the planet—and that we're producing 100 billion of these silicon workaholics a year, giving new meaning to the expression pounding sand.

Many of them don't actually do anything beyond tell you things. They don't make the fridge be a fridge; they just let you know that the water temp in the dispenser is 41 and not 43, as if that fucking matters at all. Or sensors in cars. Never mind that late at night they talk to each other, plotting ways to kill you (beware those smart toasters; they're cunning sons of bitches).

But when the chips are down (nyuk, nyuk) because you can't get your hands on enough of their components like neodymium, you got a problem. You'd have to shut down the robots that assemble cars that, although they aren't long on personality, don't complain about repetitive work, don't ever go on strike or take long lunch breaks. And the vehicles coming off the line? A thousand chips in a gas-powered car and double that in electric ones. Those rare minerals are also the reason why a bunch of those new cars aren't running around. The industrious assholes sawing the catalytic converters off those cars are re-selling them for the three critical minerals inside them.

As a soon-to-be-extinct dinosaur (Lazious Fatfuckasaurus), I am overwhelmed by all of this.

Years ago, an old appliance repair guy—they're all old now—pronounced my ancient, rarely used washing machine as 'finally fucked' (I love it when they talk technical). I asked him what the best type was to replace it.

"The one with the fewest buttons," he answered.

But that's not the way most of the world thinks these days. They want all the buttons. Which means they need neodymium, even if they don't know it.

Jack was pretty goddamn proud about going all in on neodymium years earlier. He had beaten a lot of the "big boys" to the punch because they had built mines and refineries looking for "the goddamned easy stuff" like cobalt, zinc, and lithium. The result was a surplus of this "easy stuff" that drove the price down while the commodity value of neodymium was skyrocketing, just as he had predicted.

Besides expanding my pitiful knowledge base, I had motive, your honour, in acting all keen to know about neodymium. In my vast, vast experience, the more you stay interested and talking, the less drunk you get. Jack was a good guy and pretty valuable to the proceedings. I couldn't stand the idea of losing him in a flaming car wreck on Gulf Boulevard. Luckily, to start with, Jack was one of those big men with a superhuman tolerance. He was clear-eyed as he got up to leave, assuring me it was just a slow, straight shot down Gulf Boulevard to Treasure Island.

"Thanks for helping...and for coming clean," he said, as he gave me one of his patented bone-crushing handshakes.

He had just disappeared through the palm foliage when I had a thought.

"Wait!" I called out.

His face re-appeared through the fronds. "What?"

"Maybe I'm panicking, but it's pretty easy to track the Caddy through GPS, like I said. So, they can find out you parked here but not what you did. In case they're also following your purchases, go down to Keegan's on the corner there and buy two dinners with your company card. Their lot is always full, so you had to park here."

"But I called you."

"If they're listening, they'll recognize my voice as Lawrence Palmer's."

"They'll just trace the number and find the real you, won't they?"

"Yup, but not easily. I've got an unlisted number, so it'll take a while. By then, we'll have the new phones, and it won't matter a lot if they discover Lawrence Palmer is Jake Lydon."

"Got it," he said, and his ruddy face disappeared in the foliage.

"Were you listening?' I asked Alexandra when I went inside.

"Every word."

"Annnnnd...?"

"The deal he described is mostly standard—the non-compete, the services contract, the NDA. What's weird is the power they have over the company with just a 40% minority interest. That stake would normally get you one seat on his board, maybe two. But with this, they run the show. And that ban on visiting the mines is strangest of all. It's obvious they want to keep him in the corner while they're doing whatever the hell they want at the mines."

"Was their three hundred fifty mill well-spent?"

"No idea. Seems high. I'd have to see their balance sheet, revenue projections, and P & L statement."

"I don't get why they would take an experienced mining guy and sit him on the sidelines."

"They'll put their own guy in there—if they haven't already—maybe believing that all these execs are easily replaceable."

I went back outside to smoke and finish my beer, having been banished by Alexandra from the kitchen as she was about to make dinner. In that step-saver kitchen, two's a crowd.

Just then, the palms noisily parted again, and Jack Duffy reappeared with three Styrofoam containers.

"Let's eat, kids!" he announced, sitting back down at the patio table. "And ask Alexandra to join us. Tell her I ain't mad at her anymore."

Alex had overheard and came out to join us. Jack's face exploded in an appreciative grin. While he was doing that, I faded into the vegetation like the 1919 Chicago Black Sox ballplayers melting into the corn in Field of Dreams.

"A pleasure, Ms. Simpson, to see you again," he said. "Sit down! Sit down!" he added, as he pulled a chair out and near to him, like he owned the goddamned place. "Dig in!"

We tucked into our delicious, blackened cod, hand-cut spicy fries, and creamy coleslaw that obviously didn't come from an industrial blender.

"I assume you could hear our conversation," he said to Alex. "Any comments, questions?"

"I'd rather wait to see your financials. I'm sure I'll have quite a few then." And she flashed her killer smile.

"I have some!" I announced, attempting to re-appear from the corn.

The old hound ignored me and continued with his gaze fixed. "Miss Simpson," he began, but she cut him off.

"Alexandra," she said.

"Alexandra," he repeated, savouring the familiarity as much as the Cajun-seasoned fish. "I have to tell you, I wasn't really mad at you when I called. They told me to act like I was."

"Who is 'they', Jack?"

"HDW. That financial punk from New York said that I had to stand up for the company because they were anonymous. He was on the godda—goshdarned call."

It was kinda cute watching Jack try not to curse in front of my lady. Old school. I used to try, but I gave up, mostly because she's got a pretty foul mouth of her own. Alexandra noticed Jack's struggle too.

"You don't have to watch your language around me," she assured him. "I live with this arsehole."

"This arsehole would like to know if HDW has added any more execs recently?" I asked.

"Not beyond the new finance guy, but they said they're lookin.' Said I needed a hand, what with the mines growing."

"So, who's running the show?"

"Mick. He's been pretty much doing that since my goddamn knees gave up."

"What's he tell you?"

"Not much these days. But he sounds a lot less cheerful than he used to when I do talk to him. And he's never around much. Always flying somewhere or wandering through jungle."

"Trust him?"

"With my life."

"What about Borje?"

"The same. Those boys have been with me for more than forty years. And now they're trapped...just like me. Five million apiece if they stay. Best payday they ever saw. And they deserve it; they've busted their humps for decades."

"I need to talk to them...on your burner."

"Why?"

"Frankly, it looks like somebody's keeping you out of the loop, as they say. I need to know what that loop is."

Jack considered my request for a bit. Obviously, I thought, Jack was a proud man, a guy who's sure of what he knows. Shaking that certainty was bound to upset him.

"Talking to Borje's no problem," he said, glumly. "He rarely leaves the office."

"A geologist who doesn't leave Florida. How's that work?"

"He can read an assay report from the hundreds of test holes like nobody's business. He collects information like a mad bastard.

Mostly maps—topographic, contour, vegetation, climate, demo-graphics, satellite imagery of roads and villages, drone foot- age if it exists, historical charts of past mining activity—if any, the yields they had and on and on. But then he shows a talent that I've never seen in my goddamn life. Armed with the test drill info, he sits and thinks and visualizes the whole scene. Not just the possible site but everything for miles around. And then he does this 3D-type of imagining of what's underground. Size and shape of the vein, the rock around it. Real goddamned voodoo shit. It's almost goddamned scary because he's right more often than he's wrong when he recommends a good place to dig."

"So, he says 'X' marks the spot and off you go?"

"No. That's just the start. We sit down with Bob and price the goddamned thing. Mines take years to get going. By talking with Mick who goes to these places, he estimates the cost of building out, the time and labour, shipping gear to god knows where and then we weigh that against the tonnage of the yield and the expected commodity price to come up with a gross profit figure.

Then we gotta minus the expected royalty payments to govern-ments and our contractors to see if it's worth the goshdarned, I mean the goddamned effort."

"And then, Jake," Alexandra piped up, "They have to finance the goddamned project. That means finding lenders who'll take the risk of fronting the money and the reward they can expect for taking that risk."

"Right you are, Alexandra," Jack said. "That's when I bow out and Bob takes...took...over, doing his Wall Street wizardry."

"But HDW has taken all that part away now, haven't they?"

"So what? Bob's dead, goddamnit!" Jack suddenly exploded slamming his hand on the tabletop. Our Styrofoam meal containers jumped—as we did—and I was worried he had cracked the glass.

Alexandra put her hand on his and he quietened down.

"Jack, I promise we'll get to the bottom of this," she said, softly reassuring.

We said our goodbyes and Alex and I went inside. "You were flirting!" I said.

"Was not!" Alex insisted, but she was smiling.

"Giving an old man hope is a cruel, cruel thing to do."

"You didn't seem to mind."

Alexandra is an odd and charming mixture of 1950s femininity and 'How about I bust you one on the chops, asshole.' You simply cannot be that naturally good-looking and not know it. And she uses her attractiveness as a force for good, like she just had soothing Jack. One of the many reasons I love her is that combination. Mess with her and reap the whirlwind. Jesus, I know.

CHAPTER TEN

Things to do, things to do the next morning, chief of which were getting my hands on the forensics report Kilmer talked about that Jack wanted and a (shudder) burner cell phone.

I went looking for Matt, heading south on Gulf towards 11th. Just after 14th St., I spied Bus Bench Bob who had assumed his normal position for a day of observing.

"Bob, how are you?" I asked.

"The answer to that question is of no importance to you as you pose it only as a matter of social convention. I, therefore, respectfully decline to answer."

"Fair enough. Here's one question that is of great importance to me: Any chance you've recently observed that gentleman I was with at the beach the other day? There's half a cigarette in it for you."

"There is no need for the bribery although any charitable donation is always appreciated. I must warn you however, I am not empowered to issue tax receipts."

"So?"

"As it happens, I saw the man in question this morning, as I do most mornings about this time."

Before he had answered, I saw that he had shifted his gaze from the pedestrians and traffic to a young palm tree beside the bench. I realized he was using the tree's shadow as his sundial.

"Where?"

"Oh, I see. A follow-up question, despite the fact you promised one original query."

It was difficult to tell if Bob was just slightly jerking my chain or if he saw life as completely literal.

"The gentleman enters American Grocers and leaves with a large coffee cup. He then proceeds across Gulf on the crosswalk after pushing the warning lights. I must say, given his slow pace of late, I am pleased he uses the crosswalk. I suspect he would not make it to the other side alive any other way."

"Bob, I didn't ask you if he was safety-conscious or not."

"Touché."

Bob fell silent. I lit a cigarette.

"Bob, can I ask you to speculate as to where he goes once, he's on beach side?"

"I am quite sure you are able to ask that question." So, our little word dance was to continue.

"Bob, may I ask you to speculate as to where he goes once, he's on beach side?"

"You may."

"Will you please speculate as to where he goes once, he's on beach side?"

"He continues walking across the parking lot until he disappears between two of those hideous apartment buildings, so I assume he is availing himself of the ramp granting beach access. I further speculate that, once again, given his less than torrid pace, he walks north along the sand until at least 20th. At which point, he returns to Gulf Boulevard and proceeds south, passing me about an hour after first crossing over Gulf.

"Any idea where he might be right now?"

"Also no," he said, patting the palm trunk. "My time piece is not Swiss-precise. I would speculate about half-way on his circuit."

"Thanks, Bob!" I said, extinguishing the cigarette and leaving my offering on the bench. I took off across Gulf, cut down to the beach and looked in both directions as Bob was only speculating. No sign of Kilmer. Did a mental coin toss which pointed me north.

I would be goddamned if I was going to break into a trot. Never mind the ridiculous appearance of an overweight old fuck wearing flip-flops trying to jog in sand. I am firmly anti-exertion. Plus, my cigarette pack would likely flip out of my chest pocket. I figured I could catch up to him using a double-time walk. And I did.

When I called his name, he whirled and crouched lower as if in some defensive pose preparing for an assault.

"Matt, Matt. It's me. Calm down."

"This isn't safe. I told you that," he huffily said.

"I know, but I have to talk to you."

"Make it quick."

"I wanted to tell you that I've got a line on who might be responsible for the sniper attack."

"Who?"

"Can't tell you that yet. I have to be sure, but it's not the American military."

"That's it?"

"Lighten up, boss," I said, not really liking the employer/employee shit he was pulling. "It's progress. And I need to ask a favour. I need the St Petersburg forensic report, particularly the ballistics research that your guy did."

"I'll try but I don't know…"

"Try hard. It could be important." And I turned and fell back.

At the beach cottage, formerly known as the Hovel, I received horrible news. We were going shopping! And worse, shopping for a cell phone—that portable devil's workbench that was destroying Western civilization.

I was predictably sullen standing at the Best Buy glass counter in front of a kid who may or may not have been violating child labour laws. He was blissfully describing all the different features and even the different fucking colours ("My fucking Christ, they've got yellow now!") of the various and multitudinous models in the display case. I cut him short.

"Receive calls, make calls. Send texts, get texts. That's it." My bottom-of-the-barrel request was not received well.

"Then why don't you get one of those cheap burner phones you can buy at a corner store?" he asked, as haughtily as a pimply faced, smartly dressed teenager can be.

"Why don't I, indeed," I answered and turned to go, a pissed-off Alex trailing, leaving behind a techno-apostle spared the insult of dealing with this barbarian at his gate.

"Well, that was fun," she remarked.

The phone I did get at a nearby 7-11—I think it was a Mamsung or maybe a Bapple—did exactly what it said it would, once I translated the "English" instructions into English. That's when it did get fun for Alex as she mercilessly mocked my clumsy and unsuccessful attempts to master this piece of technology. Eventually, she got me able to call her.

At issue were my fat sausage fingers trying to tell the infernal device with its roots in hell to do things, accidentally pushing the tiny buttons on the side so stuff would shut off. These same clumsy digits were incapable of actually composing a text. The gibberish I did "write" looked like it was in code and needing the Enigma machine to decipher it.

I developed a new admiration for the one skill that young people had, and I would never acquire. I had watched fascinated and envious of the ease and speed with which they composed on their phones. Using only their thumbs they could write whole chapters of books in minutes. Of course, those chapters would be chock-a-block with misspellings and devoid of even a rudimentary understanding of grammar, but they would be communicating with each other. Their audiences would also be semi-literate so they too wouldn't notice the massive failure of the public education system.

Two days later, Alex and I wandered out to the patio at 6 AM with our coffee to enjoy some quiet time with the yakking Florida birdlife. We'd have a blessed hour of peace before the Chinese water torture of the thock-thock-thock of the fucking pickleballers across the street from us, along with their squeals and shrieks, began tearing up the morning calm.

There to greet us was a bundle on the patio table. I don't know what I was worried about, but I gingerly unwrapped the old dish towel. There was an elaborate-looking rifle sight and several official-looking sheets with graphs. Accompanying those items was a shakily scrawled note that read:

> Maybe this will help. Doesn't say so, but I'm sure it was a Dragunov-SVD. He used something like this scope. Don't fuck around with it. It's roughly preset to the distance I think it was.

> Matt

I flipped through the forensics report and then took the sight to the street. Peering through it, the backstop of the baseball field at the other end of the block looked like I could reach out and grab the wire mesh.

"What the hell?" Alex asked.

"Looks like ol' Matt has a private collection that he just broke up to get this to us."

"And what's it mean?"

"Mr. Kilmer is obviously an insomniac."

"Anything else, smartass?"

"Yup. It means we're going to the scene of the crime, after we get this report and my new phone number to Jack."

"What are we looking for?"

"I honestly don't know, babe. That's why we look."

Over the past few years, I've taken to re-visiting the places where bad stuff was done—a university parking lot, a murderous wood-chipper deep in a forest, a Dominican apartment awash in blood, the site of a roadside beating death. I never find any solid clues or evidence that the cops overlooked. I don't expect to. What I do invariably get is a better understanding of what went on there, and more importantly, a great visual aid when I'm filming different movies in my wee brain about how things might've happened. But first we drove down Gulf to Treasure Island with our drop-off for Jack. We sat at the bar at Caddy's, ordered drinks, and I asked

Derek, the bartender, if there was a package for Lawrence Palmer. He retrieved a large manila envelope and handed it over to me with a big, conspiratorial grin.

Inside the envelop was a thick sheaf of paper, three years of quarterly financial statements and a memory stick. Alex looked the paper over quickly while I read the hand-scrawled note Jack had included. Along with his secret new phone number, it read:

Give me a day to figure out this goddamned phone.

I showed the note to Alexandra; she laughed. "You'll need way more time than that," she said.

Except for making airline flights, I haven't had to be any- where early in the morning for years. But the next Wednesday, I sprung— well, sauntered—into action at 6:00 to get down to the murder scene before seven, on the day of the week and at the time Bob Hale was murdered. Alex was up and caffeinated, so she had to drive. Without at least three cups in me, I would've killed us both while we were busy being hopelessly lost.

The park is about a mile from the busy, dare I say bustling St. Petersburg's downtown core to the east (although I personally hadn't seen much in the way of bustling in Florida except on its highways). The park's fifty acre-area may not sound like a lot, but you go ahead, pace out any city section by walking seven hundred yards in one direction then taking a left or right and pacing off another three hundred and fifty. Now imagine those twenty-five or thirty square blocks instantly becoming greenspace.

Crescent Lake Park is one of many, many such public spaces in Pinellas County. A shallow lake occupies about half of the park. The rest is taken up by walkways, rolling lawn and lots of Banyan, live oak and palm trees lining and dotting its non-aquatic area. Judging by their height, the trees, and therefore, the park were old. At the south end were the pickleball courts and a big parking lot that we had pulled into.

Just then, a black Nissan Z roared up to the courts and parked in the shade of a Banyan. A trim, white-haired guy got out of what was more likely his grandson's car. If the colony of pickleballers here was anything like the bunch at the courts beside the Hovel—damn, the beach cottage—he was probably a regular. One of their flock had died recently but the game must go on.

I approached the man while Alex hung back a bit.

"Excuse me, sir, I said. "I was wondering if you could help me out."

He looked at me the way most strangers do when I accost them: like I was a panhandler trying to score a butt or some spare change.

He responded with one of the two classic moves these put-upon people use: he pretended he didn't see me; he didn't break stride, kept his eyes straight ahead, and didn't say a word. The other tactic available to him was to stop, quickly and fruitlessly search his pockets, mumble an apology, and move on, content in the knowledge that he at least looked like he wanted to be charitable. This lad didn't even try to appear generous.

"Sir!" I more or less barked as he passed by invisible me. "I need to speak with you about Robert Hale. We have reason to believe you were here that morning he died."

That got his attention right quick. He stopped.

"Yes, I was here...I was....I found him," he said in hushed voice. He was shaking and suddenly looked as though he was about to cry. "It was awful. Bob just lying there. Blood...and stuff...all over."

"I'm sure it was terrible. I know you talked to the police, but—"

"If you're not the cops again, then who are you?"

"Let's just say I'm with the government."

He eyed me skeptically.

"Undercover," I added. "And you can't tell anyone. Seriously, I mean anyone. And I mean seriously."

Even though it's bullshit, I can look and sound pretty threatening. My size, an arched eyebrow, a relentless stare, and a fairly deep voice create the façade that I'm some kind of mean son of a bitch. I've had occasion to milk that fucker for all it's worth, all the while praying that no one calls my bluff.

He nodded with a nervous but sly smile. People love that secret shit. I knew he'd tell his pickle-buddies as soon as we were done, but so what?

"Now, as I was saying...I hope you don't mind going over this again."

"If I can help..."

"Great. Now, what time did you get here on the day of?"

"7:21. I know because I checked my watch as I got out of my car. Bob was always here first, setting up chairs, the coffee machine and so on. I like to get here soon after, to warm up, and maybe give him a hard time about his beloved Phillies before we'd start playing at 7:30 on the dot."

"Anyone else here at that time?"

"No. I saw Lou and JoDee pulling into the parking lot just after me."

"Did you see or hear anything unusual?"

"Not here...well, except for Bob. I thought I heard what sounded like shots, but way up there," he said, pointing across the lake to the far side of the park.

"Where was Mr. Hale when you found him?"

"Over there, behind the baseline," he indicated.

I trotted over to the end of the first row of courts. "Here?" I called.

"No, no. The middle court. You'll see."

I shifted one over. There, the surface directly around the back line was a lighter shade of green paint. Some city employee with a wire brush must have scrubbed the hell out of what would have been a substantial stain.

Standing there, I played a mini-movie in my wee brain. If no one else was there that morning but he was on the court, then Hale must've been lining up for a practice serve. He'd be facing the entire length of the park, completely unaware that a big bullet was about to smash into his face. Just then, I could hear a garbage truck, banging and crashing away across the lake. The noise was getting louder, and I could see the orange truck alongside the park and approaching us. So, I added that sound effect to my short- form documentary.

"That normal?" I asked, pointing towards the noise source.

"Yeah. Same time every Wednesday."

I had an idea. I positioned Alex where I'd been standing, begged her not to move and headed to the car.

"It's a hunch. Please indulge me, babe; this might take a while.

I'll honk the horn twice so you can sit down," I said.

I drove up 5th Street North that ran alongside the east side of the park, passing the orange garbage truck rumbling south. I parked near the corner of 5th and 22nd Ave. which was the northern boundary of the park and stood on the sidewalk with my borrowed scope trained southwest towards the pickleball courts. The trees were thick in that corner of the park; all I could see through Matt's pre-set sight was a blur of green.

No way Kilmer's alleged sniper could have seen his target, and, for that matter, no way he could've set up at street-level without attracting attention. He would've gotten the same kind of unwanted stares had he positioned himself anywhere inside the park at the other end of the lake. Even at that ungodly hour of the morning, its network of walkways was busy, busy with joggers and shufflers. The height of the trees from the roof of a two- or three-story building around there would similarly have blocked out a clear shot.

The cops had apparently found bullet casings just to the east of me in the parking lot behind a small mall facing 4th Street, one street over, so I walked there. Buildings and more foliage obscured the entire park. If the bullet had been random, the result of a gun-fight, as the police told the media, it would have to have been more 'magical' than Oswald's round.

I reckoned the shooter had to be closer. I walked back down 5th past my car and found a break in the trees in front of two small apartment complexes. I picked one and loitered around the locked entrance until I caught the door as a resident was leaving. There was easy access to the flat roof of the three-story building. In the south-west corner, I crouched down behind the half-wall that ringed the flat roof.

I could plainly see Alex through the scope.

I rushed down the stairs to the car, laid on the horn twice, then drove back to the pickleball courts where I found Alexandra sitting on a bench.

"Thanks, sweetie. Do you mind driving while I think?"

Using the police explanation as a shooting script, I tried to make a longer movie in my mind. I imagined a gang member pulling himself out of bed, moseying over to join the rest of his outfit at the parking lot where they come upon another street gang to start a gun battle, all before seven in the morning? Huh? Then they have an exchange of shots that doesn't hit anyone in the con- fined space of a sheltered parking lot? That had to be bullshit. The more likely explanation: it had been a planned diversion by one lone sniper who would've packed up quickly and hurried down to the parking lot where he fired shots randomly around the carpark from at least two handguns he had brought with him.

With that kind of planning, it also meant that picking that time of that day was no accident. The killer had obviously watched Bob Hale for his patterns for quite some time. He had finally selected Wednesday morning to coincide with the regular garbage pick-up schedule. What had Matt Kilmer said about those kinds of rifles?

"Those sumbitches are loud."

The sound of the rifle shot would at least be partially masked by the clanging din from the truck. I then brain-filmed the shooter hurriedly but expertly disassembling his rifle, packing up then rushing down the stairs and out to the street where, at a normal pace, he walked to the empty parking lot. I could see him then popping off some handgun rounds before disappearing, likely walking casually to his car sitting north of the park.

I re-shot and edited my mind-movie. It played.

If I had discovered the shooter's location, why hadn't the police? More than likely, they had and were just not talking about it. But why not? Put your PR hat on, Jake. What would be more unsettling to the public: Warring street gangs that, scarily, we all now accept as usually killing each other or an unidentified but deadly trained sniper on the loose?

We drove home. I was not any clearer about why all this

happened, but dead certain that Matt had been right. Hale's death had resulted from an organized, highly professional hit.

Kilmer was also sure the sniper had used a Russian-made rifle. So, I e-piddled around finding out about the Dragunov-SVD rifle. The weapon was accurate and lethal from distances up to two thirds of a mile. Introduced over sixty years ago, it was, sadly, still in use all around the world in wars the Russian government either started or happily jumped into, to help realize their ambition for empire or maybe just because they're dicks.

Allegedly, all the Dragunovs in the US were accounted for following the 1980s law banning the import of Russian weapons. Could you sneak one in? Of course, you could. Billions of dollars' worth of street drugs find their way to teenagers in basement recrooms all across the country. Could you also sneak a Russian in? Again, yes. That didn't immediately mean the Russians did it, but nor did it disqualify them.

CHAPTER ELEVEN

January started off shitty (for Florida) just as it had the year before, unlike the DR where I had wintered for five years and where it's hot and sunny most of the time.

Even with our new double-pane windows, the Hovel—I mean beach cottage—got downright nippley without the heat on.

Alex was listless. The near-frost nights, low 40s days, and frequent rain were keeping her indoors. She was more serious than usual. But then again, I hadn't spent a lot of time with her when there wasn't much she could do. This restlessness was all foreign to me because when I'm in that situation, I nap.

One chilly rainy night, out of nowhere, Alex asked me a question she knew the answer to.

"Want to go someplace warmer?"

"Why, yes. Yes, I do," I said. "I always do. But you? This time last year it'd have been about minus a shit-ton of degrees in Boston, and you put up with it. This is fucking balmy compared to that."

"This cold is different."

"Whatja have in mind. Mexico? The DR?"

"I was thinking St. Bart's."

"Where the rich pricks hang out?"

"They're not all pricks."

"You've been there before?"

"Yes."

"Oh, really? When?"

There was nothing I could do to make that question sound like it was casually innocent. Mostly because it wasn't. Alexandra and I hadn't spent any time deciphering our respective romantic histories. She knew mine—thirty years married then ten years wandering in a self-pitying and celibate wilderness following Beth's death, before I met up again with Alex. She had been married up until a few years ago, caught in a loveless and childless union with a womanizing cad. What I didn't know was if she had been a manizer as payback. Given her looks, her vitality, and her strong sense of fair's fair, I had self-bet that she got hers. After all, although it was likely a tremendous lapse in judgment, she did try to seduce yours truly way back when. Given the rarefied corporate air she now often breathed, it'd also be a pretty fair wager that she could've very well done her messing around in places like St. Bart's.

It took an intense conversation between me and the bathroom mirror to tamp down the impulse to cry havoc and let loose the dogs of juvenile jealousy:

Jake, can you, just this once, fight the urge to be an asshole?

I'm not sure I can, Jake. I just wanna know!

Fuck, Jake, I hate it when I have to explain the obvious to you: The past is gone and here we all are and she's with you. End of story.

What's wrong with being honest with each other?

That's a bullshit rationalization and you know it. I repeat: END OF STORY, moron!

So, St. Bart's it is, Jake. No questions asked.

"St. Bart's it is!" I announced as I emerged from the bathroom/confessional/telephone booth. "I'll get busy getting us there."

"I'm booking the hotel," Alex quickly said, eager, I assumed, to avoid a repeat of what, in her eyes, had been the Fayetteville Fiasco.

I can't say I was enthusiastic about visiting the Hamptons of the Caribbean. Any wanderlust I may have had in my younger days has been replaced by the stasis of old age. I used to love seeing different places, went to a bunch of them when I was relatively well-off. Back then, I never met an all-inclusive resort that made money off me. We'd always go away for a two-week break (no way seven days were enough to decompress from my job). It took me four days away just to unwind from being hectic, just so I could be more hectic when I got back trying to catch up with all the shit that hadn't got done.

But now, I'm looking for my place in the sun to curl up and doze off. Just like a fat old tabby, only with a beer dynamo hum.

All I knew about St. Bart's was that it's a refuge for the rich. A place where yachts jostle each other in aquamarine harbours while their owners do likewise ashore in tony restaurants, most notably, I was later to find out, at one called Le Toiny, for fuck's sake. I worked myself up to having second thoughts.

"Jesus, Alex, why would I go to a place where I just don't fit in—and don't want to?"

"They'll forgive you your financial situation if you amuse or interest them. Turns out you're amusing and interesting."

"What, sort of like having around a fluffy little chow-chow with its fur dyed purple?"

"Jake, these aren't stupid people. They're interested in brilliant artists regardless of how eccentric they might be."

"I got the eccentric bit nailed."

"And the brilliant artist part too."

"Well, ain't you sweet?"

"You haven't read the book you wrote, have you?"

"Like I said: ain't you sweet?"

"If it makes you feel any better, we can do some shopping for you before we go."

"Whoa! That's not the point. Ol' Hank Thoreau had it right: 'Beware of all enterprises that require new clothes.'"

"Fine. Stay here. I'm going."

"Excuse me while I go pack," I said.

As I always do, I wanted some background on the place I was

about to visit, so I went e-looking. It was first visited by ol' Chris Columbus who didn't hang around—presumably because there weren't any natives to enslave or murder. Europeans left it alone for about a century until the French moved in. They didn't do too much with or to it and didn't exactly prize it as their crown jewel in their Lesser Antilles collection. They couldn't grow a fucking thing there and had to deal with hurricanes and pirate raids from buccaneers with cutesy nicknames like Montbars the Exterminator, so they gave up and swapped it to Sweden of all countries at the end of the 18th Century for trading rights at the port of Gothenburg.

No doubt spurred on by the prospect of finally having a sunny place to escape their goddamned climate, those industrious Swedes colonized the hell out of the place building the port and capital city. It's a little-known fact that an early **IKEA** forerunner was established in Gustavia. That pioneering company would ship entire palm trees to customers along with detailed plans (and, I assumed, an Allen wrench) for the construction and roofing of thatched huts.

[Sidebar: It's a little-known fact only because I just made it up].

[Sidebar to the sidebar: I stole that line from a Peanuts comic].

At any rate, monster hurricanes ruined too many a vacation and, just over a century later, the Swedes sold the island back to France for, I bet, not much more than a bag of croissants and three wheels of cheese that smelled like people's feet.

The island lazed around in the sun for the next hundred years or so until it was "discovered" by the rich and famous in the 1970s. In a very short time, pricey boutique hotels, expensive restaurants, and luxury shops sprung up, along with the island's Gross Domestic Product per capita which now is about the highest in the entire Caribbean.

Around ten thousand permanent residents are spread out over the volcanic, mountainous rock. At eleven by two and a half miles, it's roughly half the size of Manhattan which, for some unfathomable reason, houses more than one and half million souls.

Our trip there turned out to be a true test of nicotine addiction (I failed). Tampa-Miami. Miami-Saint Maarten and then a puddle jumper flight to St. Bart's—although the puddle it jumped was the Caribbean Sea.

Along the way, I was debriefed about the island's vacationing inhabitants. The takeaway from Alex's insider scoop was, once there, the wealthy assume a laid-back attitude, far-removed from doing the busy-busy things that made them wealthy. I wasn't completely convinced because I knew they got to do their laying-back in 2,000-buck-a-night suites, all the while allegedly frowning on ostentation.

The small non-beachside boutique of a hotel that Alex rented didn't cost that much. I, of course, looked it up before we left. But still, for a week, the room alone cost about the same as two weeks in Cuba which included all the food and watered-down drinks you wanted and the flight to get you there.

"How many times have you been there, babe?" I asked as we were approaching Saint Maarten.

"Why?"

"I...I, uh, want to know how reliable your info is."

"Four."

I turned to face the window, figuratively and almost literally to hide my knuckle-gnawing in an attempt to resist the obvious follow-up question: "You don't say. Who with?"

"Twice with my husband," she said to the back of my head. "And twice for business. Half of Wall Street vacations there."

It finally dawned on my wee brain. "That's why we're going there, isn't it?"

"You said you wanted to go someplace nice and warm," she offered.

"That's bullshit, ma dear. There's lots of cheaper, nice warm places. You want to play amateur detective."

"I was afraid you'd get all macho protective on me again."

"Ya got me. Wanna hear my speech?"

"No."

"Fine. I'll bottom line it for you: We have to be careful; these are dangerous people."

Just then we had started our descent into St. Maarten. From my first and only vacation there with Beth—decades ago now—I remembered the final approach over the ocean was almost harrowing as we seemed to barely clear the airport security fence. I also knew it was a dangerous treat for the beach goers on the other side of that fence as some would hurry to the chain link when a big plane landed, just to be bowled over by the hot and powerful exhaust from the jet engines.

But that was nothing compared to our next airborne adventure. The short flight from St. Maarten to St. Bart's was the scariest ten minutes I had ever had flying. We swooped down to the short runway in a 10-seater twin-prop crop duster of a plane over a grassy low hill between two much more substantial hills. We were flying so low I imagined that, in the interest of public safety, there was a sign on the hill forbidding NBA players from standing there. You and the plane you're in start shimmying and shaking from the unpredictably crazy crosswinds. The screech of the brakes the nano-second after you plop down onto the tarmac is alarming, and then you hear the engines instantly cut back to avoid running out of the very short runway and pancaking into a bay that begins about two and a half feet from where the asphalt stops.

I was a tad more frazzled than Alex, the professional traveler. She had to restrain me from pulling a Pope by falling to my knees and smooching the pavement at the bottom of the stairs.

From there, after I'd had a dizzying cigarette or two, a member of the Secret International Order of Taxi Drivers took over, collecting a jaw-dropping fare price for the short drive to our hotel. In every holiday destination I've ever been to, the cabbies take care of themselves. They know you're keen to get to your resort and not really interested in spending your entire one- or two-week vacation in a sweltering airport while you dicker over the piratical fare they demand. You'll pay just about anything to get the fuck out of the terminal/sauna to get to your hotel and start drinking.

I had to concede that our room—hell, it was a spacious suite— was a far cry from the Fayetteville Quality Inn. A whole living room grouping of tropical-patterned rattan furniture, set around a giant TV. A reproduction of a Louis the Something or Other antique desk and tasteful as fuck Gauginish-type artwork on the walls. Sliding floor-to-ceiling glass doors opened onto a wide patio arranged with ornate black French bistro furniture, overlooking the distant blue water of the Caribbean.

The king-sized four-poster bed draped with gauzy white curtains looked small in the bedroom.

The can was almost the size of our entire beach hov—cottage. It had a large shower "room," double sinks, marble vanity, a bidet (but of course) and fluffy white towels 'til hell wouldn't have it. As I was laying out my meds among the collection of more elegantly bottled creams, lotions, and cleansers than I thought existed, I spied a glaring deficiency.

"So, what do you think?" Alex asked.

"Pretty darned nice, except for that!" I answered, pointing at the toilet.

"What?"

"No paper band across the toilet seat like yer classier motels have!"

"You, sir, are an arsehole."

"Seriously, Alex. Outstanding choice. But they're going to catch me; they'll find out I don't belong here and give me le boot."

"I'd tell you to just act normal, but that wouldn't help."

"So, what's the plan, Sherlock?"

"Well, first, we change and go to the pool where I'm pretty sure there's a pina colada with my name on it."

"Good—no—great plan!"

We took the flagstone walkway that connected to our patio and meandered its way to the pool area. Of course, it was of the infinity variety and of course, the deck furniture was made up of dark teak padded loungers and chairs (not white plastic). Sharply dressed servers waited upon their lazing guests and no one spoke above a whisper.

"Shit, I forgot my wallet," I said.

"Jake, Jake, Jake. We charge the room here."

"Another difference from the Quality Inn."

It takes me all of two to three minutes to slip into vacation mode after the ever-frazzling travel is done—mostly because I've been on vacation for about fifteen years, despite altogether too many attempts on my life. Alex tried to relax. I know she did. But about halfway through her giant piña colada I spotted her 'tell.' At the end of one of them beautiful long legs of hers, a foot would get to tapping, signalling that she was anxious to do something, anything. Friggin' Type 'A's, I thought. I waited.

"I was thinking that we should go to the tennis club for dinner," she finally said. "Lots of money people there."

"Sure. Another drink?" I asked, trying to get her to chill out a bit. I was thirsty. My beer glass was empty of that reticent but insouciant little pilsner from Alsace-Wherever the Fuck. Oh, who were they trying to kid? If this hotel wanted to be top-notch, they'd be serving Molson Ex. But I make allowances when I'm south to stick with beer, any beer, oh and gin and tonics. My glass, cup, bottle, or can is always empty before any drink with a fucking paper umbrella.

So, I had two more and Alex did have another coconut concoction before we had to "dress for dinner," for Christ's sake.

After our joint shower, I made one last attempt to calm her down. That involved hijinks and monkey shines—with a few shenanigans thrown in—on the king-sized bed. I was mellow as hell and she was too, judging from her contented expression. Or maybe it was boredom.

The St. Bart's Tennis Club was nearby, and we were way early for our reservation, so we made our way to the busy bar overlooking the sprawl of at least 1,025 tennis courts, some hard surface, some grass, some clay. The joint was not exactly a dive bar but nor did it exude snootiness. A good proportion of the drinking crowd wore white tennis duds, and their sneakers emitted those tell-tale squeaks on the parquet floors. I knifed my way through the crowd to get us drinks at the long bar while Alex scooped up a table by the door.

We sipped away in relative silence and studied our fellow drinkers. As unobtrusively as she could, Alex pointed out seven or eight men whose names meant less than nothing to me. Apparently, they were grande fromage on Wall Street. She acknowledged three more with slight waves and two others made their way to our table where Alex rose and exchanged air kisses. To her credit, Alex at least made the effort to introduce me and note that I was a novelist. Not that that made a bit of difference to them as they solely focused on her and suggested they absolutely must catch up. I felt like a Christmas tree ornament, and not a nice one either, but one of those shitty-looking hand-made jobbies that every year you hide towards the back of the tree.

I was working myself up to another of my world-famous angry, jealous, child pouts when Alex reached under the table and grabbed then squeezed my upper thigh which went a long way to dissipating my petulance.

"Relax, babe," she whispered. "I'm with you and I'm just on the job."

I settled the fuck down and we decided to cancel dinner in the restaurant and order bar food instead as it looked like there was a field of opportunity for our sleuthing effort right where we were. I went back to banker-watching and searching for commonalities among the dozen or so people she signalled she knew. Tall, short, fat, thin, young, old. They only shared two traits: they were men, and they were gosh-darned happy to see my woman.

Except one guy. I noticed him early on, sitting alone and staring at us. I glanced over several times, and he was still staring with an expression that screamed distaste at us for even being there.

"Alex, don't look, but there's a guy sorta behind me, at 4 o'clock to my right, who's been staring at us since we got here. Know him?"

I waited, looking elsewhere.

"Don't recognize him but he sure looks sour," she concluded.

"Excuse me. I have to go to the can. Sorry, le pissoir," I said, rising with my nearly full mug of beer.

"Jake, what are you doing?"

"I'm on the job too."

I picked my way through the crowded tables, ostensibly heading for the bathrooms. As I approached him, he looked away. That's when I tripped over a chair leg at the table in front of his and—very sadly—managed to fling half my beer onto his chest.

Not very pleased would be somewhat of an understatement to

describe his reaction. He sputtered and growled. I'll admit to maybe worsening the situation by attempting to furiously dab away at the beer with the shirttail of my Hawaiian as I apologized. "Holy fuck, buddy! I am so sorry! Goddamned clumsy of me!"

I insisted as he grabbed for some napkins.

He fought me off.

"Say, I know you, don't I?" I said.

"I am sure you don't," he said, angrily.

"No, no. I do know you! You're the fucker that's been staring at me and my date like someone's waving a turd under your nose," I said, pulling an empty chair out and sitting down. "Care to explain?"

"I don't have to explain anything to you."

"Au contraire, mon frere. I've got about a third of a beer left and after that, a pretty heavy mug that suggest otherwise."

"You are a psycho."

"Might want to bear that fact in mind as I wait for you outside." Here's the thing. I'm pretty well the opposite of tough. But I can get angry. Combined with my 6-foot, 220-pound size, I can sometimes sway a discussion without speaking.

He sized me up, I think for the first time, and I could almost feel the fight draining out of him.

"Alright, alright," he said in a normal voice. "Some time ago, Miss Simpson's firm and our firm did some business together. The results weren't satisfactory."

"Care to mosey on over to our table so you and Miss Simpson can hash this out?"

"No."

"How about a card? Ms. Simpson tries to emphasize customer service."

He produced a slightly soggy business card from his pocket. "Well, Mr. Glen St. Charles, Senior Vice President of Operations,

White Iron Group," I said reading off the card. "This has been my pleasure. Hopefully, we can hang out again."

I heard him say "I expect we will, Mr. Lydon," as I turned and left.

Back at our table, Alex looked disturbed. "Jake, what the fuck did you just do?"

"Sorry, honey. I know you meant to say: "Congratulations on making a contact" but it came out "Jake, what the fuck did you just do?" All I did was share a beer with him. He said he knows you."

I slid the dampened business card over to her.

"You just poured beer on the Senior Vice President of White Iron."

"Apparently."

"Well done. He's a dick."

"Oh, do go on."

Alex explained that White Iron Group was a very large, very private military contractor which, at one point, had more personnel in Iraq than the US government. I had heard the name before but knew little about them.

"What, like a private army?"

"No, no," she said. "They provide all the services the military needs, but they don't do any fighting. They run the cafeterias, maintain the vehicles, procure local supplies, interpreters, medical personnel, base security, a thousand different things. Same stuff they do in the US, at airports, prisons. They hired us to do an audit of their environmental and social impact overseas. Burn pits, wastage, treatment of the locals, stuff like that."

"Why the hell would they hire you? They were just asking for a shit-kicking."

"Some companies genuinely want to clean up their act. They want an outside voice telling them how. And some companies try to fool us and hope to get a stamp of approval so they can brag about it to shareholders."

"Oh, let me guess which category White Iron fell into."

"Yup. And they didn't like the results. But we published them anyway."

"That's kinda pricky of you."

"No. It's the way we choose to operate. It was right there in the contract. They agreed, even though we couldn't have been clearer that there was a risk by hiring us. We reserved the right to go public with whatever we found if they weren't up to scratch. And they weren't. Not by a longshot. American taxpayers had a right to know. They tried everything to stop us. Patriot Act, lawsuits. We won. There was a huge stink."

"Now that you mention it, I remember reading about that aroma. Looks like they're not over it yet."

"I understand it cost them a fortune because Congressional oversight demanded they make changes or lose their contracts. There were public hearings, televised."

"Well, that helps explain the Icy Death Stare. Except for one thing."

"What's that?"

"How'd he know my name? I didn't tell him." Alexandra was dumbfounded. And looked nervous. What a coincidence. I was too.

CHAPTER TWELVE

I s St. Bart's somehow better than other Caribbean islands? Same turquoise water, same weather, same hilly landscape (asterisk for the dead-flat Bahamas, Caymans, and Turks & Caicos), same palm trees, same warm-hearted locals, and the same blazingly blue sky. What you won't find is poverty, time-share salesmen, casinos, beach vendors, cruise ships, American fast-food chains, litter, garish advertising, or crime. Except for the poverty, Cuba didn't have any of those things either.

Another thing you won't find in Cuba but do on St. Bart's— besides a Kardashian or two—was unabashed luxury. The distinguishing feature of the island was the sheer volume of money flowing down the quaint as hell cobblestone streets of Gustavia, the island's capital. All the commercial establishments seemed to be high-end. With few exceptions all the hotels and restaurants were five-star. The shops were geared to those visitors who, after a gruelling day at the beach, are seized by the desire to spend five thousand dollars for a goddamned purse or a thousand bucks for a goddamned scarf. Without checking into it, I figured there weren't too many Dollaramas and likely no Walmart on the island.

Instead, there was a definite French air of très chic about the place, (or as we say in English: très chic), seeping over from its mother country. It gave the atmosphere on St. Bart's a certain je ne sais quoi (or as we say in English je ne sais quoi).

We spent the next day mostly lounging in this Gallic charm. I did, anyway. Alex decided on a long walk. I looked at all them surrounding hills and valleys and determined it was going to be a hike, so, being fervently anti-hike, I passed. We decided to return to the tennis club that evening as it seemed like promising hunting grounds to root around in for tidbits about HDW.

The joint was as busy as it was the night before, the atmosphere as lively too. That happens when everybody seems to know everybody else.

A guy approached our table just after Alexandra went off for a bout of kissy face with her old financial acquaintances who had not been forgotten. He was in his fifties, fit and trim as the overwhelming number of guests appeared to be.

"Mind if I sit down?" he asked as he sat down. He introduced himself as Lloyd, just Lloyd. "First time on the island?" he asked.

"It shows, does it?"

"I thought so. We're really just a small little community here. I wanted to welcome you."

I thanked him but was starting to feel like Rosemary being embraced by her devilish fellow tenants in the building.

"What do you do?" he asked.

"The minimum allowable. And you?" I said, even though I gave roughly the same number of fucks learning about his occupation as he did about of mine.

"A bit of commercial banking in New York. Enjoying yourself?"

"I suppose. Wouldn't have been my first choice."

"Why are you here then?"

"Turns out, my partner really has a clear idea about how she wants to vacation."

"Ah, yes. Alexandra Simpson, isn't it?"

"Yeah. How'd you know?"

"I've met her before, and I saw her come in with you. I gather she's paying the shot."

"Tell me," I said, becoming instantly pissed-off (that he was being accurate was beside the point). "Do you have any fucking idea at all why our financial arrangement would matter to you enough to say something snotty about it out loud? Or is it only because you're a compulsive dick?"

In my years in the corporate world, I became familiar with guys like this. For reasons I hope I never want to explore, they feel this need to immediately establish themselves as the #1 pecker in the order by saying asshole things meant to demean their new acquaintances.

Now watch for it, Jake, I thought, he's about to insincerely apologize.

"I sincerely apologize," he said. "I didn't mean to offend you. Here, let me make it up it you. A bunch of us are sailing to St. Maarten tomorrow for a round. You should join us."

"Long way to go for drinks."

"I meant a round of golf. There's not enough territory for a golf course on this island. Do you play?"

"No."

"How unfortunate for you."

"Not if you think it's one of the dumbest games in the world."

"Do you enjoy any sport?" he asked, gazing at my beer paunch.

"I played a little tennis, but the old grey knees ain't what they used to be."

"Then we must play day after tomorrow!" he announced. "Shall we say 9 o'clock, here?"

"We shall."

I hadn't planned or packed for anything that called for exertion on St. Barts. Consequently, I admit that my sports ensemble was perhaps a little slap-dash. My footwear consisted of my Smetchers, a cheap knock-off to replace my flip-flops when I was forced to walk any kind of distance, topped off by predominantly lime-green floral bathing trunks, and my favourite black Rolling Stones t-shirt featuring The Tongue with a fractured Canadian red maple leaf flag as background to mark the occasion of their last Canuck appearance.

[Sidebar: 70,000 of my closest friends went to that concert and all I got was this lousy T-shirt].

[Sidebar to the sidebar: I've been offered up to 200 bucks for it by strangers on a beach, in a bar, almost wherever I am. I've been mightily tempted, understanding that Sir Mick would likely approve of my cash grab].

After he got over my garb, (fighting the urge to compliment me on my eccentricity, I bet), we trotted out to the courts that remained virtually empty. Well, he trotted; I strolled. I took my time because I knew he'd be engaged in elaborate warm-up and stretching exercises to guarantee peak athletic performance. Me, I was conserving my resources.

After about two and half minutes of volleying, during which he proved to be a dink and dunk hitter whereas I like to just whale away, he shouted: "Let's play! I'll serve first!"

Guys like that aren't interested in the fun of just hitting, where you play shots that are out, return double bounces, and never dream about keeping score or serving. No, they want official games with winners and losers. The sport doesn't interest them, crushing the competition does.

Mercifully, he had a wimpy serve that, even for me, with a shitty clubhouse rental racket, was pretty easy to jump all over. I, on the other hand, could sometimes muster a slice serve that puts an ungodly spin on the ball when it hits the asphalt just right. Lucky little fucker that I am, I did a shit-ton of mustering that day and never lost serve.

Improbably perhaps, I kicked his ass. And I did it quickly, what with his anemic serves and my acing the fuck out of him when I served. True fact: I have to confess that I absolutely loved the feeling of resurrecting that adrenaline rush that comes from competing, made doubly satisfying by clobbering a dickwad.

I knew it was over when he started trying to live up to the old saying "If you ain't cheating, you ain't trying." He'd call my shots out when they were indisputably good or claim he wasn't ready after whiffing on a serve. I was actually polite at first, letting the big baby win his point, but I soon tired of caving in and went all McEnroe on him.

My shouts of "Bullshit!" and "Liar!" got the attention of glaring players on the adjacent courts.

With me up 6-1, 6-2 and him trailing 4-0 in the third set, the match was called on account of equipment failure. Specifically, his thousand-dollar racket failed to withstand the beating it took against the backstop fence post as he flailed away at it in anger.

Sportsman that I am, I jogged to the net, with a really big smile on my gob, to shake hands. In response, he turned his back and stalked off the court.

I ruled out meeting him in the clubhouse for a friendly beer and took a cab back to the hotel.

Alex wanted to know how it went. "Fucking wonderful! The best!" "Did you find anything out?"

"Yeah. Some people really, really hate to lose. Beyond that, no. Ol' Lloyd was too busy punching his ticket to Poutyville while I was kicking his preppie ass."

"Do you really have to go out of your way to seem like a boorish lout?"

Her question instantly annoyed me, both for its phrasing and its intent.

"'Boorish lout?' Where are we? In the middle of a fucking snotty Jane Austen novel? But to answer you: it's not out of my way at all. I just don't feel the need to appear polite to someone who isn't."

"Maybe it would be for the best if I did the questioning by myself."

"Agreed. Fill yer boots."

Facing the unlikelihood of a future tennis partner and now—wisely—not being allowed to mix with polite society, I went along with a temporary house arrest. Hey, it was a great house.

Her condescending question had really bugged me, a) because it was from her and her opinion of me mattered where everyone else's does not, and b) she was right; I could've made some small effort to be friendly and fit in. I also, in a way, felt for her. She had one gorgeous leg in both tribal camps: on one hand, she moved smoothly among the rich but on the other, she could dress down and curse and drink like a sailor.

During my exile off Wall Street south, I didn't have much to do and—as usual—I did it expertly and happily. Reading, jotting down notes for my book, thinking, staring at hibiscus. It was a full day. In no time, I established myself as a fixture around the hotel swimming pool, the equivalent of a scruffy mongrel stray that people tolerated around the property and eventually would occasionally scratch behind its ear.

Alex joined me in the afternoons in tropical idleness. She apologized for her to-the-manner-born behaviour while I had said I was sorry for being a classless arsehole. She had kept busy by 'accidentally' running across a slew of financial types; call her a spy in the House of Money. That's when I would spring (well, shuffle) into action, assembling the snippets of conversations, rumours, conjecture, and speculation she gathered.

The nexus for her biz-snooping was the tennis club where I'd made a spectacle of myself. She told me that the place was misnamed and should've been called a tavern. The courts went largely unused after noon, but the bar was full.

"By the way, you made quite the impression at the club," she noted.

"I try," I said. "Did that fucking asshole happen to mention I laid a beatdown on him?"

"That fucking asshole manages a billion-dollar fund at Wells Fargo. He says you cheated."

"But, of course, you defended my honour."

"Nope," she said with a smile. "I didn't argue because, in between bragging about how smart and rich he is, he turned out to be a wealth of information."

One of the first things I had noticed of my trips south was the openness of strangers on holiday. Relaxed, probably drunk, and expecting to never see you again, they would tell you shit they probably would never reveal to friends or co-workers. Once, when talking about the difference between my suburban upbringing and his childhood spent on a farm in Ohio, this guy confessed—and I swear this is true—to having had sex with a chicken. Apparently, the St. Bart's tennis club was an upscale version of that, although, to be fair, no barnyard bestiality claims had been made. At least not to me.

"So, what'd you find out?" I asked.

"For starters, he and that White Iron VP, who was the object of your beer-spilling affection the other night, came down here together for a holiday with their wives. And they have a mutual interest in an object of our disaffection: HDW."

"No shit? How?"

"HDW has money in White Iron and also does some banking with Wells-Fargo."

I had thought to bring a clean pad of post-it notes and soon one wall of our tasteful room was festooned with jottings, the way my hovel-by-the-lake would look when I was on a usually pointless research jag. But it was organized festooning based on the info provided by my sore loser of a tennis partner combined with stuff we already knew. At about eye level on one wall, a single sticky held the HDW name. Spread out in a line below were the names of what we thought were its major investments or subsidiaries and their business type, like "Orca Services—healthcare." And below that, the suspected subsidiaries of their subsidiaries.

I recognized that this was the hazy time of the hunt. Disparate pieces piled up but were out of focus like the shitty vacation photos that friends show you. It was the time when you started to lean towards possibilities, temporarily discarding or setting aside improbabilities. As a research analyst by trade and inclination, Alex was the perfect partner for trying to wrap our pea brains around the web of HDW's corporate empire. She had heard of almost every company she dug up, knew something about their industry and their major publicly traded competition.

The problem of course, was the reliability of anything she

heard. Did she just corroborate a rumour from different sources or was it the same rumour repeated by a different guy in the small universe of rich pricks vacationing on St. Bart's? When did HDW own a piece of them? Did they sell off? What percentage interest did they have in them? We really didn't have a fucking clue.

I had an idea. Of course, I didn't remember his burner phone number, so I had to call Southern Cross and ask Marjorie to put me through to Jack Duffy. All the while, I was thinking about how to phrase things, believing as I did, that his phones were likely tapped, or his office bugged.

"Hi, Jack."

"Don't ever say that to me on a plane, Ly-Palmer, you son of a bitch!" he boomed. "What the hell are you doing at Le Point Hotel and where the Christ is Le Point Hotel?"

I explained that I needed a break from the colder weather but mostly from the drunken Florida riffraff I'd been hanging around lately.

"Funny."

"Jack, do you remember when we talked about how you were re-building your network of suppliers and subcontractors?"

"Sure."

I started to make that static-y sound. "Sorr...Ja... we...brea....up."

He got the hint and hung up.

A few minutes later the phone rang in the room. Duffy assured me he was on his burner and outside.

"Now, what the hell do you want to know about those four?"

"For starters, their names."

He rattled off the list: Pretoria Mine Construction and Management, Goal2Go Security, Olrud Transportation Logistics, Darien Global Personnel.

"Any commonalities you noticed?" I asked.

"They're all goddamned expensive and snotty. I can't stand either feature."

"Anything else?"

"No, except that HDW was hell-bent on them working for Southern."

After I got off, I told Alexandra about the new arrangements.

She guessed that HDW must have considerable money in all four new suppliers. I imagined HDW's conversation with Jack Duffy. "Yeah, Jack, we know you already have a security company, but from now on, you're going to employ Goal2Go. Yeah, you did have a shipping and logistics outfit, but meet Olrud, your new supplier. And we're also happy to introduce Pretoria, your new brand-mine construction and machinery provider. Oh, and hey, Jack, we know you've had no problem getting workers through local companies but, lookee here, Darien Global will now be hiring for you. Isn't that wonderful?"

In bullshit financial business lingo, that's known as "vertical integration." It's really just a way to get one of your companies to goose the bottom line of one or more of your other companies, regardless of price or quality, by forcing them to buy the goods and services from them that they had to buy anyway.

Here's a comparison, although it's hugely improbable. Say a president insisted that foreign diplomats stay at hotels and play at golf courses that he coincidentally happened to own. And further, this hypothetical president mandated that his large security detail must pay inflated rates to watch over him when he stayed at his own properties and played golf—a lotta of golf—at his own courses. Crazy, I know, but you get the idea.

I'm Olympic-level when it comes to the search for periods of uninterrupted sloth. But only for a while. Because my wee brain never shuts the fuck up, I always get itchy to read or watch something to cram that wee brain with even more useless shit to think about.

While Alex was out doing real field work in our crusade, I had the time and the most excellent Internet service to search for the e-rabbit holes that interested me, even if only for a minute. I had an idea that Alexandra was something of a celebrity in the financial world. I googled her name and in .49 seconds I was delivered 12 million results.

I decided to narrow it down to 'news' and Greenvest, her company, and watched, mightily impressed with the slew of news stories with her name in them. I knew she had gained some deserved fame for her smarts and dedication but was only just coming to understand how well-regarded she was in investment circles. And she was not all talk; things happened when she put her exceedingly smart mind to it.

There was a clot of stories from four years ago about her involvement in White Iron's Congressional Hearing. Alex had touched off that inquiry with her scathing report on White Iron's practices in Iraq. I read a couple and was reminded of the casual interest I had had in the hearings at the time. Beyond the stories, there was video, days' worth, on good ol' C-Span.

Not that it was gripping television. I hit the first clip and saw the usual set up: the long line of tables with the long line of executives from White Iron facing the raised horseshoe of Congress members, with the media people forming a DMZ between them, crouched, or lying down snapping and filming away. The execs were all dressed in the same uniform—dark blue suits, white shirts, conservative ties. They were all older white guys. And all six or seven of them had been coached, I'm sure, to sit up straight, don't fiddle with anything, don't wear anything but a serious and confident expression. For all the world, they looked like the answer to the question: what happened to the early 1960s' vocal groups? You know the ones—identically-dressed—that lip-synced their harmonized performances on TV shows while playing instruments that weren't plugged into anything.

In the Congressional hearing room, however, the difference was that the execs were there as a show of force, mute and motionless in front of their large, tented name cards, while the singer, the only singer, was White Iron CEO Trevor Symes. He took all the questions, never involved any of his band members that I saw. He did, from time to time, turn around and consult with what I presumed was his regiment of lawyers.

The questions and grandstanding from both sides of the aisle were entirely predictable, the essence of which was either White

Iron were murderous war-pigs or a shining credit to the nation and the flag.

Symes wasn't exactly brash, but, in his opening statement, he was completely unapologetic, proud to serve his country, viewing himself as absolutely indispensable to the war effort that did not or could not commit the resources to doing the job his company shouldered. White Iron had done nothing wrong and, even if it had, they were owed the same immunity as the regular military fighting a war where the rules are different.

I turned it off after about ten minutes as the answers to either side from Symes were short, non-responsive, and maddening.

"Getting bored just sitting around the pool all day?" Alex asked, after she returned from one of her sorties.

"Fuck, no. I'm getting into the swing of this kept man routine. How about we extend our little vacay for, I dunno, a year or two? Your treat."

"I'm thinking you need a change of pace. How about New York in February?"

"That's a hard pass."

"I thought so. I'm going."

"What?!"

"I've got a meeting there…with Harrison Wagner."

"The Chairman of HDW? How the hell did that happen?"

Alex explained the previous day, someone told her that if she was looking for more financial types, a lot of them hung out at the Le Toiny. So, she decided to change her rumour-hunting grounds and went to the lounge of the hotel that afternoon instead of the tennis club. As she was leaving, the bartender had stopped her and handed her an envelope. She unfolded the letter to show me. Under the embossed black and gold HDW logo it read:

> Dear Ms. Simpson,
> Instead of bothering my people and their friends down there with questions, why don't you just ask me? I'll be available in my office next Tuesday at 10 AM. I have 45 minutes then.
> No reply required. Sincerely,

Harrison David Wagner MA, PhD.

"Holy shit," I very astutely commented. Then I stopped.

"Babe, when did we start nosing around?" I asked.

"Four days ago."

"Exactly. And you get a typed, hand-delivered, hand-signed letter from New York to a distant island in less than four days in a bar you hadn't visited before? That not strike you as just a teensy-weensy bit odd?"

"My turn to say holy shit. What's it mean?"

"First off, we're obviously being watched and reported on. Second, Harrison Wagner MA, PhD either has somebody here who acts in his name and signs for him. Or...."

"...Or he's somewhere on the island," she concluded. "We should find him."

"Easy. Let's think about it. The two of us could start a house-by-house search on foot, you know, mark the island off in a grid pattern, like we were excavating a Mayan city. Oh, and we have to rent a boat so we can canvass all the yachts. Probably take two, maybe three months. And that works only if he stays put."

"Or, numb-nuts, maybe we just stakeout that bar where I got the note."

"OK, but I'm pretty sure he won't be back there anytime soon. I think he's yanking your chain, babe. Seeing how far you'll go trying to get some answers."

"Turns out, how far is the distance between here and New York."

"Are you sure you want to do this?

"It's a rare chance to talk to Wagner. Guy doesn't talk to anyone."

"I'm going with you."

"You don't have to. Stay here for the rest of the week and fly back to Florida. I'll be fine."

"I'm going with you.... but no macho bullshit, I swear."

She looked at me with some mixture of happiness and skepticism.

"Alright," she said. "Oh, did you happen to pack your insulated flip-flops and thermal Hawaiian shirt?"

"Shit!" I said, looking down at my usual scruffy-chic and very lightweight ensemble.

"We're going shopping!" she sang.

"Shit!" I said again.

I looked up the predicted weather for New York the following week, saw that the temperatures weren't too bad—a couple of degrees above freezing, a couple below—and determined my shopping list. Online, I then found the stores in Gustavia that fit the bill. As horrified as I was by the website prices, I would at least be prepared.

"Oh, no, my friend, that's not the way we do it here," Alex said after I laid out my plan. "We're going window shopping first."

"I'm not in the market for windows," I grumbled. "Plus, how we gonna ship them back?"

The cab deposited us at the foot of Rue du Roi Oscar II and off we went.

Alexandra browsed and I, more or less, plodded along, smoking, eyes downcast, completely in character as a petulant asshole. A brief word about my notorious and tiresome cheapness. I've never had a lot of money, not as a kid and certainly not after I quit working at a regular job. I did OK for a while in grown-up employment but not nearly as OK as the people I worked for. Being in PR, I often had to accompany my boss and other senior execs on their trips. I got to enjoy a swell lifestyle far beyond my income—I'm talking limos, private jets, upscale restaurants, classy hotels—even primo Stones tickets and a lot more—without having to pay for any of it. Sort of like Pip in Great Expectations, living off the crumbs of the very wealthy Miss Havisham.

Since then, through some blind dumb luck on the stock market with our company's shares, my pension-less ass has enough to get by, but barely, and assuming I don't exceed seventy-two and a half years of age before I kick. I'm like a subsistence farmer working hard-scrabble fields while the crowd Alex was used to hanging around with these days were more like the owners of those massive agri-business megacorps.

Alexandra stopped in front of store a couple of blocks down from where we started.

"Here!" she announced. "This is the perfect place for you."

I glanced up at the sign. L'Egoiste.

Now that was funny.

"Witch! Fine, I'll go inside but understand that I'm planning to spend less time than it takes to pull off a well-planned bank heist. In. Out."

Jean-Marc, the slender, young, and immaculately dressed sales guy who glided up to us, had other ideas. Clearly, he was intent on us having the full "customer experience" which meant agonizingly slow conversation about what our expectations might be and how best he could meet our needs.

In my working days when I wore a watch, I'd consult it every five minutes if I was in a meeting, just to hurry things along and let attendees know I had far better things to do. And I did have a ton of shit to do, chief of which was not to be in that meeting. Not having strapped on a timepiece for the past fifteen years, I devised a new and even better strategy. I asked Jean-Marc every five minutes for the time. Didn't win me friends and I didn't give a good goddamn. My only thought was of escape.

"Those blue pants—36 waist by 34…. And that sweater—XXL, s'il vous plait," I said, as I quickly pointed to stuff stacked in tiny cubicles against the wall. Oh, and the cheapest running shoes you have, size 10 ½."

Ol' Jean-Marc's revenge came at the cash register as he smiled ruthlessly watching my horrified reaction as I plunked down my beleaguered Visa card to cover the fucking $785 bill.

In addition to massacring my credit limit, I had also killed Alex's anticipated pleasure in shopping with me and didn't feel great about that. Time to summon Zen Jakey.

"So, darlin,' it's your turn for a winter wardrobe," I said.

"Serious?" she asked warily.

"C'mon, ya big lug; let's go. Oh, and you're paying."

Four stores and two and a half hours later, I decided it wasn't so bad after all. Alexandra has exquisite taste and she looked wonderful in everything she picked out and modelled (although she'd be stunning in a burlap sack).

"That wasn't so bad after all, was it?" Alex said as she planted a big wet one on my cheek.

"I expect to be awakened by my own screams tonight. I need a beer."

CHAPTER THIRTEEN

We flew out the next morning, reliving the white-knuckle experience of our landing, in reverse. Alex had ignored the direct flights from St. Maarten to New York, opting instead for the one-stop route (Miami) that added almost two hours to our flying time. Seasoned NYC traveller that she was, Alex explained that we would clear customs in Miami instead of the madhouse at Newark or JFK where New York's international flights land. Also, all of our possible flights were scheduled to get in around rush hour but LaGuardia, our destination, was much closer to Manhattan saving us maybe an hour of aggravation trapped in stalled traffic whereas instead we'd have time for a drink in Miami. Damn, I've got a smart lady. P.S. She had a Mai Tai. I went with the Tanqueray and tonic (double).

I can't say it was good to be back in New York—just as I wouldn't say that about any big city except maybe Edinburgh or San Francisco. New York is the largest city I've ever spent time in, so, by my definition, it's the one I despise the most.

But it's got a lot of restaurants, Jake. So what? How many over-priced eateries can you go to in a week? But Broadway, you say. Most of their offerings are goddamned musicals. OK, then the

Yankees. It's fucking baseball. Fine, what about the Jets and Giants? They play in New Jersey. Art galleries? Can't afford a single thing, most of it is 'modern,' and I know how to use Google images. But I will give you museums and tall buildings to gawk at.

I'll go full bah-humbugger here with a fun fact: the two top-rated, most-visited attractions in the Big Apple have nothing to do with the metropolis. The Statue of Liberty stands by herself well offshore with her back to Manhattan while Central Park is the big green refuge New Yorkers seek out to escape the fucking city they live in.

Just maybe my lack of enjoyment of New York is limited by my lack of income. It takes a boatload o' cash to really enjoy New York.

I remember sharing a flight and a cigarette with broadcasting legend Peter Jennings back when I had to be in NYC quite a bit. This was the time when science understood that those little plastic signs on top of the seatbacks prevented smoke from wafting into the non-smoking section of the airplane. I asked him about his favourite job. He cited his first radio news gig in small-town Ontario. That being the case, I wondered if New York was overwhelmingly depressing.

"Oh, let's face it: with the money I make, New York's pretty easy to take," he had answered.

The real reason it's the City That Never Sleeps is because how could you with the cacophonous 24/7 sound of constant sirens and honking horns? Or maybe you're up pacing the floor at 3:30 AM, worrying how you're going to meet the $5,000 average Manhattan monthly rent payment.

Alex had picked the hotel again, explaining that it was less than three blocks from where she was meeting Wagner, with a few good restaurants along the way.

"You really do know your way around this mess, don't you?"

"It was my old stomping grounds before I moved to Boston. As a matter of fact, there are a couple of guys I want to look up; they may help us. They might talk more freely if I was alone. As long as you promise to not be an arsehole about me going."

"Fine. But maybe it makes sense for me to come with you to meet Wagner?"

Alex tried to be diplomatic, she really did, but I knew the answer.

"Thanks, but I don't think so," she said. "It…might be… awkward."

Translation: given my blunt, normally off-putting questions, building security would be hustling my ass down the elevator and out the revolving doors before the coffee arrived. Alex knew she had to handle Wagner gently, tactfully if she had any hope of getting helpful answers from him.

From the Hilton Double Tree (where there wasn't even one fucking tree in evidence), we strolled several short blocks to the gleaming One Manhattan West office building looming over that part of Midtown. I prodded her to remember the names of the four new subcontractors that Jack Duffy inherited soon after HDW opened their cheque book. I left her at the front doors, agreeing to meet up an hour later—although I did not relish the idea of stopping a grim pedestrian, no matter how spiffy I looked, to ask the time. "Excuse me, sir, would you tell me what time it is, or should I fuck off right now?"

I took in the sights instead. A cop standing beside a group of 14- or 15-year-olds passing around a huge blunt in front of Macy's. I imagined the officer debating whether or not to risk physical injury over a joint. A guy near Madison Square Garden (which is round) walking down the driver side of the line of parked cars, randomly trying door handles. Another guy on the other side of the street a few blocks down casually snapping off car aerials and windshield wipers. You know, real postcard material.

After that, I paced around and smoked outside One Manhattan West until Alex emerged through the doors almost two hours after I'd left her. I was all over her.

"Are you OK? How'd it go? Did he threaten you? Tell me, tell me!"

"I'll tell you, already. Give me a second."

"OK, but you have to promise to tell me everything; don't leave any detail out."

"Well, first I pushed the Up button for the elevator," she began.

"With quite the flair, may I add. The elevator was very quiet, and it made a very pleasant bell sound when it stopped at a floor…"

"Alright, alright. I'm hungry; let's grab lunch. What you want?"

"A drink."

"That's my girl!"

"Let's stay away from all the cheap, lunch counter places you prefer, OK? We need somewhere quiet. I know a spot."

We walked back towards the hotel, and we settled into a booth in a smallish, quietish Spanish place where I resumed my badgering questions ("No one expects the Spanish Inquisition!"). In response, she ordered drinks then she took out her phone.

"Oh, no ya don't!" I said.

"Just listen will ya?" she said, as she pushed one of them tiny buttons.

Her voice was faint but clear as she profusely thanked Wagner for seeing her, as if she'd just been granted an audience with the Pope or Beyonce.

"Oh, no, Ms. Simpson, the pleasure of seeing you is all mine," said an unremarkable but definitely creepy voice. "Can I call you Alexandra?"

"Ms. Simpson's fine."

I made the Time Out gesture and she stopped the recording. "Am I gonna have to listen to two hours of him leching after you? And isn't taping illegal here?" "Listen," she said, re-starting her chat.

"Do you mind if I tape our conversation?" the male voice continued, "For the record, you understand."

"You sly devil!" I said. "If you didn't mind him recording, then he couldn't possibly object to you doing the same, whether he knew about it or not."

She flashed that great smile of hers.

Wagner then spent the next ten minutes reminding Alex how goddamned fortunate she was to be in his presence. Now it's true that's how I think people should feel around me all the time, but I don't say it out loud.

They chit-chatted about St. Bart's for a bit, although he didn't cop to actually being there a couple of days earlier.

"Would you mind telling why you agreed to see me?" Alex asked Wagner.

"I know your work. You're thorough, you're smart. Our new PR people have convinced me that our secrecy is now damaging us whereas before it was useful. I understand that you and your friend have been asking questions of people who don't have all the information. That's neither accurate nor helpful."

Alexandra stopped the tape.

"After that intro," she said, "I was all ears, thinking this was going to be a massive scoop. But essentially, it was all just bullshit."

"Get anything valuable?"

"Hesitant confirmation of some of things that we thought. No real details. You can listen to the whole tape later for anything I might have missed. Right now, I need to eat."

"Bottom line?"

"Paella, of course."

"Fine. Other that?"

"Yes, they are invested in Southern Cross, but like I said, no detail of how much they've got in. And he wasn't very happy about me knowing."

"Ask him why he bought into a tiny pissant of a mining company?"

"Yes, sir. He said that Southern Cross had a bunch of very promising leases around their two mines. Wagner, like the rest of world now, sees the next frontier as being in rare earth minerals. Southern Cross is their entrée into that world, largely because they've got about a three-to-five-year head start in Vietnam and Brazil."

"And what about that list of new suppliers?"

"Two of the four—Olrud Transportation and Pretoria Mine Management—have his money, but he denied being involved with the other two."

"What do you think he's planning?"

"If he's got controlling interest in them, I bet he's going to roll them into Southern, which we know he effectively runs. Then he takes that one entity public as this one-stop self-contained rare earth specialist."

"So, he markets it as having great potential because of Southern's leases while the other companies—Pretoria and Olrud—stand to benefit big-time from long-term contracts with the mining operation when it strikes it rich."

"Exactly."

"What's he do with this new 3-in-1 company, swimming in cash after the IPO, besides calling it POS Mining?"

"If the point is just making money—and with him that's always the point—I'd bet he first grabs his percentage of the share offering proceeds, then sells the whole operation soon after the stock issue when investors are paying an absurd multiple based on the vapour promise of mega riches. He walks away with a giant profit but without the big headaches of having to deliver."

"Might be a plan but isn't it a big gamble that he can sell Southern's promise to investors?"

"It's safe to say it's a significant risk."

"Why would he roll the dice like that? He doesn't even have any public companies."

"That part's confusing. I assume it's for the big reward." While Alex went off to say 'hi' to some colleagues, I did listen to the entire tape.

[Sidebar to you fact-checkers: I know it's not a fucking "tape" as there is no tape. I just got bored typing "recording" and refuse to use "voice logging"].

It was, as Alex had described, far removed from the grand reveal that Wagner claimed he was going to make.

He offered no comment on a bunch of her questions, things like revenue, value of holdings, number of investors, number of employees, plans for any public offerings of their subsidiaries. Always followed by the evasive explanation that it was proprietary information. In other words, he gave the usual excuse every private company uses with any nosy media, instead of the more honest "None of your fuckin' business."

He was more than a little interested as to why Alexandra was asking about Southern Cross. She rather deftly replied that they were thinking about taking a more in-depth look at privately held mineral companies as potential investment opportunities for her higher wealth clients. Southern Cross was on her list of possible subjects. See, I would've answered: "Because someone whacked their CFO, probably the same person who was making threatening calls to my lady. Oh, and we think you're behind it, you oily son of a bitch."

Wagner then went into a short corporate-y rant about how "you people" are hurting honest and important investment in the economy with "your moralizing and pearl-clutching." He was polite about it, but there was no mistaking his hostility. Alex gave as good as she got about the value of a conscientious, fully-informed investment community that could have a role—a big role—in improving workers' lives, stopping child labour, and protecting the environment by calling the mostly foreign companies into account to behave better. She too was restrained, whereas I likely would have stormed back with "Because you greedy motherfuckers are killing people and the planet, that's why!"

What I found marginally interesting was something that wasn't on the tape. Close to the end of their conversation a female voice interrupted. Wagner admonished her, reminding her that he had said "No calls."

She persisted. "It's Mr. White on Line 2. He said it was urgent."

"Miss Simpson, I apologize," Wagner said. "I have to take this. May I have the room?"

The recording goes silent then picks up again after about two minutes. I assumed Alex turned off her phone when she left his office and back on again before she re-entered.

"Now where were we?" Wagner asked.

Then he picked up his elusive song-and-dance routine for the last fifteen minutes of the interview which I will now summarize: "Blah, blah, blah…shareholder value…Blah, blah, blah… diversification…Blah,blah, blah…New age of investment opportunity… Blah, blah blah…Responsibility….Blah, blah, blah…Accountabili- ty….Blah, blah, blah…Global presence….Blah, blah, blah…Hope I've been helpful….Blah, blah, blah…Must do this again….How long are you in New York?"

When Alexandra answered: "We're leaving tonight," his big wolfish finish was: "Pity. Maybe next time."

I could picture his leer. I desperately wanted to punch his fucking lights out for that, and for Wagner's apparent mastery of the politician trick of ignoring questions and comments by continuing to keep yakking in a breathless torrent of babble, hitting all the hallowed, pre-scripted talking points. Alex couldn't wedge a whole question into that wall of bullshit anywhere.

I was sifting through what I'd just heard, looking for anything useful, when Alexandra returned.

"We're leaving tonight?" I asked.

"No. I must've used that line a hundred times whenever I wanted to get the hell away from guys like that."

"I'll watch for you using that one on me."

"Trust me: you won't see it coming. You listened to the whole thing?"

"I did."

"And?"

"Just like you said, babe. A whole lotta nuthin.' I do have to ask about that phone call he got."

"I sat and admired the expensive artwork in his reception area for over twenty minutes."

"No sense of what it could've been about?"

"Didn't hear a thing."

"Did his mood change?"

"Now that you mention it, there was a change."

"Sounded to me like he became more subdued," I said. "He dropped the dirty old man friendliness and started to just whip through the chat."

"You're right; he did. Like he just wanted it to be over. Why is that important? Maybe he just got bored."

142

"Maybe. Or maybe he had to handle something that came up in that call. And it really bugged me that his admin introduced the guy as Mr. White."

"You're kidding, right?"

"Wagner obviously knows the guy—so it wasn't "a Mr. White" like you'd say about a stranger. And at any rate, he wouldn't have picked up the phone for a guy he didn't know. And if he was a friend, then why not "Bill on line 2"? Or even "Bill White"? And here's a call to one of the richest men in America and one of the most powerful men in the financial world, and he doesn't say "Tell him I'll call him back in twenty minutes" or even "I'll call him back when I fucking feel like it"?"

"You think of the strangest things."

"Thank you."

We had a delightful dinner at a modest nearby Italian eatery. I had no choice but to try their famous New York pizza. Mostly because the menu said: *Try Our Famous New York Pizza!* (I think it was the exclamation mark that got me). There already was cutlery on the table so I didn't risk a beating from the waiter for my outrageous non-New York behaviour as I sawed away with my knife instead of folding the slice in half and jamming it in my piehole, like a Gotham barbarian.

She reported that her old contacts hadn't been much help, other than confirming my assessment of Wagner as a [pick one or all of the following: fuckhead, asshole, and slippery son-of-a bitch.] One pension manager had been certain that HDW was into White Iron for big bucks. That was the extent of our conversation about the shitshow we had found ourselves in.

We strolled arm-in-arm back to the hotel. A light snow was gently falling through the breeze-less air, its giant flakes lit up by the streetlights. A hell of a lot more romantic than if we were marching into the teeth of a howling blizzard. In the hotel lobby, we stood side by side in front of the elevator, silently watching the descending floor numbers.

"May I come up?" Alexandra coyly asked at the ding.

"Why, Ms. Simpson! I am shocked, shocked I tell you!"

She smiled that smile, reached over, and grabbed my left butt cheek.

"OK then! Better late than never," I quickly added as I ushered her into the elevator where we more or less mauled each other all the way to the tenth floor, down the hallway and through the room door. Just like in the movies, only a lot more comically clumsy.

Fact is, I left New York a lot happier than I had arrived. Pretty exciting and satisfying city after all.

CHAPTER FOURTEEN

After all that travelling, I was happy to be back at our place. But an attitude adjustment was in order. The Hovel—Sorry, I tried, I really did, but I just can't say beach cottage; it'll always be the Hovel—was less than half the size of our suite in St. Barts. A house that tiny being occupied by two un-tiny people presented problems. Our full-sized (not even queen) bed was a far cry from the king monster with plenty of room to roam that we had had on the island. I had done the calculation and fitting a queen in our small, ironically named master bedroom would have meant wall-to-wall mattress, like a bouncy castle. Any activity in the kitchen required a finely tuned, almost balletic choreography. Barely one of us fit in the bathroom.

Get outside, Jake! The weather had turned nicer, and I busied myself outdoors, mostly keeping up with the plant life and Mitch the turtle. But I also knew I didn't want our faint trail to cool.

There were no further presents on the patio table and I wondered if Matt Kilmer had seen or found out anything further in the week we were away. I went looking for him. According to Bus Bench Bob, he lived somewhere on 11th Avenue, five blocks away.

So, I started knocking on doors about halfway down the second block off Gulf Boulevard.

Going door-to-door around here was a dicey proposition, owing to the army of salespeople doing just that. I know because we had been hit up at least twenty times with folks peddling everything from magazine subscriptions to roof repair to Jesus. Before you know it, your door camera portrait is on the local community chat forum and the vigilante hunt is on. Given my sketchy appearance, I'd immediately make their "Call the Cops Right the Fuck Now If You See This Guy" hit parade.

But that's not what happened. Two 'no' answers, one old guy who wanted to yak, and, on just my fourth door, I got lucky. Yes, the older woman who answered the door seemed wary, but when I explained I was an old army buddy of Matt's looking to surprise him, she was downright chatty over the yips and yaps of her tiny, excitable dog.

"Thank you for your service," she began. "I guess you haven't heard."

"Heard what?"

"Matt passed away almost a week ago, I guess it is now. Such a shame. He lived two doors down. Wonderful gentleman. He always had treats for my Mitzy when we'd be out walking. Such a shame."

"What happened?" I asked, expecting to hear about the sad end of his cancer journey.

"Hit and run," she said, shaking her head. "Matt didn't get around so good the last little while, but he was always careful walking. He'd always go out late at night, like clockwork, on account of his insomnia. I bet it was one of them damn Airbnbers, all liquored up. Just drove off and left him there. Such a shame."

Well, fuck, I thought. What a shitty way to go. And fuck, what are the odds this was an accident?

"People can be so damn mean," she said.

"Yes, they can."

"It got worse. Two days after it happened, I checked on his house. He had fish, you know. Back door open, the place a mess. Kids must've heard about his accident and broke in."

"Like you said. Damn mean."

I rushed home and went archiving in the local news outlets.

One Dead in Fatal Indian Rocks Beach Hit and Run—read the headline. According to police, Kilmer was "struck with force" while walking westbound along the 200-block of 11th Avenue, Indian Rocks Beach. Like Robert Hale, he too "suffered injuries incompatible with life" and was pronounced dead at the scene. A black SUV —make and model unknown—was seen speeding away from the accident by a witness. The witness, who wished to remain anonymous, reported that she had been awakened by her barking dog at approximately 2:30 AM immediately prior to hearing what sounded like a loud thud. Investigators at the scene estimated the driver did not use their brakes at any point before striking Kilmer as there were no visible skid marks. Police are asking anyone who may have information about the accident or any vehicle matching the description speeding on Gulf Boulevard in the vicinity at approximately the time of the incident to come forward.

I was tempted to come forward. I hadn't seen the "accident" or its aftermath, but I could offer up the fact that it had been a deliberate act. Then I imagined the conversation if I made the call:

"Police tip line. How may we help you?"

"Well, that hit and run on 11th in Indian Rocks? I have reason to believe it was no accident."

"I see, sir. And why do you think that?"

"Well, it started with that pickleballer being shot in St. Petersburg about two months ago."

"I see, sir. And how exactly are these two events linked?"

"Well, I have overwhelming proof—well, at least a pretty strong notion—that a New York hedge fund or a US military Special Ops unit planned and carried out the murder in St. Pete. It's the same bunch I believe that assassinated Mr. Kilmer. Oh, and the St. Petersburg cops are in cahoots with them."

"I see, sir. Thank you so very much for calling the Tips Line."

"No wait! Let me explain…" Click.

Back at the Hovel, I gave Alex the news. She, like me, instantly concluded that there was no way his death had been accidental. And she, like me, was worried.

"What do we do now? Any ideas?" she asked.

"No clue. But this shit is getting close. We can either cut and run or keep digging. One of those two. And I'm fine with either one. Care to vote?"

"Fuck 'em! We dig."

"Atta girl!" I said, but I knew there was falsity in my compliment on her determination. They'd got to Bob Hale; they'd got to Matt Kilmer. How long before they came for us? I voiced that fear to Alex. She thought for a bit.

"You know what? We may have something going for us."

"Besides our brains and your great looks?"

"Besides that. I don't think they know who we are yet."

"Of course, they do. St. Barts, New York ring a bell?" I reminded her.

"That's there. They knew Jake and Alexandra were asking questions there, but maybe not here."

Alex explained that, if "they" were tapping Bob's work, regular cell, and home phone, they'd see Bob Hale had had no further contact with her. And as far as "they" knew, Jack Duffy had only talked to the mythical Lawrence Palmer in his office, on the phone from St. Barts, and at the Beach Hovel after "Lawrence" gave him the address over the phone.

"Yeah, but a simple property search would've told them the joint was owned by a Jake Lydon," I noted. "And what are the odds of them deciding that it was a little more coincidental that Jake and Lawrence were vacationing in St. Barts at the same time?"

"You cover that right now by calling Jack on his office phone to tell him that the Lawrence you is leaving town because your sublease is up, and the owner wants you out."

"Fuckin' Canadian slum landlord."

She then pointed out that my only contact with Matt Kilmer had been in person.

"Likely whoever's doing this doesn't have all the resources and manpower of the FBI. What are the odds of them physically following Matt whenever he went to the beach or the grocery store?"

"Wait, whoa. Then how'd he get dead? They had to stake him out to figure out his insomniac late night walk ritual."

Alex thought.

"It's possible they got interested in him after he last saw you."

"The ballistics guy with the St. Pete's cops!" I said in my 'Eureka' moment. "He sent the forensics report to Kilmer, probably used e-mail. Somehow, that rang a bell with them."

"You think the police department's involved?!"

"Or just one guy there. Maybe the same guy that ended the Hale investigation."

"Jake, we can't worry about that right now. At the heart of all this is Southern Cross and HDW. That's what we have to figure out first."

My wee brain hurt. The more we looked at what had happened and how it could've happened the wider the possibilities became— the ol' ripples in a pond (well, at the moment, more like a fart in a bathtub). But it felt good to have Alexandra fully engaged, as they say. In my past hapless misadventures, she's been either absent or on the outside while I was busy running at windmills. But she's real smart and real analytical, applying judgement and insight and all the things I lack as I tend to just stumble around and bump into shit. Finally, an adult in the room.

And she was right. We weren't exactly in any kind of position to dive into the St. Petersburg Police Department on the chance that something or somebody was rotten inside the 1000-officer depart-ment. And yet, the most immediate, right-at-hand possibility of who actually was doing the killing was a police force member or members thereof. With surveillance resources and weaponry—and the people who know how to use both—they had the means and opportunity. But at that point, there was just no way to discern motive.

Same way the two of us weren't about to see just what the hell might be going on with the American military as Kilmer had hinted. While the prospect of them going rogue on their own citizens might be a juicy, moveable feast for conspiracy theorists, it was pretty easy for me to, at least temporarily, park the notion that Special Operations ordered and carried out a hit on Robert Hale. I couldn't say with absolute certainty they hadn't, but it just wasn't the sort thing that we could easily investigate. I could not see myself crossing the causeway and driving up to the gates at MacDill Air Force Base to ask the guard there, "Say, buddy, can you ask around, see if any of the SOCOM folks in there are murdering private citizens in Pinellas County? I'll wait."

Nope, Alex was right—as per usual. We needed the why and the answer to that had to lie somewhere in Southern Cross Mining. Unfortunately, our logical starting point was dead. We were get- ting desperate for an answer, for a hint of an answer as to why Bob Hale was upset enough to be blowing the whistle on a company where he'd been a loyal and crucial principal for decades. He hadn't been specific with Alexandra and Jack said he didn't have a clue about what was bugging his partner.

Obviously, I needed more information about what just the hell was actually going on with the mines in Brazil and Vietnam. There wasn't much of a chance of doing that by talking to the Florida people. Jack Duffy couldn't fly. Bob Hale couldn't do much of anything. Borje—unlike Elvis—rarely left the building, and I didn't think Marjorie, the pleasant middle-aged admin/receptionist, led a double life as a jet-setting mining exec.

I had to talk to Mick Rogers, Southern Cross's operations guy for an idea of what was happening on—or under—the ground.

But before I did that, I decided I should talk to somebody who hadn't figured into any conversation so far: Bob Hale's widow. Maybe Bob had confided in her. I called Jack and asked him to make introductions because, otherwise, why would she talk to me?

"Sorry, bud. I'm no goddamned help on that front," he said. "Alice is too goddamned sweet to accuse me, but I'm pretty sure she blames me, somehow, for Bob's death. After all these years, we were pretty close but, at the funeral, she barely said a word to me. I called a couple of times after to see how she was doing. She wouldn't even pick up."

"Fair enough. Can you at least tell me about her?"

He described Alice Hale as a quiet, old-fashioned, and very religious. She had worked as a teacher in their early years; she had to support Robert as he chased his dream of finding valuable shit underground. With a few lucrative strikes and at Bob's insistence, she had quit working. At home, she had busied herself with church and charity work. In their move to Florida, Alice had requested a house in one of those gated communities with shared facilities like a common pool, gym, and clubhouse. Places like that always have a Homeowners Association that organizes events like potluck dinners and Mahjong leagues and all sorts of other activities. Jack gave me her address and phone number and wished me luck.

I didn't look forward to confronting the widow Hale. I can force myself to be nice and diplomatic and empathetic; Alexandra naturally is all those things. We decided she should pose as a claims specialist with Southern's insurance provider. It took only a couple of hours to even have fake business cards done up at one of those quick print outfits, after Jack told me the name of their insurer. And off she went.

I was weeding along the shaded side. I knew she had returned and judging by the sound of slammed cupboard drawers and doors, she was angry.

"I felt like shit the whole time!" she said when I went inside. "Here's this darling woman utterly destroyed by her husband's death and I'm vulturing around trying to pick up scraps of information."

I didn't say anything beyond telling her that I understood. It was an unsavoury but sometimes necessary job in the process of building a storehouse of useful knowledge. I offered to get her a glass of wine.

"OK, but I feel like I should shower first."

The glass of pinot had a calming effect as she recounted her visit.

"Seriously, she was a sweetheart. She gave me tea—in real China—and scones. Real old school. Had macramé coasters and friggin' doilies on the arm rests. I mean, she's maybe ten years older than me and the whole time I felt like I was visiting a great aunt."

The net result of her visit with Alice Hale wasn't much. Yes, she was angry at the "new" Southern Cross, in general and by association, with Jack. She was also pissed off and worried about the lawyer's kiss-off letter leaving her with zero money after Bob's dedication (and her support and understanding) over the years. She was relying on the death benefit from his company insurance plan. Yes, Bob was worried, maybe a bit more than usual. Yes, he did mention that the source of his anxiety was a "real problem" with the paperwork coming from the mines and unaccounted for costs. No, Bob didn't go into detail because, generally, he was loathe to bring his work home.

According to Alex, about the only negative thing she said was that Bob had commented he was surprised that "Scandinavians could be so deceptive."

That took me aback. I knew of only two Nordic entities involved with Southern Cross Mining: one was a person—Borje the Swede, the other a company—Norwegian-based Olrud Shipping. Which one was Bob referring to? And what did that mean?

Alexandra was happy to be back to her computer and her phone and away from the sad side of using bullshit identities to dig into damaged humanity. Instead, she threw herself at looking into Harrison Wagner and his secretive empire, with real focus on two companies of his that Wagner admitted he had money in and that had had contracts with Southern: Pretoria and Olrud. I asked her, as well, to find out whatever she could about his personal life. She didn't want to, believing that those details had little bearing on the companies he assembled.

I happen to think that CEOs are (mostly) human beings. Often, the companies they run take on the boss's personal characteristics. So, stuff like their childhood background are important to me. Not just the basic facts about where they grew up, where they went to school, where they worked, but the remembrances of fellow classmates and teachers, teammates, early co-workers, shit like that. Was the guy or girl popular and well-liked or were they generally thought to be an asshole? These days, thanks mainly to The Google, you can find out a lot of this stuff, particularly with celebrities in any field.

Articles—especially puff pieces—often give their tastes in music, movies, and books and you learn something. Same with favourite pastimes, even where they like to vacation (if at all), the type of house they live in and so on. Do all that and a portrait emerges.

But, Jake, don't you just arrive at superficial pictures that can verge on the stereotypical?

Why, yes, I do. But you can't tell me there's no difference between someone who loves thrash metal and someone who routinely listens to recorded whale sounds. Someone who prefers lava surfing in Hawaii or would rather attend quilting demonstrations, watch C-Span or reruns of Starsky & Hutch. Is he or she someone whose idea of a night out is tacos from a food truck then a row of tequila shots in a dive bar, as opposed to, say lamb shank navarin paired with a cheeky 2018 Chateau Pontet-Canet Bordeaux at La Sirene Soho?

It's all indicative of personality and character and often predictive about current and future behaviour and decisions. In other words, I wanted all this stuff so I can build a pretty good idea who we were up against. Plus, I'm a nosy little fucker.

It's been proven again and again that CEOs also have way more than their share of sociopaths among their ranks. Apparently being remorselessly batshit crazy is a sought-after trait in the corporate headhunting biz. Imagine the interview:

1. Is there any time when you didn't lie or cheat to get what you wanted?
2. Has there ever been an occasion when you actually considered other people's feelings?
3. Have you ever thought you might be wrong about anything?
4. Can you possibly think of a time when you sincerely apologized for something you said or did?

A "yes" to any question and the candidate will be disqualified.

But, Jake, isn't this just a bunch of armchair psychoanalyzing bullshit dreamed up by a fucking amateur?

Why, yes, it is. But if I have a knack for anything (and the jury's out on that) it's for figuring out people and why they do the things they do.

I understand Type 'A' personalities. Alexandra's one. I was one —well, a solid 'A Minus,' OK, a 'B Plus'—when I had a high-paying job. That normally means you're dedicated, you put in the work, you give a shit, and you can't relax. But it's a fine line between Type 'A' and Type 'Somebody Should Consider Locking This Guy Up.'

The burner phone rang. "What's up, Jack?"

"It's not fucking Jack!" roared a loud voice with a thick Australian accent. "Mick Rogers! Duffy said you needed to talk to me."

"I do. Thanks for calling, Mick. But I'm having trouble hearing you," I said, trying to ignore the loud laughter and crowd noises in the background.

"I'm in a pub in bloody Amsterdam. The Old Sailor. Jack said you'd like it."

"Sounds like I would."

"Why don't you find out for yourself? I'll be here for another day and a half."

"In the bar?"

Mick laughed, deep and rich like Jack would.

"No, ya bloody fool, in Amsterdam. Otherwise, I'm off to Vietnam, if you fancy that."

"Can't do this over the phone?"

"Going by me dealing with Jack on his shitty little secret spy phone, fuck no!"

"Well then, see you in Amsterdam!"

"Ace! Whaddya look like?"

"Old guy, long, grey hair, Hawaiian shirt," I said, supplying my standard self-assessment.

"Got it! Hotel Barbizon. Ta!" and he hung up. I had to break it to Alex.

"Babe, remember when we planned to have dinner tonight?

"Yeah. I was thinking Guppy's."

"How about we have dinner in Amsterdam instead?"

"What the hell are you talking about?"

"Just spoke to Mick Rogers. That's where he is. I've got to talk to him. I'll be gone two days—three, tops."

"When?"

"Now. Otherwise, it's a trip to Vietnam."

Alex declined to come with me, electing to spend two solid days devoted to her business. I didn't feel at all that good about her decision which she sensed and, once again, told me to knock off my protective "macho bullshit."

There was an 8 pm flight to Dutchland out of Tampa through Atlanta on Air France. I calculated drinking and then recovery time with Mick and booked a return two days later. I wasn't looking forward to two days of road ass nor was I looking forward to at least ten and a half smoke-free hours of travel, but there seemed to be little choice. I had to talk to him. And all that was predicated on being able to confide in Mick and that he'd do the same for me and be forthcoming.

I found my trusty bowling bag that Alex had hidden in a closet, jammed my New York wardrobe into it, and added my meds. I passed on the insulin because it needed refrigeration, reasoning that I wouldn't go blind or lose a foot in two days. Plus, I had the rest of my mobile pharmacy to protect me.

The sun was setting behind us as we drove across the Tampa Bay causeway. The darkening waters of the bay gave way to all the twinkling lights of Tampa's sleek waterfront. I reminded myself that every city from a distance looked better at night with the lights on.

We hadn't said much on the 45-minute drive and, obviously, both of us were sad. Despite what ol' Billy Shakespeare might say, these days, there was no sweetness attached to the sorrow of us parting.

At the curbside, we looked into each other's eyes and at about the same time said: "Be careful."

CHAPTER FIFTEEN

As suave as I might want to appear when I travel, I am doomed to be a fucking bumbling old incompetent. I can never get the automated check-in right and so must wait for an airline per- son whose only job is to smile and help out morons such as yours truly while the line of impatient would-be passengers at the kiosk grows longer and more pissed off. Ditto for the passport scan at security. At both stops, I was told a QR code (whatever the fuck that is) on my phone would make it all easier. I denied I owned a smartphone because I knew the device I carried was dumber than a sack of Jakes. It and me had barely learned to receive and send calls and messages, nothing more.

Nine times out of ten, I'll set off the metal detectors because I apparently had never been told that I was supposed to empty my pockets. At customs, I always invite further scrutiny because of my shabby personal appearance and the expression on my face which evidently screams: "This man looks like he's done something horribly illegal!"

All that to say, I didn't get to off-handedly tell a fellow passenger: "Yeah, this afternoon, I thought I'd fly to Amsterdam for a late dinner." If I had been able to pull off this casual boast, that passenger would've still known I was a fucking idiot because, with the ten and a half-hour flight time and six-hour time difference, we'd be getting in around lunchtime the next day.

My fully flustered self finally settled into my window seat where I promptly grabbed the next seat's belt buckle which, against all odds, I couldn't get to marry with my buckle. Mercifully, they'd left the middle seat empty and, just as mercifully, the half-bottle of NyQuil I'd chugged in the departure area and the two quick gin and tonics on board fully kicked in. I lost consciousness, leaving my fellow passengers with the joy of beholding my drooling, snoring, open-mouthed near-corpse.

I know I make being a fucking useless moron look easy, but believe me, it's exhausting.

I groggily came to about an hour before landing, popped a Nicorette, popped open my shitty laptop and learned what I could about my destination. The Barbizon was on the lip of the famous Red-Light district while the Old Sailor was centre-west in Europe's fun zone. The temperature was in the mid-40s, skies were sunny, and the local government was trying to discourage "nuisance" tourists who come to the city just for the plentiful sex, drugs, booze and maybe a bit of rock n' roll.

The coolly efficient—that's to say really Dutch—customs officer wanted to know where I was staying and for how long. I told him. Then the cagey bastard asked: "Business or pleasure?" I panicked a bit. I normally would answer "Pleasure," but here was afraid I'd be arrested and deported. "Business," I said. He waved me on with a look that said "Yeah, sure, buddy," only in Dutch.

We made the short drive into the city centre from the south-west, along a wide expressway that turned into several wide boulevards. On the way, we passed over a score of the several hundred thousand canals on a bunch of the approximately two million bridges that span them. The architecture was mostly low and dense. The four- or five-story new shit was uniformly boxy, grey, and ugly. As we reached the District, the old stuff, with tons of red brick, gabled roofs and whimsical trim was uniformly beautiful. Clearly the 17th century lads had it goin' on.

Within seconds of entering the spacious, high-ceilinged lobby of the Barbizon I was startled by a loud voice reverberating around the expanse.

"Oi! Lydon!"

The shout's source got up from the plush armchair and stepped towards me, right arm extended.

As we shook hands—I was coming to believe that owning a bone-crushing handshake was a hiring criterion at Southern—I sized up Mick Rogers.

A shorter, leaner version of Jack Duffy. Copper-coloured skin set off by lively blue eyes and tousled straw hair. He was only a little younger than Jack but looked at least fifteen years his junior. "How'd you know when I'd be com—" I managed to get out before he cut me off.

"Figured you'd be on the Atlanta flight. On it me-self a lot. Let's get you checked in, yeah?"

Without waiting for an answer, he grabbed my trusty bowling bag and headed for the front desk.

"G'day, Alice," he said to the receptionist whose face lit up.

"Mr. Mick," she said, her face exploding in a giant, red-lip-sticked smile.

"You got a reservation for Jake Lydon. Get him a better room, will ya, love?" he said. "At my rate. Ta!"

In no time, I had my room key. Mick and I rode the elevator to an upper floor.

"Stuffed, are you?" he asked.

"Pardon?"

"Knackered."

"Oh, you mean tired? No, slept a lot on the plane."

"Fancy a cold one then?"

"I'm waaaay beyond fancying a beer. I'm desperate for one."

"That's right! Jack said you were a Canuck. You bastards can drink. And not that horse piss the Yanks love. Learned that during ten bloody cold months in the Yukon and a bloody summer was supposed to be in there somewhere!"

"And I'm hungry too."

"No worries. I know just the place. Molly Malone's."

"I was kinda hoping for Chinese. Haven't found any decent Chinese in Florida."

"There is none, but sorry, that's not on, mate. I've got a month of Asian—really good Asian—food comin' up. Get your fill after I'm gone. I need some Brit shit. Now!"

We headed out from the hotel and must've walked for a good minute and half—maybe two. We turned up a street lined with narrow red-brick buildings butting up against each other all down the block on one side and overlooking—surprise, surprise—a canal on the other. I was tipped off to our destination about half- way down the block by the orange, white and green flag hanging from the second story. As we approached it, a further hint was the bright green façade sticking out from its red-bricked neighbours.

"They set up a patio—they bloody well all do—in the summer," Mick explained, as I imagined the furniture and the further touch of green from the presently naked trees sprouting from the cobblestone.

How do you not want to go into a place with this sign on a chalkboard by the front door:

If you're Hungry
We'll feed you
If you're Thirsty
We'll get you drunk
If you're Lonely
We'll get you drunk

Even at lunch time, the place was rowdy and, I presumed, Irish as fuck. Right down to the red-haired bar tenders who either were imported, like the beer, from Ireland or were graduates of the Dutch Actors Studio.

We snagged two stools at the end of the bar and wedged ourselves into them, only briefly staring down the rows of glasses, bottles and taps before we were served by a green-vested man who introduced himself as Sean (but was probably Wilhem). Mick ordered a Guinness while I, somewhat sacrilegiously, did not. Recalling my teenaged hitch-hiking trip to the UK, I had a Harp lager.

"Cheers, mate," Mick said as we clinked the heavy cold pint mugs. We then undertook the ritual—not unlike dogs sniffing asses —that I'd noted and liked in England. Brits and many of their colonial offspring called it taking the piss; we know it as trash-talking. Basically, it's just guys giving as good as they get. He made fun of Canadians; I trotted out every Aussie stereotype I could think of.

Even though we were shoulder to shoulder, we had to aim all this good-natured viciousness loudly just to be heard above the lively din.

[Sidebar: Travel tip for soft talkers: Stay away from Molly Malone's in Amsterdam! You won't be heard any easier than if you were standing in front of the speakers at a Who concert.]

Going by the sidelong glances, I realized what he was doing, because I do it too. Underneath the frivolity and superficial joshing, his eyes were searching, gauging, seeing what there was to learn and if he could trust me or not.

In between all the shit-talking, we found time to order food (bangers and mash for him. I had fish and chips. Thanks for asking).

"We can't talk here," Mick announced, as if he'd only just noticed the noise in the packed pub.

"I know," I said. "Just like you wanted."

He smiled but didn't say anything; he knew that I knew.

Outside, Mick immediately took out his phone—something he hadn't done so far.

"Sorry, mate," he said to me. "Bit of business."

He punched a number in, said: "Yeah...yeah...Hmmm... yeah...I don't fuckin' care. Just do it! Understand?" and hung up. He then proceeded to make three more calls, all with same tone and length, with one in Spanish or Portuguese before ending with one more call, only speaking in a sweet, cajoling voice this time. I didn't feel badly about listening, mostly because I didn't have a choice. He was loud enough that I expect I could have overheard him from the other side of the canal. Or the city, for that matter.

I don't know how many living Australian spies there are, but Mick would not be a leading candidate. He talked loud, he laughed loud, he even seemed to move loud. He made Jack Duffy look like a stern librarian or a horse whisperer on the job.

"Where do we start?" I asked as soon as we were back in his room.

"With a cold one," Mick immediately suggested. "I like the cut of your jib."

Mick ordered up six beer from Room Service, to go along with the two Heinekens he fished out of the mini-bar. We settled in and proceeded to fill in some of our backstory as it related to Jack. As an eighteen-year-old, Mick was bound for Banff, Alberta and a summer job in a hotel there, ("Christ," I told him. "I wish our immigration laws had been just a little bit tighter."), when he met Jack, Borje, and Bob in a bar in Vancouver. They were heading back to their small copper mine near the Yukon River and persuaded the kid to join them as they could always use an extra hand.

"Why bloody not, I thought. Fuckin' clown show when I got there," he recalled. "Had to get my hands dirty right quick, learning the ropes."

I could see it. Chances were, Mick had always been energetic and engaging. But also smart, smart enough to keep a million details in his head, confident enough to make snap decisions on the fly about what needed to be done and when, what people to contract, how to treat the workers, who needed to get paid when and on and on.

Mick explained that they had set out with a target— 'x' number of tons of raw ore that should yield 'y' number of tons of copper, based on Borje's estimates. Multiplying that amount by the projected copper price on global commodity markets gave you a gross revenue target that either justified or pissed on the idea of opening a full-fledged mine.

"But there was no bloody way in hell we could've hit that number without expanding," he said. "And that meant more people, more machinery, more trucks, better roads, a dock on the river and lots of other shite."

"That'd be costly."

"Bob went back to beg for more money. Borje went with him because his work was done. Just Jack and me. We went deeper, ran a few more adits—sideways tunnels for you bloody civilians. The copper was there! Just like Borje said it would be, zinc too. We just didn't have the bloody horses to get it out and down the river. And then Bob came up dry looking for investors."

"That was the end of it?"

"Yeah. I showed our reporting results to a larger competitor upriver. They jumped. So, we sold the claim for a lot more than we paid for it; I hear that bloody mine is still producing."

"Must've pissed you off."

"To be that close to a strike? Yeah, it did. Maddening, but exciting…and it still is. I was hooked."

"So, you went back to Pennsylvania with Jack?"

"Fuck no! In Vancouver, Jack and I got on a plane—several of them—and went to bloody Borneo and their first mine, looking for… cobalt, I think it was."

"The Yukon to Borneo move, that's a change in scenery."

"Palm trees not bloody pine. But the same mozzies."

"Tell me about the mines you've got going."

"We got Terra 2 in Bahia State near Paratinga, about a nine-hour drive from Brasilia, the capital. In Vietnam, there's Pleiku in the Central Highlands."

"And they're successful?"

"That they are. Might be handy for you to know what the bloody hell was going on in their early years. We actually got going in both places about five years ago after about a year of prep work. We were starting to produce on a limited basis with the half-arsed refineries I got rigged up. Promising as hell, just like Borje predicted, but the banks were drying up on Bob. It was the Yukon all over again."

"Dark times," I said.

"Then HDW showed up with their money bags about two years ago. And with that money came the freedom to expand. We got going right off. We changed from underground mining with all its bloody shafts and tunnels and went to open pit."

"Meaning you just scrape away the mountaintops."

"Yeah, more or less. It ain't pretty if you fly over it, but they're both in the bloody middle of nowhere; nobody flies over them. It is a lot more efficient and cheaper way to upscale. And a hell of a lot safer for the workers."

"But what about the damage to the land and the people?" I asked, listening to my inner Alexandra voice.

"We meet or beat all standards and laws," Mick said, reverting to a bit of corporate-ese.

Mick could see his simple company bullshit wasn't working on me.

"Look, mate, mining anywhere for anything is ugly, but without it, we are all well and truly fucked. Breaking eggs to make omelettes and all that."

"And HDW has made all the difference to the omelette."

"Whether Jack would admit it or not, Southern Cross was circling the drain. And that would have been a bloody shame. I had a vested interest in making sure that didn't happen, because Borje was right—he's always been right. With the new bucks, we finally have a chance to play with the big lads. And there'll be a lot more where that came from. With the size of the claims, we'll be producing on a large scale for a long bloody time."

"You're pumped."

"Bloody right, I am! I had a pretty clear idea of what things were costing, what big expenses in workers and equipment had to be made. I've always known how much we needed to reach the potential. Bob agreed. Jack—bless him—wanted to keep doing what he always did."

"Which was?"

"Pray for a fuckin' miracle. Just trust that things would somehow work out. They mostly had in the past, but not this time. This time, Jack was all in and it was shit or get off the pot time. That new money was a bloody life saver."

"Did it come with strings?"

"Here's a big string: we're finally getting paid well. And regularly."

"You weren't before?" He burst out laughing.

"You having me on? With Jack, it was always feast or famine, mostly famine the last few years. Jack didn't tell you, did he?"

"No," I had to admit. "Any tough conditions from HDW?"

"Not really. It's meant more reporting to New York. That was the mine comptroller and Bob…and now the comptroller and a guy they replaced Bob with. I just keep my head down and do the bloody work, like always."

"It also meant inheriting new subcontractors."

"Yeah, pain in the arse at first. But they're OK; they've got the same marching orders as we do."

"Jack has a different opinion."

"Jack was happy with the hand he had. Didn't mean they were the best, just what he was comfortable with. All the new ones cost more but they're upgrades. I should bloody well know."

"What about the stories of aggressive tactics by Goal2go with the workers and the locals?"

"Some of that's exaggerated by the bloody protestors who are turning up these days, but you're right. Goal2Go's more…"

"Ruthless?" I suggested.

"Steady on, mate. I was going to say more efficient. But that's where I miss Jack the most. He was bloody marvellous with the tribes and the workers. On the one hand, he made the site tick along real smooth which made my job easier. But on the other, he gave too much away, overpaid the workers which was harder on Bob then, and me now, because I'm the one who had to tell them their wages were being lowered."

"So, what happens to you now?"

"Three more years, mate. I was promised that they wouldn't open up any new projects, that I could just focus on expanding and running the jobs in Brazil and 'Nam. Sure, they're big projects now, but I can do that with me eyes closed."

"What about Jack. Think he can go the distance?"

"Dunno, mate. You have to ask him."

"Any chance you get a piece of his share if he leaves early?"

"Look, five million is more than enough for me," he said, laughing.

"And what do you do with that pay-off?"

"Take the money and run back to Oz." Here he looked away. "Got some land near Perth, going to put up a sweet—" Then he snapped back to focus those lively eyes on me. "Hold up there. You're doing it again, mate."

"What?"

"Getting me to talk and giving nothing back. That's usually my game."

"Guilty," I confessed because what else could I say? He had me. The least a kidder can do after being found out by the kidder he was trying to kid is cop to it.

"So now your turn, mate. Jack said you believe Bob was murdered."

I had already decided what I'd tell him about my theories and the facts that Matt Kilmer and I had unearthed. I would keep Matt and his notion of a government-ordered hit out of it. So, I gave him a truncated version: Bob wanting to turn whistleblower, the threatening calls to Alexandra, finding the sniper site, our adventures in St. Barts and New York around HDW.

Mick listened but almost impatiently. I do tend to spin things out, dress them up.

"How did you know?" he asked when I appeared to be done. "It's a good bet that when a finance guy dies violently, it has something to do with finances. And the big changes in finances at Southern came from HDW."

"No, no. I meant how did you know it was a sniper?"

"I know a little bit about guns. I saw the police ballistics report that determined it was a large calibre armour-piercing cartridge.

So, I went to the crime scene. I ruled out the stray bullet idea but found where the sniper took his shot."

"You saw the ballistics report? How?"

"I'd rather not say."

He changed the subject immediately.

"Any idea what Bob was going to go public about?" he asked.

"No, beyond it had something to do with accounting and the mines. So here I am."

"I don't know what to tell you, mate. I don't make money; I spend it. We have a mine comptroller on-site. He tracks what I'm spending and, more importantly, what I plan to spend based on the need and the target. Then I tell Jack or Bob what I need and, with HDW now, poof! The money appears. I can tell you, nobody's robbing the till at my end. I'd know about it. You should come with me to 'Nam, see for yourself, fill your gob with some great food at the same time."

We did make it out for an evening at the Old Sailor. Bigger than Molly Malone's, it was just as quaint but louder. Mick and I reverted to shit-talking each other over more beer. We apparently amused the fuck out of each other, and it was all pleasant as hell again. We wound up supporting each other, arms laced over shoulders, on our meander back to hotel the way you see a team trainer escorting an injured player off the field. Only we were both injured. Oh, and dead-drunk. One of us was singing Aussie rugby songs whose lyrics, if I remember, were mainly comprised of "Oi! Oi! Oi!"

Next morning, I woke up late and to a championship hang- over. I caffeinated the fuck out of myself and was about to leave to take on (and likely lose to) the day when I spotted a note that had been slipped under my door. Even though the change in elevation induced instant vertigo, I bent to retrieve it. On hotel stationery, it read:

Hope you got what you came for. Cheers, mate. Mick. P.S. All this beer jabber stays between us, right? Take care of yourself. Oi! Oi! Oi! Ya Canuck bastard!

I left the hotel to wander unsteadily around the excessively quaint, excessively neat cobblestone streets in search of greasy eggs and greasier bacon. I didn't find the Dutch equivalent of a diner right away, but I did find myself on a particularly narrow and yet still excessively quaint, excessively neat cobblestone street where the red brick facades were punctuated by rows of door-sized plate glass windows. Super sleuth that I am, I deduced it was one of the more overt signs of the Red Light District: its infamous walk-by brothels.

Half the windows had curtains drawn because, I assumed, there was a lack of commerce at that time in the morning, while the rest featured attractive and scantily clad women bathed in— you guessed it—red lights. They lounged or strutted around. One of them yawned, another did her nails.

I didn't stare, not because I don't find attractive and scantily clad women appealing but because I felt badly for them. Toss aside all the intellectual and moral pro and con arguments and the fact they didn't need or want my sympathy, I just wished they could find other employment—and I bet many of them felt the same way.

A male passer-by had noted my head down posture and, either because he was a hawker for one of the brothels or just a fan, stopped me.

"They don't bite," he said in clipped English. "Well, unless you pay them."

"No thanks," I mumbled and went on my way.

Fearing I would wind up permanently dazed and confused in the labyrinth of identical streets (and canals!) I turned around and made my way back to the hotel but by another route where I found a bustling bistro or café or some such overly chic place. It was their chalkboard sign out front advertising 'American or English breakfasts' that caught my bloodshot eye.

I found a chair at an overly chic black wrought-iron table and went for more coffee and the English breakfast, which, if memory served me, was even greasier than its North American counter- part. I threw in a side order of bacon, the other part of the magic animal, to go along with the sausages, and another fried egg.

While I waited and for most of the meal, I thought about my whirlwind rendezvous with Mick. As I expected—but couldn't explain—the injection of cooking grease in my innards had result-ed in my wee brain de-fogging a slight bit.

I normally don't parse drunk talk, but I had no doubt that, behind his off-hand delivery, Mick chose his words carefully. Something in his lively eyes that, even through a film of beer mucus, showed deliberate, calculated thought.

We had gotten along well. You can't fake having a good time for that long, especially when loads of alcohol are involved. The majority of our time was spent in two loud bars where the conversation had to be superficial and intermittent. That was by his design. What there was to learn lay in the several hours in his hotel room. We may have had a pleasant beer dynamo hum when we sat down but we weren't shit-hammered.

Mick Rogers was nothing if not adaptable. His whole working life was one of being flexible to changes in real-time and reacting to shifting conditions on the ground. He couldn't afford a minute to sit back and deeply analyze a situation; he had to decide. Not unlike an air traffic controller. None of this 'on one hand...but on the other...' horseshit. Yes or no, right the fuck now!

Certainly, the massive infusion of cash from HDW represented a big change for him, but a change for the better, if he played it right. Unlike Jack, he saw the boatload of moola as an opportunity to make his job easier, his targets more attainable, his—and therefore, Southern Cross's—achievement grander. So, he signed on to it, even if it required new subcontractors and more stringent scrutiny which he could slough off to the mine comptrollers, and ultimately, to Bob Hale.

Armed with the promise of no new mine projects to undertake over the next three years, Mick could see his way clear to enjoying the time building onto what he had envisioned with all the resources he'd need and then fucking off back to Australia.

A by-product of the new regime was the marginalization of Jack Duffy, the man who'd hired him and ran with him for over forty years. Mick seemed fine with that. He had affection for his mentor and friend but, being adaptable, he was dismayed that Jack had remained with what he saw was the "old ways are the best ways" philosophy in an industry that had changed dramatically. Had Jack really remained enrolled in the old school that had been let out years earlier or did Mick just fuck him over as a condition of the pay-off? I didn't have an answer.

Concerning to me was Mick's relationship to Bob and Borje. I didn't get any sense he had one, even though they'd been comrades-in-arms for decades. He also had skipped over my simple yes or no question about Jack's bonus money should he decide to fuck off early.

But most alarming was Mick's reaction to the theory I'd supplied about Robert Hale's death. He didn't have one. No astonishment, or anger or even spirited disagreement. Instead, he wanted to know the details about the sniper and his bullet.

I cleaned every scrap off my plates and left, a mass with the density of plutonium roiling around my belly. I just wanted to nap. Sort of like how an anaconda must feel after swallowing a goat. But I had to postpone my dozing until after I had packed, checked out, and was uncomfortably settled in the airplane seat.

My wee brain hurt, and it wasn't only from my beer intake over the last twenty-four hours. I did the only sensible thing: I fell asleep. For seven hours.

I woke up refreshed and having almost emerged from my Holland daze, but suddenly worried and powerless at that moment, to do anything about it because one question didn't just linger but screamed out loud, over and over again.

If Mick was accepting, maybe cosy-cosy with the new HDW people in the field and the moves they were making, maybe he was in on the whole deal. Maybe he was just peachy with whatever they were doing and how they were trying to cover it up—whatever 'it' was. Had I not just tipped my hand to being on to them?

Settle the fuck down, Jake. 'Maybe' was the only sane answer at the moment. Just as easily, I said to myself, Mick had only wanted solid evidence behind my conspiracy theory before he bought it. He's a practical guy and wouldn't immediately get swept up by the outlandish scheme from an utter stranger without proof. Maybe.

CHAPTER SIXTEEN

Finally, back in Tampa, it was a joy to be cabbing it across the causeway. It felt like I'd been away from Alexandra and the Hovel for weeks. Gosh, I was looking forward to some sanctuary as I marshalled my resources—my code phrase for doing fuck-all but thinking.

The Tucson was in the driveway but the kitchen door was locked. Alex was probably out walking or down at the beach, I thought. I fished out my key, jiggled the sticky lock for bit. My reward for entering was almost taking a cast iron frying pan to the side of the head. Alex was poised behind the kitchen door, more than ready to use the stovetop weapon.

"Geez, babe," I said. "A simple 'Welcome back' would've been just fine."

"Sorry/not sorry," she said as we embraced. "You told me to be careful."

"Careful, sure, but not homicidal. What's up? Did something happen?"

"No, no," she assured me. "First time alone in the place. Strange sounds, animals out there, people talking. Stuff like that."

We were close to the street and on a corner lot. Indian Rocks is a vacation spot, so the ever-younger holidayers don't go to bed at nine like us old farts. I was very familiar with late-night golf carts stuffed with drunken teenagers and blasting hip-hop. Same for the racoons and possums rummaging around in the dark in our sheltered jungle of a backyard—but without the hip-hop. Cuter n'hell, yet unnerving when you first hear or see them.

"How'd it go over there?" she asked when we were settled into our assigned patio stations accompanied by two tall Tanqueray and tonics loaded with our squeezed limes (for the scurvy).

"Honestly," I began, trying to verbalize the events of the last two days. "I'm not sure. Amsterdam's absurdly quaint and has great bars. Mick was forthcoming to a point, but overall, I came way with more questions than answers. How'd you make out—besides pining for me?"

"Got caught up at work. Turns out the place isn't crumbling without me. Did some digging around on those two subcontractors, Pretoria and Olrud."

"And?"

"Not much on the financial side. Both are private—surprise, surprise. We know that HDW has a piece of them—Harrison Wagner confirmed that—but we don't know how big those slices are. Pretoria Mine Management has been around for years. Started in South Africa just after the war. Jan Vandegrift is the CEO, quite young. They can do pretty well everything around a site from building the actual mine and refinery to sourcing the specialized machinery. They were a big name in the mining industry until about five years ago."

"What happened?"

"There was a major disaster at a mine they built in Zimbabwe. Eighteen dead. The lawsuits and fines, never mind the cost of the re-build and their loss of reputation really hurt them. They still must be of considerable size because they claim operations around the world working for some of the major players. But not nearly as big as they were.

"Olrud's been around for a lot more years. Norwegian family business that started, it looks like, just after the steam engine was invented. Chairman is Halle Olrud, with several other Olruds in senior roles. They used to have their own fleet of ore-carrying ships but have sold off most, if not all of them, and shrunk the company. Like Pretoria, they're a lot smaller than they were in their hay day. Over the last little while, they've started leasing, not only ships but rail cars and trucks that often are needed for the so-called last mile to a remote mine site. Oh, and warehouses and storage facilities."

"What are they storing?"

"Mainly the minerals that were mined for, either waiting to get shipped to end users' manufacturing plants or to other refiners for more processing."

"Anything there with those two?"

"Nothing that stands out. I spoke to Sasha at the office. She knew both of them and said both of them are well-regarded even though they're now mid-sized. Sasha's been analyzing the industry for decades, and said that, a few years ago, rumour had it that the pair of them had financial issues. They had heavy capital costs and became overextended which isn't unusual if you're on the wrong side of the boom or bust mineral world. When mining companies suffer, you do too."

"So, you're needing investors, but you still want to be private and you're desperate enough to overpay to find them. Perfect for the likes of HDW to swoop in."

"Looks like that's what happened."

"Any chance you had a look at Darien Global Personnel and Goal2Go?"

"No. I can, but maybe you could tell me why."

"I don't know."

"That's a big help."

"If I take Mick at his word, nobody's siphoning money, meaning there's no simple embezzlement. So, it has to be something going on with the mines themselves that Robert Hale was threatening to uncover. Those two companies sound like they're respected and reliable. It's just a wild shot that it might have something to do with the other two."

"Were you tempted to go to Vietnam with Mick to see for yourself?"

"You know, I was. But I also knew it would be pointless. As pointless as me looking under the hood of a car. I wouldn't have a fucking clue what I was looking at."

"Did you think that might be the reason Mick invited you?"

"Thanks…but now that you mention it…"

It's true there had been points in my semi-wild night in Amsterdam when Mick and I had been dancing and we both knew it. Why couldn't his bogus invite have been another two- step, just one that I hadn't seen?

"Any progress on a deeper profile of Mr. Wagner?" I asked.

"Just started. What's next for you?"

"I need to see Borje."

But first, there was going to be a tricky phone call with Jack Duffy. I had to report in, and I had to hide or at least dampen down Mick's apparent enthusiasm for the new way of operating under HDW's regime.

Jack didn't want to talk, leastways not on the phone.

"It's about four o'clock," he said. "I can knock off work, because…well, I've got precious little goddamned work to do anyway. Meet me at my place."

I drove down Gulf to Treasure Island and the address he gave me. It was a modest four-story building but on the water. His third-floor corner unit was nice, his wide balcony overlooking the Gulf was nicer. He shepherded me along the wraparound deck and stopped.

"There she is," Jack said, leaning over the railing and pointing at a small marina on the other side of Gulf Boulevard.

"There who is?"

"The Coddamn," he said proudly. "She ain't new but she's a beauty. 2005 twenty-five-foot Scout Abaco, twin 115 horsepower Merc outboards. The latest Garmin fish finder and chart plotter sonar gear, Raymarine autopilot."

Oh, swell, I thought. A boat nut.

I ended his technical rhapsodizing by asking if it had a shitter.

"And it's got a shitter!" he roared and clapped me on the back. "So, how'd you make out?" Jack asked after we'd settled in the patio furniture with our drinks.

"Good, I think."

"Not surprised that you can't be sure. Mick can be a bit...slippery. Probably helps him in his job. Did you learn anything?"

"Nothing that jumps out. Mick's pretty pleased with the progress."

"He would be. I suppose that's a good thing. I just hate the goddamned open pits and all the water they're using."

"I know you do; he does too. My main takeaway is that Mick has a ton of respect for you, for Borje...and for Bob. He really wants these mines to produce. I don't think he ever got over having to walk away from the Yukon."

Jack looked out over the water and a smile crept onto his face as he remembered.

"Heard about that, did you? Yup, that was a goddamned shit show," he said with obvious fondness. "You see anything sketchy going on?"

"Not that I could see. He swears that nobody's stealing cash; I want to believe him. So, it wasn't a rip-off that Bob was going to blow the whistle on. Have any thoughts what else it could have been?"

"None. I've been racking my brain. It's allegedly my company, but I'm just as in the goddamned dark as you are."

"Could it have been the environmental damage?"

"Don't know how. Bob hadn't been overseas in a while so he couldn't have seen the goddamn mess."

"Well, it's got to be something to do with the mines. I should talk to Borje."

"No time like the present," Jack said. And with that, he went inside, found his phone, and called. When he came out, he told me that Borje would meet me inside at Caddy's in fifteen minutes.

"Bee hates coming here, and he really hates the smoking," Jack explained, as he fired up another Camel.

I left my car at Jack's, walked over to the restaurant, and

grabbed a table inside. The cavernous, breezy joint was done up in full Florida beach bar decor. Pastel colours, plastic furniture on the painted concrete floor, walls festooned with neon or tin beer signs, compulsory Tampa Bay Bucs regalia, and mounted stuffed fish. It was a gorgeous day (again), so the place was empty inside while the picnic tables in the sand were jammed with drinkers trying to find some shade under the forest of Land Shark umbrellas.

As I got my near-sub-zero Yuengling draft in a chilled mug, a figure who'd just entered made straight for my table.

Intimidating isn't the right word. Maybe imposing. Tall, slender, obviously fit, he moved with a casual grace as he crossed the floor. His wispy blonde hair was tinged with grey, his face almost classical, high cheek bones, broad forehead, a strong jaw, aquiline nose, serious mouth, but above all, alert blue eyes that darted, always studying, always curious.

What struck me immediately was that those eyes of his would not meet mine. I've known people like that, people who, for different reasons, find it difficult to look directly at another human being.

"Borje. Jake Lydon. Thanks for meeting me," I said as I got up and offered my hand. His handshake was weak, indifferent, not, I sensed, because he was shy, but because he viewed it as an unnecessary formality.

He declined my offer to buy him a beer, saying: "I don't drink alcohol."

[Sidebar: Why do many teetotallers insist on telling you about their abstinence when a simple "No thanks" works just fine?]

"I am not sure why I am here," he said as he sat down. He was a soft talker and his English was perfect but formal which shouldn't have surprised me given his long history in the States. "But Jack said I must talk to you."

"I need to understand how Southern Cross works, how you do things," I said, getting to the point. Small talk and tall Borje didn't mix.

He paused for a while, organizing his thoughts about his company.

"It starts with Jack," he began. "Do not be deceived by his

manner; it would be a mistake to underestimate him. He sees possibilities, before they are even possible. We have mined for very
different minerals because he can imagine the need far in the future.
It is a very long time and much work before a new mine opens and
produces, so he must be right years earlier."

"So, say he's right, then what happens?"

"He asks me for a general idea of which mineral is where, how
much there might be, and off he goes with Robert to develop a business case. They must estimate world prices five, ten years into the
future, and also the costs of expanding any mine. If they agree it
might be worthwhile, I am instructed to select a specific area,
sharpen my estimates about yield, about the challenges of building.
That takes the longest time, as I must collect all the data—the
results from the test holes, topography and so on—to build my
picture."

"Then what?" I asked when he finished his explanation. All the
while he'd been fidgeting and alternating between gazing out the
window or around the restaurant.

"If Jack is satisfied with my picture, he negotiates with governments for the claim. Always the claim is very much bigger than what
we can do. He works out arrangements with the local population,
starts Mick off doing the things that need to be done while Robert
secures the rest of the financing. You see, it is all Jack. And he is
seldom wrong. Seven or eight years ago, he picked Brazil and
Vietnam—a world apart but both countries have giant reserves of
neodymium and no one truly who was going after them."

"Then why isn't Southern a roaring success?"

"The problem is the money cannot keep pace with his
ambition."

"And now it does."

"Yes."

"What now for you? Mick told me there would be no new
projects for three years."

"I am becoming accustomed to doing not much…at last. But
what they said was no more projects involving Mick. They have
ambitions elsewhere to expand and much work has to be done

before Mick takes over. They have said I am to select five more sites which is what I am doing now. I do want to see at least one more until the end."

"Where?" I asked.

"In the north of Sweden. I believe there is very much rare minerals near Kiruna. I went there. I want to prove it and then retire."

"Sweden? I was told you didn't travel to sites."

"It was a vacation to see family at home. I do not visit work sites. After many years, they are always as I imagined them to be, so what would be the point?"

"Are you that good?"

"I am that good," he said, not in the least bit boastfully, any more than if he'd been bragging about the sun rising in the east.

"Then, excuse me for asking, but why are you still at Southern Cross? I'm guessing your talent is known in the industry. You must have been recruited by the big boys."

"Yes. But I know that none of them would give me the freedom that Jack gives me to work the way I do. They all say they would, but that is not what I have seen. And there is such a thing as loyalty. Jack took a chance on me. I will always be in his debt."

"Tell me about Bob. Were you close?"

"I liked Robert very much. We were the same in many ways. Just as Mick and Jack are the same. They are impulsive, loud, very emotional. Robert and I are...were..."

"Counterpoints?"

"Yes. Thank you. We were counterpoints. The other two are good with people. They like talking to them and joking and..."

"Drinking."

"Yes. Robert and I preferred our reports and spreadsheets."

"Did you get any sense that Robert was nervous or worried towards the end?"

Borje sat back.

"You must understand that all four of us have been nervous or worried for decades. Each one must deliver, or the project falls apart. Jack must predict the mineral and the demand. I must tell him exactly where and how much can be produced. Mick must build and operate the correct facility and Bob must raise the money we need to pay for it. After a time, it was merely the way we were accustomed to working. I think we all became very good by always being under pressure."

"Like lumps of coal being squeezed into diamonds?"

Here, Borje broke into a slight chuckle—his equivalent, I guessed, of a thirty-second raucous, roaring belly laugh.

"A dramatic comparison but, yes, I think."

"How did everybody cope?"

"Mick, he drinks. Jack drinks and gets married. Robert and I go back to check and check again the numbers."

"But both you and Bob, the other two as well, couldn't be under the same pressure anymore with the money coming in from HDW."

Borje quickly glanced from side to side at the empty restaurant, and he leaned forward, knitting his long fingers into a steeple. His quiet voice dropped to a whisper.

"You know about that? We were instructed that was a very big secret."

"Sorry, Jack told me. It was important that I know."

"You do not work for them, do you?"

"Fuck, no. I think they may be up to something. That's why I asked about Bob's state of mind lately."

Borje stared out the window.

"You must understand: Of all of us, I would say that Robert was the most nervous. All the time. It did not seem to matter if things were going well or poorly, he would worry. And if it was not about a big thing, he would worry over a small detail."

"So, no change in him?" "No...not that I noticed." Borje looked at his watch.

"Can we be finished now?" he asked. "I am expected at home." He left quickly, ignoring my half-assed attempt at a thank you and a handshake. I stayed behind, went out on the deck to the uncovered smoking section, ordered another beer, and watched a spectacular sunset.

But I didn't really see the celestial show. My wee mind was

racing about the brief interview I'd just had. If I had to engage in my bullshit psychoanalysis, Borje was way more firmly on the spectrum than I was. Obviously at a genius level of intelligence, he was also one of the most socially awkward people I'd ever met. I'm not exactly graceful when I meet strangers, but I can do it, the way I could do math in high school; I just hated it, almost as much as I hate fucking socks. It wasn't only his avoidance of eye contact. His body English spoke volumes, as he nervously fidgeted, shifting his positions as if he were sitting on a cushion of thumbtacks, clearly desperate to be anywhere but in front of me.

That, or he was just really shitty at lying. I reminded myself of Bob's comment to his wife about "deceptive Scandinavians." Was this what he meant? For an answer, I walked back, and pounded on Jack's door. When he finally opened up, it was obvious that in the hour I'd been at Caddy's, he'd passed the time by getting wired to the tits. He was almost incoherent.

"You again!" he roared. "C'mon in, lesh have a little drinky-poo." With that, he turned and headed back to the living room, ricocheting off the hallway wall.

Fucking marvellous, I thought, this'll be fun.

"Jack, listen to me. I can't stay. I just have two quick questions."

"C'mon, shit down. I'll answer over a drink."

"No, Jack," I insisted. "I just want to know if Borje ever looks you in the eye."

He squinted at me and puzzled over the question as if I'd asked him to name his Grade Three teacher.

"You're right, goddamnit! He never doesh. I don't think he'd recognize me in a goddamn crowd!" he added with a loud guffaw.

"Good, Jack. Now…Question 2….Did you tell him that I thought Bob was murdered?"

Again, he thought as hard as he was able to in the moment. It was a heroic struggle.

"Poor Bob," he said.

"Jack, did you tell him?"

More agonized thought.

"No," he announced. "....I mean Yesh, goddamnit. I'm shure I did."

"Thanks, Jack. Now go to bed!" I ordered.

"Okey-dokey," he answered like an obedient nine-year old, albeit a shit-faced one, and trundled out of sight.

Well, that was a colossal waste of time, I thought. I needed those two answers to be definitive. Best bet: Borje's evasive mannerisms were a built-in feature, not evidence of him having bull-shitted me. That didn't mean he wasn't busy being a deceptive Scandinavian, merely that his nervous habit wasn't the obvious tell. More importantly, if Jack did suggest that Bob had been deliberately killed, then why hadn't Borje at least mentioned it in relation to his good friend? I'd try again in the morning when Jack's booze cobwebs—hopefully —had been brushed away.

CHAPTER SEVENTEEN

I called Jack on his burner the next morning. I let it ring twenty times but no answer. Somewhat alarmed, I then called the office.

"Marjorie, it's….Lawrence…Palmer," I said, momentarily forgetting my bullshit name. "Is Jack around?"

"No, dear. I haven't seen or heard from him today."

"When he shows up, could you let him know I need to ask him one more question for the article."

She promised she would. And I was left to stew for a while. In mid-stew, my phone rang again.

"Jake! Helluva nice goddamned day, isn't it?" roared Jack, far more cheerily than I thought he would be after tying one on the night before.

"Sure is."

"Want to play hooky with me?" he asked.

"What'd you have I mind?"

"Let's go fishing. Whaddya say?"

"Can I bring Alexandra?"

He paused.

"Naw. Not this time. Boy's club."

"But I told you I'm not crazy about fish—"

"Stop being such a goddamned ninny! You can drink beer and watch. C'mon!"

I used to think I was a pretty good cajoler, but this guy was world-class.

"OK, sure. I can be at your place in a half hour."

"The hell with that! I coming to pick you up. There's a church across the street from you. On the other side of it is an inlet with a little marina. I'll see you in fifteen minutes. Bring beer."

He hung up. Like I said, world-class.

Between our twenty miles of a barrier island sand spit and mainland Pinellas County is a stretch of water dividing us; at points, it's a half mile wide, at others, only a couple of hundred yards. That whole uneven strait has been engineered, with sea walls on either side and a series of man-made inlets and bays lined with houses. As Jack had told me, one such inlet was on the other side of the church across from me. I was waiting on the dock there for about a minute when Jack and the Coddamn chugged along- side me. He didn't tie up but kept jockeying the boat to close the gap to the pier.

"Permission to come aboard, Cap'n?"

"Granted, swabee!"

Unsteadily and ungracefully—the only two ways I do things—I stepped onto the slightly bobbing deck and collapsed onto a cushiony white chair, reaching for my cooler.

Jack declined a beer as he had a cupholder full of Jack Daniels on the go. Fully in command, a soggy Camel clenched between his teeth, he backed the Coddamn up and wheeled it around, getting clear of the dock. Unlike his office, the boat was spotless, mostly white with blue and gleaming chrome trim. Its huge black outboard motors burbled away as we slowly headed north.

"So where are we going?" I asked.

"Gonna see how the other half lives," he said.

True to his word, Jack eased past mansion after mansion in Belleair, the next town up from IRB. He'd occasionally motor into the bigger inlets and perform a tight turn while I gawked at what real money looked like. Every few McMansions was a modest, older bungalow which, Jack explained, was likely being bought for about a million dollars to be torn down and replaced by a new barn "inches from its goddamned neighbours."

We crawled up the east side of the strait past Clearwater then turned around and headed south.

There are only two outlets from the barrier island to the open sea of the Gulf of Mexico, one at the south end at John's Pass near Jack's, the other one in the north just before Clearwater. Beach.

I assumed we'd be turning into that pass at Clearwater Beach to take us out into the Gulf so I could watch him fish, but Jack guided the Coddamn past its mouth and continued along the sheltered strait back towards IRB. I was puzzled.

"I thought we were bound for Mexico," I said.

"Not today, I'm afraid. Maritime forecast said the sea's way too goddamned rough for this old girl," he said, patting the dashboard.

"Just our luck."

In a wide, open stretch of water he put the boat into neutral while we sat and smoked and drank and drifted.

"Ain't this the life?" Jack said.

"That it is."

"Wouldn't it be great if all this goddamn mess was behind us and we could just relax?"

"That it would."

"So have you found anything more?" he asked.

"Not really. Just to confirm part of our conversation last night: You did tell Borje that I thought Robert was murdered."

"No…I didn't say that. I didn't tell him."

Rather than argue with semi-drunk Jack over the different answer drunk-drunk Jack had given me the night before, I changed the subject.

"Did Bob tell you about the suspicious bookkeeping at the mines?" I asked.

"He did. You've got to understand that Bob could be such an old woman about his precious spreadsheets. It turned out to be an honest goddamned mistake. I didn't even mention it to you because it was nothing."

"Tell me about this honest mistake."

"About three months before he died, he came to me all hush-hush and told me there should be more mineral coming out at both mines. A lot more."

"Why did he think that?"

"He knew the amount of royalty payments we were making to the Brazilian and Vietnamese governments. They're based on the tonnage of ore extracted and partially refined. He goes to Borje and asks about the size of the veins, the purity, and our refining capacity. And he concludes that we should have more mineral."

"Was he wrong?"

"Of course, he was goddamn wrong! He was a goddamned whiz in the money business, but take away the dollar signs in front of the numbers and he was lost. He worked off those spreadsheets, not in the real goddamned world. Shit happens in the real world—a run of bad weather, machinery breakdowns, worker shortages, a hundred different things can mess up his goddamned theoretical projections."

"Makes sense," I said, and it did. "So that was the end of it?"

"You don't know Bob. Dog with a goddamned bone; he wouldn't let it go."

"What happened?"

"So, he comes to me a couple of days later, said he picked a two-month period, looked at the royalties paid based on tonnage and then compared them with the shipping invoices from Olrud for those months. Their bills are also based on the tonnage shipped. They should be the same as the weight that was loaded at the mines. They weren't. Based on that difference, Olrud charged us almost 50% more. Bob was in a goddamned panic."

"Why did he think it was such a big deal?"

"He thought Pretoria was under-reporting to the governments to save royalty costs. We've never fucked around with money we owe host countries; I just don't allow it."

"Was Pretoria fucking around?"

"No. One goddamned phone call to Mick cleared it up. I called him for an explanation because he handles both the mine reports and the site bills. He swore that Pretoria was playing it straight and that he'd get the comptroller to look into the bills. Then he calls back to say that Olrud had overcharged us by mistake; they had apologized and sent new invoices that agreed with the royalties, along with a refund."

"So simple bookkeeping error?"

"Simple goddamned bookkeeping error. End of story. Christ, I can't believe I just spent that much time talking about it. Anything else?"

"Yeah, as a matter of fact. Did you get anywhere with that ballistics report?"

"Not really. Steel comes from iron ore. The traces and proportions of goethite, ferric oxide, lepidocrocite, and magnetite suggest it came from Western Australia. There must be ten companies bringing that ore up so no telling what mine it came from."

"Where could it have gone to make the steel?"

"Most likely China. They send over 80% of their iron ore there. No chance nailing down where exactly it got turned into bullets."

"So dead end there."

"Does that mean we're at a standstill?" he asked.

"There are a couple of things I want to look into but, yeah, for the moment."

"Let me know what's going on, will ya?" he said, but I got the feeling that, for some reason, he was almost relieved that we seemed to be spinning our wheels.

I hopped out at the marina, thanked him for our three-hour tour, and for not shipwrecking us. It had been a good time, but Jack had puzzled me; his behaviour had been so un-Jack. He'd been subdued, almost wistful, instead of his usual full bore, hard-charging self.

It was only a half-block walk home, but I had a head full of bees (and alcohol). The queen bee was a math question. What was the statistical probability that the same accounting mistake was made at two different mines bringing up the same mineral at the same time? And a follow-up question: had I just been handed the first decent lead about what might've been going on at the mines or was Jack right in insisting that it was trivial?

I was completely mystified and so was Alexandra when I got home, looking more confused than usual.

"So, tell me what happened," she said.

"Hard not to have a swell time with Jack. Say, darlin,' you wouldn't happen to know off-hand, why a mine might underreport what it was extracting and shipping, would you?"

"Not off-hand," she said. "No, wait. They might lie to the governments to cut down their royalty bill. I'll ask Sasha tomorrow. Why do you ask?"

"Just a little detail that neither Jack nor Mick had bothered to mention earlier."

CHAPTER EIGHTEEN

The next day, while we were waiting around for her mining expert to call back, Alex filled me in on the research she'd done while I was cruising with Jack.

"Goal2Go is a mid-sized security firm," Alex explained. "Head-quartered in Atlanta, it operates mostly in the Southeast. Started up just a little over three years ago. They began with con- tracts for college football games. I guess that's where the name comes from. Looks like they supply security guards at any place people gather. Doesn't seem to matter what size of crowd—high school dances, shopping malls, rock concerts, racing events. CEO is listed as G.H. Keitel."

"George Keitel?" I asked.

"Dunno. The entry in the corporate records just said 'G.H.' Why did you say George?"

"The name's familiar," I answered. "Just can't place it."

"Anyway," she continued, "They don't seem to have much of an international presence. A few contracts for soccer stadiums in Mexico and Costa Rica. No mines anywhere that I could see."

"Any idea where their start-up money came from?"

"Nope. But it doesn't look like they would've needed much.

They hire locally, as required, based on the signed contracts."

"What about Darien Personnel?"

"They're sort of like an office temp agency, only for the construction industry. They find tradespeople, mostly labourers for building sites and mines. Owned by Daresh Patel, based in Panama, but with offices throughout Central and South America. They're also in the Far East that they service from Singapore. They get paid by the number of heads they find and how long they stay."

"Big company?"

"Not really. Like Goal2Go, they hire locally. They need a small group of managers to run everything."

"That's gotta be a tough business though. Lots of paperwork, high turnover."

"Probably, but going by the way Mr. Patel lives, it's also a profitable one. I found all sorts of articles about his flashy lifestyle—houses, cars, boats, grand parties, a string of pretty young women, and such. He seems pretty wired into the power players wherever he operates. For sure, he pulls some levers in Panama given all the photos of him with politicians and generals."

"Any scandal?"

"Loads. But all personal and gossipy. Nothing criminal."

Sasha did call back with her theory about why a mine might underreport the amount of ore it was bringing up. Same theory as Alex's—to fuck governments out of the royalty payments they were owed. She actually did have examples of companies who'd tried that. It hadn't gone well for them.

We decided that Southern Cross would have to be foolish to try it.

The mind is a wondrous thing. Mostly because you wonder just what the hell is stored up there.

I remembered a line Arthur Conan Doyle has his Sherlock Holmes say when his sidekick Dr. Watson expresses astonishment that the famous detective didn't know the earth revolves around the sun:

"I consider that a man's brain originally is like a little empty attic, and you have to stock it with such furniture as you choose…"

My chaotic brain is stuffed with not useful facts but the jumbled bric-a-brac of arcane trivia and strange remembrances. At the oddest times and through the oddest of associations, things pop up —memories, pictures, sometimes, just a name—that I wasn't thinking about or didn't even know I'd retained. Leastways for my wee brain, the harder I try to recall something specific, the more elusive it becomes, staunchly refusing to be unearthed. And then, maybe hours or days later, it emerges, more or less shouting: "Hey, fuzz-nuts! Remember when you were trying to remember this?"

One such event happened a couple of nights later when I couldn't sleep. I opened a beer, then my shitty laptop on the patio and began idly flipping through news stories. It's a dark and quiet time then. A warm night, the slightest of breezes. The hubbub of the day was muted. No traffic, no conversation and laughter, just an occasional barking dog or a siren, because apparently bad guys, like rust, never sleep.

The name George Keitel was silently yelled out from the rickety windmills of my mind. And then, it came back to me. I was sure he was one of the executives from White Iron that, thanks to Alexandra, were getting the snot beat out of them at the Congressional hearings.

I dug up the video I had watched. Sure enough, the Committee chairwoman introduced each silent witness from the military contractor. Among the geek chorus, George Keitel, Vice President, the Americas. I flipped to Goal2Go's website and there under the Executive Team section was the same stern-faced George Keitel who according to the brief bio beside the photo "has thirty-seven years' experience in the US military and private sector, primarily focused on security and protection services." White Iron was not named directly, but obviously his time there would have formed a goodly portion of his credentials.

This was getting a tad too complicated for my wee brain. Could it really be that HDW, who we knew had a slice of White Iron, didn't also have some relationship with Goal2Go that was being run by a former senior White Iron guy?

But, Jake, Wagner had denied it.

Gee, Jake, what are the odds that a hedge fund owner told a lie? Say it ain't so. But, Jake, why would he lie about it? He admitted to having money in Olrud and Pretoria.

That's the complicated part, isn't it?

For Christ's sake, Jake! How about you get a life, finish your beer, and go to sleep?

The next morning over coffee, I told Alex about my sudden and previously less than total recall.

"Did you come across Keitel when you were kicking the shit out of White Iron?" I asked.

"You say he was in the Americas? Sorry, no. Wrong hemisphere. We were hired to focus on the mid-East. That's where the media heat was."

But she agreed that it was likely that HDW had invested in Goal2Go despite Wagner's denial and that their apparent hardball tactics at Southern Cross mines were in keeping with the allegations of White Iron's fast and loose predilection for unchecked violence.

When Alex and I were first talking about her mining report, she had shown me some of the jerky phone videos of security guys aggressively breaking up a crowd of protestors near Southern Cross's Brazilian mine and read accounts of how they'd done likewise in Vietnam. At the time, I didn't know they worked for Goal2Go; they didn't wear uniforms with any markings.

Security guys are about the only contractors who get to boss their bosses around. A plumber can recommend you get a new toilet, but he can't force you to buy it. Lawyers can't make you take their advice. But a star's bodyguard, the President's secret service detail, or a large but minority investor can override your decisions all in the name of either keeping their employers safe or keeping the money tap turned on. Goal2Go was hired to protect the mines and then was given—or took—the leeway to decide how. And what they decided to do was to be complete assholes to the local population and to their land.

One immutable law of nature is that nuthin's easy. Before us was the ol' riddle wrapped in a mystery hidden in an enigma. Were we pulling strands together to weave a coherent narrative or were we grasping at straws? Fucked if I knew. For a fact, we had a bunch of crimes—the murders of Robert Hale and Matt Kilmer, the attempted intimidation Alex faced. And those were just the ones we knew about.

But beyond that, we also had a shitload of sketchy behaviour. The relatively sudden cancellation of the investigations in Hale's death by both the St. Petersburg police and the FBI, the uncon- firmed investments of the shadowy Harrison Wagner, the possible rigging of two critical mines' results half a world away from each other, the surveillance by someone of not only me and Alex but the four principals of Southern Cross Mining.

And what of that quartet? Each, in their own way, was bril- liantly capable but idiosyncratic, each holding a piece of the puzzle —whether they knew it or not. And each with different histories, motivations, and perhaps, loyalties, but welded together for decades in the age-old, nerve-wracking hunt for buried treasure.

And we had one near-certainty: Somehow, money—great gobs of it judging by the lengths people were willing to go—lay at the heart of everything, as it often does.

Jake, step away from dealing with minerals in distant lands and money passing through distant hands. Shop locally. Take a look at the police behaviour after Hale's death. I had a general idea why the investigation had been called off but no picture as to how these things are stopped. But someone close to me did.

I called my daughter, Halley, who's a detective in Toronto Police's Homicide Division. I asked her how a murder investigation gets called off.

"Dad, we don't vote on it. We have a chain of command and limited resources. Every police department's the same. The Chief of Detectives decides whether to continue an investigation or not after he or she listens to the investigators assigned the case. What stage are they at, anything promising. Working theories and so on. Then we go back and back again, reviewing all our notes, re-interviewing witnesses, analysing the forensics again and again. Looking at tips we might've tossed out earlier. Then we do it again. But the longer a case goes on, the colder it gets."

"How long does that take?"

"Could be months."

"Ever had it happen to you?"

"Sure. A couple of times. Pissed me off each time. You don't want to admit you've come up empty. You get over it and move on because it's not that rare and because there's always another case. I read a recent FBI report that said that, on average in the US, homicide departments have just over a 50% clearance rate."

"Holy shit! Half of all the murders don't get solved?"

"Looks that way. We get about 80% in Toronto, but we aren't patting ourselves on the back. It means one in five murders wind up in the cold case file. That's families, loved ones, entire communities that don't get answers. And it means, the killer is still walking around."

"But you re-open if new evidence comes up."

"Of course....What have you got yourself involved in now, Dad?"

"Nuthin.'"

"Da-aaa-aad," she said, stretching one syllable into at least three.

"OK, OK. There's a murder down here that I heard about.

Police closed the case but it's bugging the shit out of me."

"So, what does Alex think of your pleasant little hobby while you're on holiday in the south?"

"We're a team on this one."

"Bullshit!"

"Call her and ask."

"Dad, I'm a cop; all I do is check things."

"Check away. And while you're doing that, contemplate, if you will, how wonderful it feels for a father to have his own daughter call him a liar."

There was a long pause during which I guess she was doing a bit of contemplating. She knows me well enough to understand that I take just about nothing personally. It may be a character strength or a weakness, but I really don't give a shit what anybody says about or to me. Asterix for Alex; what she says matters.

"Fuck, you're good," she finally said, realizing I was playing her with my guilt schtick.

"Thank you."

I got off the phone even more mystified. Robert Hale's murder case was shut down in a couple of weeks. Why? Why was everybody keen to buy the magic stray bullet from a gang member's gun when everyone associated with the case had to know it was bullshit? Even I had figured it out, for Christ's sakes. Did they reckon it was a one-off, targeted hit that left no usable evidence but that was unlikely to repeat? While they had the how and where, there had been zero apparent progress in finding the all-important who and why. Was that why they closed it down and went on to other events where a human being decided to extinguish the life of another? Maybe it was that simple.

I knew of only one person who could, for sure, give me some answers: the Chief of Homicide Detectives. I also knew that, if something sketchy was going on, the annoying, insinuating questions of a fucking Canadian nosy parker might not be all that welcomed by the Chief of Detectives, particularly one who was maybe connected to some homicides of his own.

I figured the ballistics guy who had helped Matt Kilmer might be more willing to talk. I remembered his name typed below his small, neat signature on the ballistics report.

I called the listed number for the Forensics Services Unit and asked for Quentin Purdy.

"I'm sorry; Mr. Purdy doesn't work here anymore."

"What happened to him?" I asked, somewhat alarmed.

"He retired."

"Oh…do you know how I can contact him?"

"Who's calling please?"

I hung up.

Curiouser and curiouser, I thought.

He had a relatively uncommon name, so it didn't take long to track him down to a small, neat bungalow in North-East St. Petersburg. The house was among leafy blocks of small, neat, older bungalows, most, like Purdy's, with tidy gardens and closely trimmed grass. His home was grey stucco with white shutters.

A very large Black man answered the door when I knocked. He filled the doorway. He wasn't fat, more like chunky and prodigiously muscled. Maybe 6'5 or so, weighing at least 300, mid-fifties, tightly cropped hair without a hint of grey.

"Mr. Quentin Purdy?"

"Can I help you?" he asked in a deep, low voice drenched in the same irritation I display when a stranger—always selling something I don't want—decides it's a swell time to knock on my fucking door.

"Mr. Purdy, I'm sorry to bother you, but I have to talk to you,"

"About what?" This said with more irritation.

"Matt Kilmer."

The instant change in his demeanour was remarkable. Gone was the irritated homeowner confronting a stranger at his door. In his place, a nervous, maybe frightened man.

"You shouldn't be here," he almost whispered, looking around me.

"Why not?"

"You just shouldn't."

"Should I be going to the *Tampa Times* instead, maybe speculate to a crime reporter that a certain St. Petersburg ballistics guy—recently retired—illegally sent a report to a private citizen in Indian Rocks who wound up dead under mysterious circumstances a few days later? Would that be a better use of my time?"

"How did you—?"

"How about we go inside?"

I wasn't about to push my way past him, any more than I could push my way through a medium-sized mountain. He paused and, crammed with reluctance, opened the door.

The place was spotless and crowded with overstuffed furniture.

One wall surrounding the small fireplace was devoted to Ohio State football memorabilia. Pennants, team photos, a framed jersey. Dead-centre in the display was a picture of a helmetless and fearsome Quentin Purdy in a lineman's three-point pre-snap squat. There were a number of trophies on the mantle and one section of the wall featuring Westfield High football with a slightly younger Purdy in an equally scary pose. Every guy I know bullshits about their alleged glory days in high school sports. Quentin had the receipts.

"Let's go out back," Purdy said.

In the kitchen I was introduced to Jeanine, a gracious woman who offered me iced tea.

The patio doors opened up to a fairly large lot that dwarfed mine and humbled my landscaping effort. Lush weedless lawn, sculpted flower beds in full bloom and set off by the all-important superior edging. We sat down on two comfortable padded chairs and were uncomfortably quiet for a while as we sipped the tart iced tea.

"Great job on the yard," I said. "Who's the gardener?"

"We're a team," he answered proudly.

"You played ball?" I said.

"Four years on the O-line at Ohio State," he said. "Three as a starter. Left tackle."

"Go, Buckeyes. Looks like you could still play the blind side."

"Thanks," he said, with a wistful smile. "I blew out my knee badly in the second last game, and I mean, man, I destroyed it."

"And that was it?"

"Before I got hurt, I was projected to go as high as mid-fourth round in the NFL draft. After, I slid to 6th or 7th round maybe, with an outside chance that there might be a couple of teams willing to gamble their late-draft pick on my full recovery."

"What happened?"

"Everybody passed on me. I supposed I could rehab and work like crazy to catch on somewhere, Canada maybe, but the math was against me. Did you know that every year, 35,000 college juniors and seniors are eligible for the NFL draft? About two hundred are picked, and most of them will never see an NFL field. I knew my time was over."

"Sorry," I said, thinking about the crushing of bodies and dreams in the sport I love.

"Don't be. Most people don't get treated like a hero for four years. Imagine the thrill of a hundred thousand fans in the stands going crazy over you and their team. And they just invited me back to Columbus for the 100th Anniversary of the stadium this summer. We're going."

"What happened after the injury?"

"I was on a free ride in school. I majored in Criminal Justice Administration—my dad was a cop in Houston—so I made the switch to ballistics. I figured the guns weren't going anywhere in this country, so them being involved in crimes wouldn't either. Studied my ass off. Worked my way up. And now, this house is paid for. I've got two great boys—one on a ball scholarship at Baylor, the other is in pre-med at Columbia. He gets that from his mom; Jeanine's a nurse."

"Not that you need or want a compliment from me, but well done. You've earned your retirement."

"It wasn't my idea!" he blurted out and then seemed to regret it.

"Let's stop for a minute," he said, composing himself. "Why am I even talking to you?"

"It's pretty simple. I was a friend of Matt's. I think he was murdered, and I think it's connected to that pickleballer in the park."

That got his attention right quick.

I ploughed on, giving him the bare bones of what we'd found. I deliberately left out any mention of HDW and the New York money, limiting it to a mining exec being killed to prevent any whistleblowing.

Quentin leaned back and took it all in. You could see his eyes darting as he analyzed each sentence of the plot as I outlined it.

"And Matt got involved how?" he asked.

"Looks like he was just a concerned citizen. Based on the reporting and then his contact with you, he thought the whole thing was being hushed up to avoid panic over a professional assassin being on the loose."

A sickened expression crossed his face.

"So, what you're saying is that I caused Kilmer's death by sending him that ballistics report."

"No!" I quickly added. "The son of a bitch driving that SUV caused his death!"

"Any idea who that son of a bitch was?"

"No. Obviously somebody with an outfit that has professionals and resources."

"Somebody like a police department? That's what you're getting at, isn't it?"

"Possibly. They do have the ability to wiretap and bug offices, they do have SWAT sharpshooters…and they know how a smart criminal can get away with a crime."

"I've worked with St. Pete cops for twenty-seven years. I have never seen or even heard about anything like that. Sounds like complete bullshit to me."

"Maybe it is. Let's talk about your forced retirement."

"That ballistics report I sent to Matt. I e-mailed it through the department server; they had the record of it. Which meant they had me."

"Why was that such a big deal?"

"That's what I thought. Kilmer was ex-ATF. I confirmed that. Didn't see the harm. The man was a colleague. His expertise might be valuable in the Crescent Lake case and in the future. Lord knows, we could use it."

"I gather the department did not see it that way."

"No, sir; they did not. They gave me a choice: keep quiet and take the early retirement package with full benefits under the guise of streamlining operations or get arrested, likely convicted, and lose everything. It wasn't a tough decision."

"Why do you think they played hardball with you? They could've let slide you sending that ballistics report. Kilmer was dead. No harm, no foul."

"I did break the law. But yeah, they could've let it go. But there was other stuff."

"Like?"

"I hated that they were shutting down the Crescent Lake case. That stray bullet theory—I don't know where that came from—but it was just plain wrong right from the start. The shells they found were from only two handguns. They were scattered all over the parking lot like the two shooters danced around in about ten different places and didn't hit either one of them. Gangs don't fight that way and, besides, they empty their clips."

"None of which could've found a path to Kilmer on the other side of the park."

"Exactly. And even if one, by a miracle, did get down there, either of those two calibres couldn't have possibly done the damage that the victim suffered."

"But a high-powered rifle using an armour-piercing cartridge from the roof of that apartment building up 5th would."

"You found the spot too?"

"I did. Clear shot."

"I made a stink; Ted Myers, the head of forensics and my boss, told me to shut up about it. Then they found out I went to the outside. Myers is buddy-buddy with the Chief of Detectives in Homicide. They fish together. He said the decision to drop it came from higher up. I think the PR people were involved. Lot easier to blame Black gangs for it which pissed me off. Still pisses me off. But that was that."

"So, case closed."

"That's not exactly right," he said. "That was another weird thing. We were told they were shutting down the investigation, but they haven't officially closed it."

"What's the difference?"

"You close a case, and all the information goes to the state archives—notes, incident reports, forensics. The public can access the files. They obviously didn't want that. I've seen that trick before."

"What's the name of the Chief of Detectives?"

"In homicide. Lionel Henderson. Why? What are you going to do?"

"I don't know…something."

"Whatever you're thinking, it isn't Lionel Henderson. I've worked with him on dozens of cases; he's the real deal."

"Friend of yours?"

"I wouldn't say that."

"So how well do you know him?"

"Well enough to know he's a good cop," Quentin emphatically said, getting all bristle-y. I'm pretty sure there are few human beings who would want to be the cause of pissing off Quentin Purdy while sitting three feet away from him.

"Look, I can't help you," he said. "I'm proud of the life Jeanine and I built. I won't threaten that. I can't threaten that. You understand."

"I understand, Quentin." And I did.

He got up and I followed in his wake through the house, thanking Jeanine for the iced tea along the way. On the front porch, just before he clasped a giant mitt around my hand, he said: "I wish you well. Good luck."

I drove away thinking that it'd be pretty swell to have an ally like Quentin Purdy. Smart, committed, with a decent outrage quotient. But he had already answered the questions I had. Now, he just wanted to help. I had no right to endanger him any further.

CHAPTER NINETEEN

I drove home to find my yard and driveway filled by two cop cars, a large black van and some obligatory nosy bystanders peering from behind yellow police tape. Panicked, I jammed the car into "P" on the front lawn. Halfway up the driveway, I eluded the police, got under the tape. Two people in hazmat suits were poking around the side window. I found Alex talking to two cops at the patio table. I rushed to her, and we hugged and hugged.

Despite making the Wizard of Oz's cowardly lion seem like Braveheart, I really don't care all that much about my personal safety. I mean, how could I? I smoke, for Christ's sake. But the thought of Alex being hurt or worse made me crazy.

"Are you OK? What happened?"

"It appears," a policewoman piped up, "as though someone fired a shot through your side window into the living room. First glance, it looks like a stray."

"You could have been sitting in the La-Z-Boy!" I said.

"But I wasn't," Alex said. "I was in the kitchen when I heard the shot. I'm fine."

But she wasn't. She was trembling.

"What do you want to do, babe?" I asked, as the last of law

enforcement cleared out. "You say 'quit' and I'll quit. If you don't feel safe here, we can pack up and be gone tomorrow. I've got no dog in this fight."

"But you know—we know—the people that do."

"Look, we can stop at the *Times* offices for a sit-down with a reporter our way out of town. Give them everything we got and see what they do with it. Something will happen."

"Sorry, Jake, this is our home. I'm not running away from it." I loved her for her defiance, but I was scared shitless.

Stan and Laura from next door came by, just like they had last year after I was forced into some gunplay. They wanted to see if we were OK and to ride our ass a little. Both motives deserved a margarita. Or two.

"Listen," Stan said. "This is quite the tradition we've got going. You guys get shot at and we come around for margs."

"I wouldn't mind if we skipped the bullets part," Alexandra said.

"Have it your way, but it just wouldn't be the same," Laura said.

Our little incident was duly reported in the local paper the next day. While the article stressed the likely random nature of shot, someone at the paper made sure to mention the shooting at the very same address a year earlier.

Funny how publicized calamity always attracts a crowd. Complete strangers felt entitled enough to wander up our driveway to examine the window damage for themselves.

I varied my response to them, alternating between the direct: "Get the fuck off my property" and the more nuanced: "Police said the guy might still be hanging around," while glancing nervously up and down the driveway.

One such gawker turned to be our insurance agent. He introduced himself as Don Cooper and I liked him right away. Not only because he was about my age and had a deep, booming voice, just like my insurance guy in Canada, but because he was wearing Florida business attire—a faded Jimi Hendrix T-shirt, old jean cutoffs and flip-flops. I remembered Alex telling me that she had only dealt with him by phone and that his voice had cinched the deal for her.

Cooper told us that, unfortunately, because of our deductible, the policy wouldn't cover the window's replacement.

"Oh, I see," I said. "Just deny, deny, deny. Is that it?"

"Wait a minute," he said after a pause. "Any damage inside?"

"Bullet tore the shit out of the place."

"Then I might be able to do something," he said.

"Then I might be able to offer you a beer."

"What kind?" he asked, which startled me. It was the sort of question I have never knowingly asked of anyone offering me a free beer.

"Yuengling."

"That'd be fine."

"Lemme get this straight: if I had said Bud Light, you'd be outta here?

"Like a shot," he said, smiling.

He then went on to briefly illuminate me about the taste of beer being influenced by the variability of the malt, yeast, and hops, side-tracking a bit to tell me about why he had a preference for a glass as it protects the aromas of fruit, leather, floral scents and oil or some other such bullshit.

"Oh, for fuck's sake, do you want a goddamned beer or not?"

"Please, but what's the damage inside?"

"Go see for yourself."

"I can't believe the destruction that one bullet did," he said as he emerged from the house with a beer and glass in hand. "The panelling, that Tiffany lamp. Must've ricocheted to take out the TV."

We three sat down at the patio.

"Too bad it's not Molson Export," he said as he poured.

"How the Christ would you know about Ex?" I asked while Alex rolled her eyes.

Don explained that, as a student at the University of Michigan, he and the lads used to take the train from Ann Arbor to Toronto where the drinking age was lower, and the beer was better.

"But you're just sucking up to a client right now, aren't you?" I asked.

"Yup. I mailed your policy to your Canadian address, remember? I know you folks in the Great White North love your beer. But truthfully, Export really was the best of what we tasted. And we tasted a lot."

We were on our second beer when an attractive red head pulled up in our driveway on a bike. I was about to shoo her away when Don Cooper boomed out "Hi, honey!" So that's how we met his wife, Ellen, whom he described as an amazing artist. Alex was intrigued to learn that Ellen taught a ceramics class at the Beach Art Center across the park from us.

"Sign me up," Alex said, to Ellen's delight.

"Hey! You could make me an ashtray," I suggested.

"Not that kind of ceramics," Ellen said. "More creative sculptures."

The next morning, there was a knock at the side door. While answering it, I couldn't help but notice that the sunlight through the windowpanes had disappeared. I thought that perhaps a surprise eclipse was going on.

Quentin Purdy stood in the doorway.

"Remember what you told me when we first met, on your front porch?" I asked.

"Yeah, I said that you shouldn't be there."

"Well, bud, my turn to say it."

"Yes, I should. I read about the gunshot. You're sticking your neck out. That isn't right. Now shut up and show me what happened."

When a guy that big and with some history of doing violence to his opposition tells you to shut up, well, sir, mum's the word.

We moved to the side window where we regarded the bullet hole —and the trampled coleus underneath it—like it was the fucking Mona Lisa, before he went closer and poked around.

"When you're taking a shot through glass," he explained, "the biggest factor determining its direction is the angle of obliquity. If its angle of obliquity is dead-on at 90 degrees, certainly less than 15 degrees, the projectile will pass directly straight through. At any angle greater than that, the bullet will generally start to yaw and be deflected. In this case, from the damage to the glass, it appears to have been fired at about a 45-degree angle."

All the while staring at the window, he backed up to the areca palms bunched up along the driveway. He then turned around and started rummaging through the palm leaves.

"No damage I can see to the palms," he said, turning back to us, "so the shooter was probably standing about here."

"What's that tell you?"

"It wasn't a stray bullet. Were you ever in the front room?" he asked Alexandra.

"No. Kitchen, Back bedroom only."

"Did the Sheriff's Department find the bullet?"

"They must've," Alex said. "There's a hole in the wall by the front door."

"Show me, please."

With the two of us and the giant of a ballistics expert in there, our tiny living room was officially full. He studied the gash in the panelling by the door jam.

"So, it hit the panel and block wall at about this angle after passing through double panes. There's not much of a hole in the concrete block so I'd say it was a smaller calibre—maybe a .32. You can see that the slug tumbled. Unlikely to be identifiable."

"I heard one CSI guy say it was pretty mashed up," Alex offered.

"Were you ever outside?" Quentin asked.

"Sure. All the time, back and forth."

"Show me."

We filed back outside. Alex pointed out the patio table, the shed door, and her reading spot on the other side of the house.

"Any conclusion?" I asked.

"This was no professional. First off, if a pro wanted you dead, you'd probably be dead. With your activity outside, he could've just waited a few minutes for a clean shot. So many questions. Why would he fire so obliquely? If he's the same guy from Crescent Lake, why did he switch to a smaller calibre? Why wouldn't he have used the same weapon? We didn't find it or any casings there. The site was clean."

Quentin looked around.

"From the roof over there," he said, pointing across the park at the two-story municipal building. "If you can see the top of that roof then he can see you."

I had a thought. "Could it be a pro trying to look like an amateur?"

"That's what I'm thinking. The angle suggests he was deliberately firing away from the kitchen. It's just a truly bad shot for no reason. What did the Pinellas County Sheriff say?"

"Not much," Alex said.

"Can't we get the police report?" I asked.

"It just happened," Quentin explained. "The incident report isn't available to the public until the case is resolved. That could be months, assuming it's ever resolved."

"Know anybody over there?"

Quentin didn't answer, no doubt fully aware that he'd already been busted once for shipping unauthorized info to people.

"He was trying to scare you," he said instead.

"It worked. I'm scared," I said.

At his car, I thanked him for coming.

"I'm not done," Purdy said. "There might be somebody I know at the Pinellas Sheriff's who could get me the police report."

"Quentin, I'd rather you didn't. This is getting way too dangerous."

"I said: I'm not done."

"Do you at least own a gun?"

"You kidding me? This is Florida. Of course, I own a gun. Do you?"

As soon as he left, I hurried inside and e-rummaged around for his phone number.

"Hello, Jeanine?"

"Yes."

"This is Jake Lydon. We met a couple of days ago at your home. Old guy, long hair, Hawaiian shirt, loved your iced tea."

"I remember."

"Listen, Quentin just left my place and I'm worried."

"Why?"

"I don't know how much he told you, but there are some nasty things going on."

"He hasn't filled me in completely. I know there's more he's not telling me."

"He's already been very helpful, but he just shouldn't be involved anymore."

"What do you want me to do?"

"Convince him to let it—all of it—go."

"You don't know Quentin when he's made his mind up."

"That's why I'm calling. He won't listen to me, but you probably have a better chance at persuading him to back off."

"I'll try."

"Please do. For your family's sake."

CHAPTER TWENTY

T here's an ebb and flow to being involved in shit like this. The trick is to assemble as much information as possible and that takes time. Slow boring time when you're working in isolation building a picture, moving it from abstract to hyperrealistic. Alexandra is a champ at doing this. I just didn't want to press her so soon after the incident—which we referred to as The Incident.

A few days passed without us even speaking about the case.

The rising sun's rays shot through and illuminated the Spanish moss draped on the Live oaks in the park such that it looked like tinsel. The sun even lit up the twitching tails of the squirrels effortlessly scampering along the power lines in search of who-the-fuck knows what. We were on the patio enjoying the silence and our coffee when Alex brought the whole Southern Cross Mining mess up.

"Want to hear what I found out about Harrison Wagner?" she asked.

"Dirt! We want dirt!"

"Not much to find," Alex said. "There's even hardly any pictures of the guy. He's not your average multibillionaire. It's like he's trying to be Howard Hughes."

"These days, with social media and everybody being a goddamned citizen journalist, that can't be easy."

"I know, but there's just not much. No page six material. No social events, no known charities, still married to his high school sweetheart."

"What about her?"

"Mary. Low-key as well. She has a foundation. His name's not on it. Big gifts to PBS and NPR, a couple of international aid charities."

"Kids?"

"Two boys. I guess one's a fuck-up with the fast cars, big parties, rehab stints, splashed all over Page Six. The other you wouldn't call a trust fund baby. He's a high school swimming coach in California."

"How's Wagner live?"

"For all his money, modestly. He's got a place in Weston, Connecticut, as a matter of fact, near Keith Richards'. It's nice but, really, it could be Keith's gatehouse."

"Any idea of what he's worth?"

"Not definitely, but more than Keith. Estimates are all over the map because all his investments are private. Forbes has him at $10 billion. Bloomberg guessed twenty-five."

"What's five or fifteen billion between friends? Tell me about the scandal."

"He was a top broker at Lehman, had a big book of clients and was doing really well. This was at the height of the dot com bubble in the late 1990s. But I guess a couple of clients lost a bunch of money with him."

"That couldn't have been unusual—especially then. Just sore losers?"

"No, there's more to it. They claimed they never authorized all the buys and sells Wagner made. Lehman looked into it. Saw that his trade orders had their forged signatures. Plus, quite a bit of money was just plain gone. So, they marched him out of the building."

"Lose his broker's license?"

"For two years."

"No arrest, no lawsuits?"

"That might happen today, but I guess Lehman made it right and it went away."

"So, slap on the wrist. Then what?"

"He dropped off the radar for a few years. Licking his wounds, I suppose. Then HDW hit the sweet spot when the hedge funds were all just taking off. He started out with a lot of his old, big-money clients who went with him, but he really hit the jack- pot when he guessed right on the subprime fiasco. He dodged that and bought into a lot of private companies who got beat up after 2008. He proved two basic principles in investing: Wall Street has a short memory and money follows money."

"Anything on the personal side?"

"Not much. There was a profile in *Vanity Fair* a few years ago, entitled *The Billionaire You Didn't Know About*. It wasn't very compli-mentary."

"Oh, do tell."

Alexandra went on to describe the portrait painted in the maga-zine piece. The writer had done her homework, tracking down some of Wagner's classmates from high school and university. Wagner had grown up middle class in Syracuse, New York. In high school, he was described by a former friend as a "hustler," operating a lawn mowing business and delivering newspapers. Soon, the friend said, he had more requests than he could handle, to the point that he formed a company, hired friends to do the delivering and cutting, quit manual labour himself while paying his workers less than what he had been making. "We did the work while he made the money," the friend recalled. HDW Enterprises Inc. dissolved in acrimony just before he was accepted at Cornell, majoring in—surprise, surprise —business.

His roommate at the Ivy League school said Wagner wasn't really diligent about his own coursework, instead putting his efforts into "dressing and speaking well" and writing essays for other students. That business changed because of demand and so, following a pattern, he began buying and selling ghost-written essays by other students, while defending his dishonest scheme by claiming "It's just a piece of paper everybody gets anyway." He didn't get his own piece of paper because he was kicked out, under a cloud of secrecy. Rumour had it, he was busted in his second year for the plagiarism ring but threatened administration with a real blow to the school's reputation by revealing the extent of his operation. He was allowed to withdraw.

Another rumour had it that his departure was the result of a possible sexual assault of an Ithaca bar server.

Wagner finished his college career at SUNY-Potsdam with a degree in Business Admin. A fellow classmate remembered him talking endlessly about his desire to get out of "this two-bit school in a two-bit town" so he could move to New York and conquer Wall Street. "We had no doubt that was exactly what he would do."

Two days after graduation, Wagner left upper New York state, bound for Manhattan. Wagner then worked for a series of broker-ages while obtaining an MA then a PhD in Business from an online university.

A senior trader at Schwab recalls Wagner as "a brash kid who could talk a mile a minute. Given enough time, he could persuade you that Rhode Island was bigger than Texas." Another, this at Lazard Freres, said "He had that certain something—some might call it a killer instinct—that we look for."

That is, until the scandal when everybody, overnight, lost his Rolodex card.

Although it was much more recent history, the article was thin on detail about HDW and Wagner's emergence from the wilderness. The writer actually had found less out about HDW's dealings than we had. She did suggest that as Wagner's power and influence grew alongside his bank account; few people would go on the record, obviously fearing the guy.

When Alex finished her tale, she asked what I thought. "Doesn't sound like a guy used to losing."

"And he really hasn't. But, Jake, I've been around these guys for most of my adult life. He's just not that unusual. They're all aggres-sive; they all cut corners to make the sales, and they all live large."

That made sense. In sports terms, in every small town everywhere, there are a few, maybe only one athlete, who absolutely dominates their high school football and basketball standings or junior hockey league. They get to the pro level, and, with few exceptions, they almost look ordinary. Everybody in the bigs is that good; everybody has that combination of talent, discipline, and ambition.

"So how did Wagner become a superstar, like Brady, Gretzky or Jordan?"

"The big Wall Street money makers push right up to the line. Looks like Wagner never minded crossing it."

"My, my, such a cynical outlook," I said.

"Pretty clear I've been hanging around you too long."

A quiet week passed. No drama, no incidents involving the police.

Until I got this e-mail:

Would you come to see me please? I'm in town to do a little deep-sea fishing. I'm staying at the Don Cesar. Meet me in the Rowe Bar in an hour, ask for Ray Sanders' table.

The sender was Harrison Wagner.

I was tempted to reply:

Fuck that. C'mon over to my place. We can examine the bullet hole in my window together.

But instead, I wrote:

Sure. Alexandra will be with me.

His reply:

I prefer if you come alone.

As always—well, almost always—Alexandra was understanding. She suggested I go along with his wish for a one-on-one. I could tell she was on the verge of providing me with grooming and wardrobe suggestions, but quickly recognized the madness of her folly and abandoned her attempt to improve me.

After choosing an unsuitably shabby outfit, I quickly went online to learn about our planned meeting spot. The Don CeSar was the grandest grande dame of old hotels on Florida's Gulf Coast. It had a colourful past that included an original owner dropping dead in the lobby after its opening in 1927, purchase by the US Army when it was transformed into a war-time hospital then a VA centre. Deserted for years, it fell into utter disrepair and became a candidate for the wrecking ball until it was snatched up for peanuts and lovingly and very expensively restored to its original Art Deco glory. Our rendezvous point was to be in the Rowe Bar, which, going by the images, was an airy but expensive-looking place that reminded me of St. Bart's.

Driving down Gulf I determined my approach to the multibillionaire. I decided to start off by being annoying, quickly moving up to enraging then reaching for open hostility.

Against all evidence, I am selective about who I piss off. Top of the list are criminals and bullies who do cruel, unkind, or devious things to people. Next are phone/cable salespeople, then any stranger who decides, unprompted, that it's their moral duty to point out one or more of my "offensive" habits. I also get amped up by any fucking braggart who feels compelled to tell me—or deliberately imply—that they earn more, travel more, live better than I do. Or is healthier, holier, or more enlightened than I'll ever be.

OK, OK, maybe I'm not that selective after all.

But I do tend to go easy on telemarketers because it's probably the only job they could find at the moment, and I am crushed if I annoy or anger Alexandra. Most times.

With Harrison Wagner, I figured: What the fuck? Why dance around what had become obvious—well, to me anyway? But I wanted to open with at least one unobjectionable comment: a compliment for his selection of an alias: the combination of names of the founders of McDonald's and KFC.

[Sidebar: I can look at a Sudoku or a simple math problem and be completely flummoxed, but give me some trivia-based shit and I'm a god-damned grandmaster].

Up ahead in the distance, the famous Pink Lady loomed, separate and distinct from the unremarkable condo buildings sitting at a discrete distance from it. Its eight stories of painted stucco would be almost laughable in Chicago or Toronto. But here, girded by tall, stately palms and bathed in Florida sunshine, its pink- ness was perfectly placed, its towers and minarets crowning the spreading wings.

Walking through the Don's opulent lobby, I attracted my share of stares from guests who had to be wondering how the garish old hobo managed to get past security. In the bar, I was guided to Ray Sanders' table which had an expanse of glass overlooking all the moneyed merriment going on outside.

"Mr. Kroc and the Colonel would be pleased," I said as I shook his hand.

"I value my privacy," he said with the approximation of a smile and the plain voice I recognized from Alex's recording.

"You gotta tell me how you do it," I said. "My adoring fans and the paparazzi are driving me fuckin' nuts."

His appearance was as non-descript as his voice. Pastel blue golf shirt, tan slacks, he was average height, not muscled but fit. No chains or jewellery or expensive watch, just a simple wedding band. Obviously well-groomed, with short, styled brown hair and smooth, manicured hands. His face was not handsome, but it wasn't ugly. Call it late middle-aged ordinary, and with no hint of a sunburn which I would have expected from a day fishing in the Gulf.

"So, how was the fishing?" I asked.

"I'm going out this afternoon. Care to join me? I understand the wahoo are biting."

"Thanks, but I don't enjoy mindlessly killing something for kicks."

"Suit yourself. I gather you've never experienced the thrill of the struggle."

"No, I gather I haven't. Care to let me in on why I'm here?"

"Right to the point. Good. The point is, Mr. Lydon, you and

Ms. Simpson are deliberately trying to make my life difficult."

"How we doing?"

"You must stop."

"Aww, Harry, I just met you and already you're trying to eliminate some joy in my life."

"You don't know who or what you're dealing with," he said, his lips getting just a little bit thinner.

"Au contraire, mon frère, I know exactly who I'm dealing with: a greedy little prick whose fanatic—some would say rabid—thirst for fucking money compels him to do a bunch of illegal things. Am I getting warm?"

Given the sudden crimson colour of his face, either someone had just jacked up the thermostat to about 105 degrees or Mr. Wagner was about to blow a gasket. He then displayed a pretty impressive level of Zen-ness by taking deep breaths and settling himself the fuck down.

"Mr. Lydon, as you must know, you are an irritating little man. Ordinarily, I would simply remove you from my situation. I chose not to. Rather, I'm going to explain to you what is actually going on."

"All ears."

"You don't exactly understand money because, I believe, you never had much of it until you latched onto Ms. Simpson."

"Ooo, that hurt, Harry."

"Do you any idea what fifty million will buy?"

"Let's see. About 5,000 water wells in Africa. Or thousands of yards of concrete to cover dirt floors for countless Central American families."

"Yes, that. My wife's foundation does that, thanks to me. Personally, I could buy a big house on Long Island that I don't want and would hardly ever be in. Or I could buy a couple of companies in emerging industries, so they emerge faster."

"I know what you mean, Harry! I do figuring like that all the time! 50 bucks for a lunch out with maybe one drink each or a two-four of beer and a bucket of KFC to have at home for days. Same principle. Only with a whole lot fewer zeros."

"I started out needing other people's money," he said, ignoring my lippiness.

"Like from the clients you ripped off?"

Not too surprisingly he got all bristle-y at that and became almost emotional again.

"That was bullshit! Those stupid rich people wouldn't listen to me. They wanted to play it safe, protect their little stash. So, I went ahead and invested their money the way I wanted and made them a lot more. That was my job."

"Everybody made money?" I asked.

"Virtually everybody. I lost a couple of my bets; that's what happens on the stock market. They went after me and Lehman. I made it all up to them."

"I'm thinkin' you just didn't pay yourself the regular commission when you were playing around with other people's dough."

"Goddamn right I didn't! I would have seen less than half a percent on their piddly safe buys. When it was all me; I made them the money."

"And then got fired for it."

"As I said, I vowed right then that I'd get my own money. And I did."

He had a point, a slender one, but only if you subtract such nasty realities like laws and company rules. It struck me that that's the way he worked, that's the way he saw himself. Maybe not above all those annoying regulations, but separate from them. Operating on a different plane. A lot of sports and music or movie stars live like that. And I bet every eventual dictator or corrupt politician starts out believing that they're just different, somehow special enough to ignore convention or statutes. Look at it this way: Not too may car thieves don't steal cars because they think: "Gosh, I better not; there's a law against that." They think: "I want that car. Why shouldn't I have that car?" Then they get away with it, so how about boosting another one? And another one. Is that hubris? Maybe, but it never seems to start out that way. And you only get to call it hubris during the post-game show if the guy gets caught or killed. And not everybody does.

"The problem with the stock market and American business," Wagner said, "is the quarter-by-quarter sickness. Everything matters in three months. Sales departments rush to book orders that may or may not exist. Executives claw to report results that'll give them bonuses or share options. Then they have their little conference call to give analysts guidance about the next quarter. They miss their guidance by a tiny bit and their stock gets hammered."

Wagner was on a roll.

"Take some international event or a trend. The financial press instantly analyzes it, then announces "Fear of recession in China sparks market sell-off"! Or "Major supply chain problems send jittery investors to the exits." And what happens? Stocks plunge, but less than 24 hours later, stocks rebound. "No wait. It's not so bad after all." What happened to the fears and long-term problems? Poof! They apparently just disappeared."

I had to admit, he had quite the flair for sarcasm. And he wasn't done.

"It's like the guy shouting "Fire!" in the crowded theatre. Everybody stampedes then stops and goes: "There's no fire after all!" and they all rush right back in, only looking for better seats. Meanwhile, overnight, companies lose or make billions in so-called value. Are they really worth that much less or more than the day before? Think the Chinese are doing any of that? They've played the long game for five thousand years. They must shake their heads while they kick our asses all over the world."

"Meanwhile, you just sit back and keep making money."

"Do you know what that money buys me?"

"More than anything you want or could possibly ever want?"

"It buys me safety and control."

"Not so much for the Botocudo and the Montagnards."

"Who?"

"The local people in Brazil and Vietnam. You know, just some of the folks you're fucking over just so you can be protected and in charge."

"There is a price to pay for progress in the real world."

"And you don't want to pay it, no matter who or what gets trampled along the way."

"Spare me the damn kumbaya moment. You can't possibly be that naïve that you don't know there always have to be winners and losers…in everything. I know what side I'd rather be on."

"With your billions, why don't you just stop?"

Wagner looked at me genuinely puzzled, as if no one ever suggested it before or he hadn't ever thought about it.

"Because there are billions more," he simply answered.

"In mining?"

"Yes. About five years ago, it occurred to me that our—the western world's—failure to corner the available supply of rare earth minerals was an epic tragedy. The demand for them was going to explode and keep up for at least the next one or two generations, likely longer. China had the supply, but logically, there had to be more outside China. No one was really going after it, except the Chinese. They say the demand for rare earth minerals will increase by 600% over the next fifteen years. The race is on and we—this country, the West—cannot afford to lose it. Otherwise, we'll be at their mercy for generations while they become the only superpower. And, by the by, think they treat workers any better in the countries they are exploiting?"

"So, you're on a one-man crusade to humble China? How noble of you."

"There is nothing wrong in making a profit while I do my bit. I am assembling private companies that I can manage and provide the investment and the access to capital to make a dent."

"And somehow little Southern Cross was the key?"

"To start. I hired a mining expert to do some left-field thinking to find small, private miners who were likely prospects. He went back fifteen years through records of claims made for rare earths around the world and Southern Cross popped up. No one had staked claims that big but with such a poor record of royalties paid. And no one was showing such profits for selling those claims when they couldn't finance their own projects. Which means they were onto something."

"Four people could do all that?"

"One person could do all that," he corrected me.

"Jack is that valuable?"

"Jack?" he actually snorted. "We don't need Jack. His time is past. No, Borje Hallstrom is the real unique talent. Thanks to him, the mines are producing high-quality neodymium. Thanks to him, Southern made gigantic claims that will pay off for years. And thanks to him, we have identified at least five new sites that we're moving on right now."

"What about Mick Rogers?"

"He's adequate, but good logistics managers are a dime a dozen."

"And Robert Hale. Was he dispensable?"

"That was unfortunate. But I had nothing to do with that."

Wagner was staring right at me, his gaze not dropping, almost daring me to challenge him. I didn't. Christ, I wanted to, but I didn't have all the facts. And he hadn't given the slightest indication that he was lying his fucking head off.

"Anything else you'd like to ask me?" he asked.

There's something really eye-opening and unreal about meeting a person like Wagner who lies and rationalizes as easily as they breathe. You soon understand that conversation of any kind—even hostile ones like this one—are completely pointless. So, I thought, what the fuck?

"Yeah, now that you mention it. Any idea what's going on with Southern Cross? I'm betting you're doing something shady at the mines that Hale found out about and had to die for."

I'll give him credit. His face didn't redden to that crimson shade it had sported earlier. I thought it might. Nor did his voice crack or raise in volume. But he clearly was making some kind of an effort to not lose it on me again.

"I believe I already answered your question," he said drily. "I believe you didn't."

"I think we're done here."

"OK. What about the name of the person that's been threatening my lady or the guy who put a bullet through my brand-new living room window?"

"If you'll excuse me, Mr. Lydon…" he said rather forcefully and picked up his phone. "Thank you for coming here…. I hope you'll understand my meaning in our little chat. For your sake," he added.

"I'll take it under advisement," I said. "And thank you ever so much for wasting my gas and time to come down here just so I could get bullshitted in nice surroundings."

And with that, I got up and left, marched out to the car, and just sat behind the wheel for a bit, shaking. I wasn't aware of any DIY manual that explains how to successfully 'poke the bear' without the aforementioned bear tearing you to shreds.

I thought of a couple of things as I drove home, one specific, the other very general.

Specifically, why, when I brought up Bob Hale's murder, did he instantly deny any part in it? I hadn't accused him of being involved. Hinted at it maybe, but he could've let that slide.

Generally, I considered the universes that people create for themselves. I do it, you do it and, for sure, Harrison Wagner had done it. In those worlds, we seek to fashion a customized logic and rationale that justifies why we do the things we do. For the vast majority of us, this handy self-delusion is harmless; maybe a little damage to other people's feelings. Sometimes, we feel bad enough about doing so and will try to rectify it. But that's not the case with sociopaths and garden variety narcissists like Wagner. They couldn't give a shit about the garbage they spew and the damage they do in the pursuit of whatever their selfish hearts desire and their minds can explain away.

That's the category I decided Harrison Wagner occupied. I don't know a lot of billionaires. (No, wait; I know three, two of whom I helped put in prison. But that's a different story). However, it's clear that the richer you get, the more armoured and enamoured you become with the rightness of your actions. You have people who work for you that tell you you're a fucking genius and you have the bank account scoreboard that proves it to you. You also have the fierce determination to protect yourself and your money at all costs.

"How'd everything go?" Alex asked when I got back to the
Hovel.

"Swimmingly," I answered. "Liar."

"I may have called him out."

"About what?"

"Pretty much everything."

"Do you have any idea what you're doing?"

"You might've asked that before I left."

"And the answer would've been...?"

"I'll take 'No fucking clue' for 200, Alex."

"Now he knows we're not giving up."

"And I know he was lying about Hale. We're on the right track.
For sure."

"So now what?"

"I'd give worlds to know. I think the best bet is to lay low for a
while. At least give him the impression that we're backing off."

"And are we?"

"I don't honestly know, babe."

FOR THE NEXT SEVERAL DAYS, we were marvellous at resuming what
might be called a normal life. We socialized with Stan and Laura.
We played tennis on the courts across the street—despite the inces-
sant 'thock-thock-thocking' of the pickleballers playing across the
walkway that meandered through the park. We walked the beach
and/or watched sunsets. We ate and drank at Hurricane Eddy's
which, even though it didn't have the dive bar delights of the now-
deceased Red Lion, was serviceably close to the hovel and offered
chilled beer mugs and decent food.

But it was disheartening though, to see only glimpses of the lives
we thought we had designed. Most times, we looked over our collective shoulder. For a guy hanging around the park and watching our
house, a car repeatedly driving slowly by. We didn't see either and
breathed a little easier.

I insisted that Alex go to Ellen's 7 pm ceramics class at the IRB
Arts Center; I reminded her about making me an ashtray. Then I

sat around being nervous while I tried to watch a documentary on our coastal seas. Usually, I can depend on David Attenborough's soothing voice to put me under in less than fifteen minutes, but not that night. Just before 10, I elected to brave another Alexandra lecture about my "macho bullshit" and went to meet her and escort her home through the darkened park.

To my surprise, she seemed happy to see me and we chatted away as we strolled hand-in-hand along the pathway. The park was dead silent and suitably spooky looking, with the old Live Oaks all black and gnarled, their dripping Spanish moss ghostly lit by the distant streetlight.

Just past the public washrooms, four big guys jumped us.

CHAPTER TWENTY-ONE

Two goons came from behind. They pinned our arms behind us and zip-tied our wrists while, simultaneously, the two in front plastered over our mouths with duct tape before we could cry out. I'm not exactly a small man but I was obviously not a match for the giant behind me; no way could I break his hold on me no matter how hard I tried. Quickly, our heads were covered by thick hoods, and we were hustled and dragged the fifty or so feet to the end of the park. Car doors opened and we were roughly forced inside.

Start to finish, our kidnapping hadn't taken a minute. Hard not to admire the military precision with which it was carried out. They weren't amateurs; these lads have done this before, I thought.

I tried to imagine our route. A quick left onto 16th, then a right. We were heading north on Gulf Boulevard towards Clearwater.

I squawked, feigned suffocation. A guy reached under our hoods and tore the duct tape off.

"You OK?" I whispered to Alex.

"Yeah, under the circumstances."

"Lean forward; it won't hurt as much."

I counted time while I guessed at our direction. A right—we were heading inland over the Belleair Bridge. Then another left, again going north. After a while, another right, going east again. There was no racing in the street, no high speeds, and they stopped at red lights.

My hood did not admit even the slightest glimmer of light, so it was hard not to feel disoriented and maybe like a caged bird when the blanket is dropped down at sleepy-bye time.

After a series of short left turns near the end of what I had I reckoned had been less than a half hour, the car stopped. We hadn't crossed a long, uninterrupted stretch of causeway so we were still on the Pinellas County side of Tampa Bay.

We were hauled out of the car. At this point, my arms had stopped hurting and felt nothing but numb.

"Watch your step; you're going up," we were instructed, the first words spoken by our captors.

We ascended a short shaky stairway—eight steps—just as the whine of jet engines engulfed us.

"Looks like we're heading out of town," I said. "At least we got to skip the security and ticketing bullshit."

"Just shut up, will you!" I was told, as my head was forced lower to get inside the plane's cabin. That was Alexandra speaking.

In the aisle, a voice, obviously the boss man, said: "We are now going to free your arms. You are to bring them in front of you, held together by your hands and we will tie them."

Thus trussed, we were plunked down in what felt like backward-facing seats but not belted in. I felt the presence of two men sitting across from us. You'll be happy to learn that I resisted the temptation to blurt out: "Do anything you want to the girl but, for Christ's sake, leave me alone!"

The jet backed up, turned, and began taxiing to a runway. We stopped, the engines gaining power. After just a few minutes, the pilot floored it. We shot down the runway and rose quickly.

"Alex, stop struggling," I whispered. "We have to do something."

"For once, I'll go all Zen on you. If we're fucked, we're fucked. But they could've killed us any ol' time they wanted. There has to be a reason they didn't, and they won't now."

"Quiet, you two!" barked one of the kidnappers.

"Why don't you go fuck yourself?" I suggested, a millisecond before Alex elbowed me in the ribs. No response from our captors.

"See?" I whispered to Alex. "These fucking morons were told that we're supposed to be alive when we get to where we're going." Just then, the side of my head exploded in pain. Under my black hood, I saw stars. My skull hurt like a son of a bitch, and I felt like passing out. The butt of a gun will do that.

A voice growled: "My orders didn't specify what shape you'd be in."

"Let's all just be quiet, shall we, and enjoy the flight," I managed. I figured an hour or so went by when I heard the plane throttle back and begin its descent. A smooth landing and within minutes the plane shut down.

We clumsily made our way out of the plane and down the steps where, at least, we could hold the railing. We were marched for a bit after our precarious stumble down the jet's stairs. Then forced into steel chairs Our legs were zip-tied at the ankles.

Our hoods were whipped off. As my eyes got accustomed to the light, I looked over at Alex, her eyes full of dread. I suppose mine would've showed the same except I have this annoying habit of being a smartass in sketchy situations. I smiled; she weakly smiled back.

I could see that we were in an office with big glass windows looking out at the inside of a brilliantly lit, cavernous aircraft hangar.

The office door opened, and I found myself staring into the face of George Keitel, CEO of Goal2Go Security. Gone was the blue businessman's suit from the website photo, replaced with a black turtleneck that had some kind of shoulder patches, baggy desert-camouflaged pants and sandy-coloured combat boots. He wasn't near as tall as I imagined.

"Mr. White, I presume," I said.

"Very good," Keitel said with a chuckle. "*Reservoir Dogs*. One of Harvey's best roles."

"Now let's see how smart you really are," he said as he perched on the edge of the desk in front of us.

"Alrighty," I said. "Did you know that Alabama refused to pay a million dollars to buy the entire Panhandle from Florida in the 1890s? Crazy, huh?"

"Try this one: Care to hazard a guess why you're still alive?" he asked.

"It's sort of a mystery to me now that you mention it, what with my smoking and diabetes and all...oh, and the people I've been forced to hang out with."

With her legs bound, Alex was still able to fetch me a sorta kick in the shins.

"Guess again," he said, chuckle-less this time.

"OK. Try this: Wagner doesn't want to take the chance of you disappearing us, especially after your colossal fuck-up with Bob Hale and then Matt Kilmer. Alexandra here is something of a public and media figure and would immediately be missed. My daughter is a really good homicide detective and I know reporters. I bet you already have all that info. What Wagner's really hoping for is that we'll be scared shitless enough to shut the fuck up forever. I'm also betting he doesn't know you're playing G.I. Joe-Special Ops right now and would be some kind of pissed if he found out. How am I doing?"

"Close enough. What you didn't include is the fact that I'm considerably less patient than Mr. Wagner, and with considerably more physical resources to protect my mission. And that it's always easier to beg for forgiveness later than ask for permission. Oh, and one more thing: I need to know if you want to be responsible for Quentin Purdy's death or not."

I wasn't particularly enjoying his icy glare. He was as deadly serious as fucking cancer. We, for the moment, were being spared. But the time for bluffing and threats was done. While I'm not fond of ever doing so, sometimes you really do need to know when to fold up.

"Purdy'd be so much easier to make go away. St. Petersburg can be a dangerous place you know but—Jeanine, is it? —would be devastated," he added.

Those details were unnecessary. I had made my mind up. "Congratulations, dickwad," I said. "War is over. We surrender."

I leaned forward, grabbing the edge of the uncomfortable metal chair and stared at him.

He kept studying my face, betraying no surprise or suspicion at my announcement, but obviously looking for some clue about the truth of my statement, determining if I was just trying to fake my way out of our imprisonment.

"Wise choice," he said, obviously having decided I wasn't bullshitting. "And you, Miss Simpson?"

"Same."

"But tell me," I said. "Do these yahoos work for you or are they loaners from your buddy, Trevor Symes at White Iron?"

Keitel didn't answer but I made him pause. He turned to one of his camouflaged minions and said: "Take them back. Safely."

We were stood up and our ankle ties were cut. Two of the pseudo-soldiers produced our hoods.

"Oh, for fuck's sake," I said. "We don't need those. We're in Atlanta now and going back to a hangar at Clearwater-St-Pete airport then taking a chauffer-driven limo to Indian Rocks."

Keitel smiled then slightly shook his head and the hoods disappeared.

"I remind you, Mr. Lydon, We have a deal" he said. "One, I must tell you, that I'm personally quite eager to see you break."

"Got it."

And with that, we were hustled back into the plane.

Again, we were sat down, side by side, facing two of the guards. Their camo and combat boots just looked incongruous, almost ridiculous, amid the luxurious tan leather and chrome interior.

The engines roared to life, we backed out the hanger, whirled and taxied to our runway. After only a brief stationary period, the pilot hit the throttle and we were shooting down the concrete, lifting off and ascending, it seemed, straight up.

As happens during a climb, we hit more than a little bit of turbulence. Beltless, I hung onto the bottom of the seat and leaned my bulkitude into Alex's side to lessen her being bounced around until the ride smoothed out.

Alex and I were quiet but we sorta held hands, pinkies actually. The silence, however, was killing me.

"Say, buddy," I said to the big lug in front of me. "Does your momma know that you're murdering US citizens for a little more money than when you were in the Army?"

Rather than answer, he half-stood, leaned over and, lightning-fast, clocked me on the other side of my head with the butt of his ugly, black AR-15-type gun. Fuck! That was a new definition of pain for me. I briefly blacked out.

"Hurts more without the hood, don't it?" he said.

The fucker was right. "Your boss said—" I began, but he cut me off.

"You were there, asshole. Major Keitel said 'safely.' You're safe.

Look around; you've got four armed guards."

That brought a few chuckles from our nasty entourage and me silence.

My silence continued for the rest of the flight. From the look on Alex's face, she was fine with me as a mute.

We landed and taxied into another hangar, the plane's sharp nose pointing at a big black Escalade.

[Side bar: Why is it always a big SUV and why are they always black? How about a green Impala?]

As the twin-engine whine died down, we rose. I stopped briefly in front of the pilot standing by the cockpit door and thanked him for a great flight. Geez, he looked surprised.

"What were you at, buddy? 30,000?" I asked.

"35,000," he answered.

"You were honkin'."

"Almost flat-out," he replied.

A rifle muzzle prodded me along and down the stairs whose railing we could at least clumsily grip this time. Without direction, we walked by the sleek nose of the jet. I gave the co-pilot a friendly, two-handed Forrest Gump-type wave.

The streets of Clearwater were almost empty and quiet. The

giant backlit signs of the fast-food restaurants beckoned no one. We pulled up to the hovel and the car doors opened. A guy in front cut our zip ties, we got out, and they sped away. We walked up the driveway rubbing our wrists. The hovel was unlocked, in darkness except for the light from the TV I'd left on.

"What the fuck did you think you were doing back there?" Alex demanded as soon as we were inside.

"Oh, you know me, babe, I was just trying to lighten the mood," I said, followed immediately by the universal 'shush" sign with an index finger to my lips as I looked around.

She nodded.

"We need a drink—or two—and I need a butt."

"First good idea you've had in a while, Jake. Except for the cigarette."

I grabbed a cold Yuengling and the flagoon of white wine from the fridge. She took the Pinot from me and shakily poured a generous—oh, let's call it philanthropic—amount into her waiting glass, and we headed outside. It was a warm, breezeless night and the backyard was dark as the solar lights had taken the rest of the night off. It was after 1 and we were guided to the patio table by the halo of the streetlight.

We sat and gulped; I fired up a lung dart and greedily inhaled.

Our hands finally stopped shaking.

"You think they planted a bug?" Alex asked in a whisper.

"I do. They seem pretty big on surveillance."

"That's creeping me out."

"We just have to be careful for a bit. They'll leave us alone," I said, with more hope than certainty.

"Because you were serious with your answer?"

"I was. I am. We have to be out."

"Then what was that crap with the pilot?"

"Oh, just idle curiosity."

"Bullshit."

"OK, I thought we likely went to Atlanta, Goal2Go's headquarters, but I didn't know for sure. It definitely was a big city with all the lights I saw when we took off. Keitel didn't confirm or deny it and I wanted to be certain. I can figure out airspeed on that kind of jet. It's a Citation. Probably about an hour to Atlanta. Orlando's too close, if they were going almost full out, like the pilot said."

"But it might be the same distance to Miami. Or Jacksonville for that matter."

"See any water when we took off?"

"We wouldn't if we took off in the opposite direction. You still don't know for sure."

"Well, Miss Negative Nellie, that's why I was going to check their flight plan."

"Now how would you find that? I've been on these jets, a lot of them don't even file."

"Back in my PR days, I did some work for Nav Canada, the outfit that runs the air navigation system up there. They have a Challenger to check on radar and lights at the airfields that don't have air traffic controllers. I flew on it a couple of times and they always had to file because they were flying above 18000 feet. Which we just were. It's international law. And besides, you don't just show up at night unannounced at Hartsfield, the busiest airport in the goddamned country, and demand to land. We didn't circle so they knew we were coming. And we were, like third in line to take off, so they knew when we were leaving."

"Great. But how does that get you a flight plan?"

"It doesn't. N65180T does."

"The plane's tail numbers."

"Yup. I memorized them. They were written under the cockpit window. That'll also get us the owner and probably the owner of the hangar."

"Jake, this doesn't sound like idle curiosity."

"It wasn't. But I had a final think on the car ride here. Figuring out all this flight stuff is just me fucking around, proving what I already strongly suspected. It doesn't change the situation. We just can't fight these guys."

"You are serious."

"Yes. Because I'm seriously afraid. Look, we're just two in a long line of scaredy cats. Do you think drug cartels or street gangs, or the

Mafia kill absolutely everybody who might stand in their way? They don't. What they do is scare the shit out of them enough so that the authorities can't find co-operating witnesses or informants or neighbours who saw something."

"You're OK with being intimidated, just because we're not alone?"

"No, I'm not OK with it!" I said, getting amped up a bit. "But these guys aren't fucking around, babe. If we keep up the heat, they'll decide it's worth taking the risk of killing Purdy. Or you. I will not do that. Especially to you. I just won't. Call it macho bullshit all you want."

She reached over and grabbed my hand, squeezed tightly. "No, babe. I might call it love."

"Bingo, my dear," I said, as I drained my beer. "Another round?"

"Nope. Bed. I want to jump your bones."

"Well, if you insist. But we have to be quiet. The very walls have ears."

"Shit, the microphones. OK, that's beyond creepy."

"I'll find the bug tomorrow."

"I'll help."

So instead of shenanigans, we slept like the dead—grateful we weren't.

CHAPTER TWENTY-TWO

T he next morning after coffee, we went looking for electronic
listening devices, after taking a vow of silence during the
hunt. We first scoured the patio area, eaves, BBQ, our furniture,
nearby plants. Nothing. Inside, we found a bug right away. A giant
palmetto roach that expired under the couch. We also found an
electronic one very quickly. It was attached to the plate holding a
thick scented candle on the coffee table. It was actually comical
watching Alex pantomiming, all excited and pointy when she made
her discovery.

"Another coffee, my darling?" I asked and we reconvened on the
patio, after shutting the kitchen window and door.

"What do we do now?" Alex asked.

"Keep looking. These guys are pros; that was way too obvious."
We resumed the soundless search. Alex found another bug, this on
the underside of the counter lip on the island between the kitchen
and living room. I spotted one more, behind the TV stand double-
sided taped to the wire harness for all the equipment. And that
seemed to be it, mercifully none in the bedrooms or the crapper.

The question was: What do we do about them? Keitel et al were
looking for proof, one way or the other, if we were being good little

doggies and backing off on our half-assed investigation or if we wanted to risk reaping the whirlwind by continuing to nose around. We voted to noisily destroy the obvious decoy in the kitchen sink after loudly staging our "discovery." But we wanted to leave the other two in place, so Keitel would be convinced he was getting the straight goods about our co-operation. We also pledged to spend a whole lot more time outdoors while being a whole lot quieter indoors.

It was passing strange trying to live a "normal" life inside the hovel, but we managed. Much knuckle-gnawing ensued as I chafed against my natural inclination to be a nosy little fucker. I resumed, as best I could, writing my second novel; Alex conducted her long-distance management of her company but, to my ear, she sounded reserved and uninvolved.

We had become almost expert in our routine of chatting aimlessly while we were inside to deceive anyone listening to the two bugs we hadn't drowned, then closing the kitchen, bathroom, and bedroom windows when we went outside so that we could say whatever the hell we wanted to. Even getting good at that was depressing, to know we weren't in the clear.

We walked the beach. We made love—quietly. We even entertained. Stan and Laura from next door came by, armed with a bottle of Cazadores Reposada and an overpowering thirst for my margaritas. We had a raucous and splendid evening, waging our spirited war against sobriety and the scurvy. In mid-revelry and unplanned, Don and Ellen showed up on their bicycles and joined in. Ellen didn't drink but Don sure did. Because he wasn't a margarita or major brewery fan, I introduced him to the joy of tequila Caesars while riding his ass about being a craft beer snob.

Outwardly, we had to have looked like a normal retired couple doing normal retired couple things, only with lots of alcohol.

I sank deeper into researching and writing my book. I was grateful for this immersion. Long-form writing is—and has to be—involving. You have to be with your characters, in that place at that time, otherwise you're just fucking around. Alex, to her credit and my good fortune, was likewise, self-sufficient. She went to a nearby gym regularly, she'd jog, she resumed attending Ellen's Wednesday evening ceramics classes where she turned out some interesting, colourful pieces. I assumed (but didn't dare ask) if they were meant to be abstract.

When we were together, on walks or at the patio table, we never mentioned how our winter down here had unfolded. But from time to time, Alex or I would catch the other's eye and know, really know that we had been beaten.

It had been almost two weeks since our impromptu late-night visit to Atlanta. Sun-drenched February was about to slide into sun-drenched March. And nothing, despite our activity, felt right. Nothing felt completely real.

Until this: an online headline in the *Tampa Bay Times*: *Former Police Employee Shot in Home Invasion.*

With growing dread, I opened the story link.

The bare facts of it: At 2 AM, February 23, Quentin Purdy, 58, the recently retired Manager of Ballistics with the St. Petersburg Police Forensics department, was shot three times by two assailants in what police were calling a home invasion of the Purdy residence in the 1400 Block of 51st Street North, Harris Park, in St. Petersburg. Paramedics rushed Mr. Purdy to St. Anthony's Hospital where it was determined he had suffered serious, possibly life-threatening injuries from the gunshots. More to come.

Looking back, I don't think there had been any event in my sixty-five years on the planet that outraged me more than the possibly fatal wounding of this gentle giant. A stand-out football player, sure, but beyond that, a stand-out public servant. And way, way above and beyond that, a stand-out husband and father.

I needed to put my rage somewhere. And I knew exactly where. I found George Keitel's direct phone number on his website, then punched it into the handheld.

"Purdy?! What the fuck?!" I more or less yelled when he picked up. "We had a deal, you dwarf douche!"

"That had nothing to do with me," he said calmly. "Or you."

"The fuck it didn't!"

"Settle down, Lydon. It would seem that Mr. Purdy was pushing the issue of his forced retirement with his former employer. We are not happy about what happened either. Steps are being taken."

He let that sink in.

"I repeat," he said, "Nothing to do with me or Wagner. Or you. In the meantime, you must remember that we still have a deal."

"I know. I've been a good little boy."

"So, I understand. But I wanted to make it crystal clear. You still have a girlfriend, don't you?"

"Yeah."

"Then we still have a deal."

The motherfucker hung up before I could get the last word in, which was going to be motherfucker.

Alex and I looked at each other. I knew what she was thinking. Sitting on the sidelines had been a bitter experience for both of us.

Fuck that; we were coming off the bench.

CHAPTER TWENTY-THREE

B ut where to start? Where to start?

"First, I have to see Quentin," I said.

"Jake, I understand, but they won't let you in. He's got to be either in surgery or the ICU."

The news of the attack on Quentin was updated that night. Mr. Purdy had survived surgery and "an extreme loss of blood." Police said that, although the investigation was in its preliminary stages, they had not determined if any items had been stolen but speculated that because Mr. Purdy evidently had returned fire, the attempted robbery was not completed. There were, as yet, no witnesses beyond Ms. Jeanine Purdy who had been awakened by the gunfire. She told police she saw two males fleeing the house, before tending to her husband's wounds, likely saving his life.

Thank, Christ, Quentin had survived!

That news made turning our attention to our half-assed investigation a little easier. We first summarized.

Alex pointed out that nothing had changed since we had the shit scared out of us. "They" were a whole lot bigger, nastier, and better equipped. They were relying on spy-grade information. The size and extent of their enterprise was a mystery. Yes, we had found out about HDW and its reclusive chief, traced his connection to Goal2Go and followed their link to White Iron, the giant secretive military contractor with the gung-ho CEO. Somehow that shady network had become involved with mining for rare and increasingly valuable minerals through Southern Cross which operated apparently sketchy mines on two continents.

But wait; there's more! As they say. Both investigations into Robert Hale's death at the hands of an obviously trained sniper—one locally, one by a national agency—had been inexplicably dropped. There had been no further look either, as far as I knew, into the alleged hit and run that had killed Matt Kilmer a few blocks from the Hovel. And now, we were all supposed to buy the latest theory from the St. Petersburg police that Quentin Purdy was near death from a home invasion where nobody saw nuthin' and nothing had been stolen.

As tempting as it was to just roll all the events into one giant ball of wax, it was Alex who put the kibosh on that idea.

"I'm thinking there are two separate streams going on here. One is HDW and all the money and military stuff over the Southern Cross mines. The other is what's going on with the St. Pete police."

"And the FBI in Washington," I added.

"We need more facts. We can dig around online and still look like lazy snowbirds."

Alexandra quickly voted to look at how Southern Cross's mines operated and their HDW connections which meant I got the Goal2Go-White Iron connection and the St. Petersburg police. George Keitel—Born 1966, Brunswick, Georgia. Other than the standard short bios that were paraphrased from each other on White Iron's, Goal2Go's and business websites, there was exactly one media story about the low-key exec. This from the 1989 archives of the *Banner-Herald*, Keitel's Georgia hometown newspaper. The paper was proud of their native son who'd graduated from University of Georgia with a degree in Business Admin. Having completed ROTC training and joined the Marines, he was then posted to Camp Pendleton, California as a lieutenant in the Military Police, honourably discharged after four years with the rank of

Major. In other words, he could go into an American Legion but wouldn't be allowed in a VFW bar as he'd never seen action in a foreign war.

I also got re-interested in White Iron, starting off with reading all the archived news stories around the time of their pee-pee-whacking at the congressional hearings.

As one of the country's largest private contractors—an anodyne label that revealed nothing—White Iron was largely made up of crews of ex-military personnel.

During the hearings and in interviews, CEO Symes staunchly denied that White Iron was anything but a purely support operation overseas which had "No combat role whatsoever." He did admit to "being forced to assume defensive postures"—whatever the fuck that meant—although I imagined it implied that they'd shoot at any folks threatening American bases.

Any attempts to be more definitive proved to be futile. The Patriot and Espionage Secrets Acts were used like bureaucratic whack-a-mole clubs on any efforts to find out just exactly what White Iron was doing overseas. But rumours persisted, articles were written, attributing all sorts of nasty doings—everything from over-the-top "enhanced interrogation" to off-the-books assassinations, kidnappings, and raids. As one of the anonymous sources in an article, an alleged former White Iron soldier, said: "We could go places and do things that the regular Army just couldn't."

What to believe? The corporate scrubbed-clean version or a bunch of online stories with unidentified sources?

Oh, let's guess some, all or even more of these alleged events were going on during the dirty business of making war. This was the real "don't ask, don't tell," as no legislator of either stripe seemed to push for answers, at least not publicly.

The White Iron website was particularly pleased with itself for hiring so many former military people. It also went out of its way to decry the use of the word 'mercenary.' For sure, if you're a White Iron employee working in a cafeteria kitchen in Fallujah, you couldn't be called a gun for hire. But if you were being paid to kill people on behalf of a government, well, if the combat boot fits. It got me thinking about why would you go from being a soldier to a soldier of fortune? As with just about everything, there were, as near as I could tell, a bunch of differing motives. A desire to keep using all the training and skills they'd been given at the government's expense. Disaffection with that former government employer was, apparently a big factor. So was a shit-ton more money and, presumably, a better benefits package.

I realize I'm wandering into John Lennon's Imagine territory, but I do wonder what would happen if you could somehow cancel the siren call of "serving your country," because just saying that phrase out loud ensures that morality, ethics, philosophy, con-science have fuck-all to do with anything. If they did and it all was a matter of personal choice, there would probably be more fighters in the National Hockey League than in all the standing armies on earth. Maybe all you really needed is a quiz when they enlist. A quiz with just one question: 'If it was entirely up to you, would you go into another country and kill strangers for no particular reason?' I'd also recommend keeping a close eye on everybody who answered 'yes.'

Mark Twain, as usual, said it best:

Man is the only Patriot. He sets himself apart in his own country, under his own flag, and sneers at the other nations, and keeps multitudinous uniformed assassins on hand at heavy expense to grab slices of other people's countries and keep them from grabbing slices of his. And in the intervals between campaigns, he washes the blood off his hands and works for the universal brotherhood of man. With his mouth.

It seemed to me there was another, more personal reason that wasn't often raised. Maybe they came back home and found they couldn't re-adjust to civilian life after the things they had seen and done fighting overseas.

There was also no escaping the fact that a certain segment of this outfit simply reveled in the true macho bullshit. They liked nothing better than to hang out with their bros, play with guns, swear a lot, and swagger, all the while convinced of the rightness of their "mission." Stateside, they very likely would join secret militias, where they'd give each other imaginary ranks, swaddle themselves with Army surplus hardware, and play war games in the Michigan wilderness, endlessly waiting for their ruthless and illegal government to just try and take their guns away.

The hardcore among them, however, thirsted for the real thing. They wanted to make war in a foreign land. Oh, and some of them rather enjoyed "legally" killing other human beings.

Hoorah.

Meanwhile, Alex was also on the phone a lot—sitting outside around the corner on the shaded reading patio—talking mostly to Sasha Brownlee, her mining expert in New York, trying to figure out just what the fuck was going on with the antics at Southern Cross' two mines.

I couldn't wait any longer. I decided to take my chances and drove to St. Anthony's hospital in St. Petersburg. As Alex had predicted, when I got to ICU, they refused to let me in as only visits from family members were allowed. A nurse rejected my claim that I was Quentin's adopted brother. But Jeanine intervened, nodded to the nurse through the big window of Quentin's room and met me at the door.

"Jeanine," I said, as she warmly clasped my hand. "I'm so sorry this happened."

"It's not your fault; you tried to warn him. He's been asking for you."

I was quickly introduced to his sons, both large, good looking men, and we stood around for a bit, staring at the man-mountain overwhelming the hospital bed, surrounded by an array of beeping monitors, hooked up to a variety of plastic tubes. At first, his eyes were closed, and he was motionless. But then, his eyes opened, and, with a finger, Quentin motioned that I come closer.

"Some gun expert you turned out to be," I said. "You fucking missed."

He smiled weakly and tried to speak.

"Not gangbangers," he said in a hoarse whisper. "These guys had uniforms.... All in black...ski masks."

With that, Quentin drifted off again. I left, thinking about what

I'd just learned, besides being overjoyed that Purdy was still alive. He had confirmed what I had assumed. Street gangs don't wear uniforms. Would cops be dumb enough to wear matching ensembles if they were trying to look like the home invaders they arrest? That didn't make much sense. Alexandra and I had just had a recent experience with freelancing military types who seemed quite at ease with uniforms. But Keitel had denied the involvement of his pretend soldiers in Purdy's shooting.

When I got home, Alex was at the patio table, thumbing through papers. I asked her about any progress.

"Sasha and I looked at this every which way," she said. "You know how we discarded the notion that Southern Cross was under-reporting their results? We've changed our minds. But it's not just to screw over the Vietnamese and Brazilian governments on royalties."

"Why did you pull a 180?"

"Olrud's shipping bills. Why would they claim their over-charging was a mistake and apologize?"

"So, Jack wouldn't find out about and stop it."

"Jack was powerless; he couldn't affect anything. And the two governments would never have access to Olrud's invoices."

"So why do it?"

"We could come up with just one explanation."

"Which is?"

"They're manipulating the world-wide price for neodymium."

CHAPTER TWENTY-FOUR

M y first reaction to Alex's theory was complete and utter disbelief.

"Oh, come on! Southern's tiny."

"They're not going to be small for long. Those two new and improved mines are almost in full production. Combined with the size of their claims, they're about to become a player. The demand for the neodymium they're mining is huge and growing, so even a small decline in its availability, drives up prices. The actual refined amount outside China right now is small, but the estimated reserves where they're working are massive. They're building up a secret inventory to sell at the higher prices over the next few years, if they're smart and play it out slowly. The price will keep shooting up because it still can't keep up with demand. At the same time, their newer mines come fully online."

I asked if she had any idea what it was worth.

"A lot. With its value forecasted to at least quintuple over the next ten years, a ton of the stuff will probably cost over a million dollars."

I imagined the bed of a small pick-up truck filled with a million-buck cargo.

"But China could flood the market at any time," I pointed out. "Sure, but why would they? If they did, the prices would plunge."

"Do nothing and say nothing and watch the money roll in for their inventory."

"It gets better. Remember, our bet that Southern Cross would probably go public?"

"Sure."

"Sasha and I think they'll issue their IPO at the same time as the mineral price surge."

"So, with 40% of the company, HDW reaps a whack of the IPO proceeds," I said.

"I'd bet all the proceeds. They can do that by structuring the share classes to cut out Jack, Mick and Borje."

Mining along with high technology may be the only two remaining pure, lawless, Wild West outposts on the stock market frontier. In mining, you get wildly optimistic readings of assay reports or a description of the bazillions worth of mineral X or Y still underneath the planet's surface while neglecting to mention your infinitesimal role in the hunt for it. In the tech world, you goose sales and order confirmations or are forever "poised to be a leader."

Yes, there are laws against groundlessly hyping share prices but then there are batteries of lawyers who figure out how to get around those laws. They march right up to the legal line and use the weaselly words that play to the get-rich-quick fever dreams of speculators who only later find out that they bought vapourware or iron pyrite.

Here we had the exact opposite. Southern Cross' mines were producing a whole lot more than they let on.

"Looks like we've come up with our very own conspiracy theory," Alex said.

"We should patent the fucker."

We sat back and, I think, we were both trying to visualize the scale our theory represented. Multiple companies, multiple countries around the world and god knows how many people who all handled the mineral, were somehow involved at every stage and who, improbably, had stayed quiet for at least a year after the mines started to go full bore, probably longer.

Then I thought of the quasi-military muscle that had been used on Bob Hale and Matt Kilmer.

"It all makes sense," Alex concluded. "But there hasn't been even the slightest whiff of this—in the press or financial circles. I just can't get over that fact."

"I can see it. With Goal2Go and White Iron riding shotgun—pretty powerful incentive for silence."

"Yeah, but there are so many people who have to be corrupt to pull this off."

"Maybe we're looking at this all wrong. We see all these companies in five distant countries, and we think, what a huge machine. But really, if we think about it, maybe there aren't that many bad guys."

"Let's see if we can count 'em up."

"I'll start: How many people from the government watch dogs?"

"Sasha said there's a government guy on-site who records the tonnage coming out of the on-site refineries. He or she might be the same person validating its purity after testing. Then there's another pair of officials at the ports confirming the weight that gets loaded onto the ships."

"So, you have to bribe only four, maybe six civil servants, all of whom make shit salaries. Doesn't mean the whole government is corrupt. Just a few guys involved in the testing and weighing. Oh, and Mick and/or the comptrollers throwing petty cash around for the bribes."

"Someone at Pretoria had to know what was going on at the sites. Then what?"

"Olrud has to be involved because their ships are being weighed."

"But again, not all of Olrud—or Pretoria. Maybe Wagner gets to one senior guy who turns around and gets one or two at the operations level, the guys who handle the paperwork."

"So how many so far?"

"Say fifteen—give or take."

"Then there's the real baddies, at HDW, Goal2Go, and White Iron. So, at the very least Wagner, Keitel, and Symes."

"Underneath them, there's that quartet of goons that we met. Probably a few surveillance and electronics guys, maybe a couple in Finance."

"Don't forget the St. Pete cops and the feds in Washington."

"Again, maybe one guy in each."

"Total it all up and it might be less than thirty people, every one of whom has a good reason to shut the fuck up."

"You didn't mention Southern Cross except for Mick."

"Jury's out on Borje."

"And Jack?"

"I vote no," I said. "He's got a long history of doing the right thing."

"I agree."

"Ok, we have some idea what's happening before the ore reaches the warehouses. What about when it gets stored or shipped for further refining? Doesn't anybody keep track of it?"

"Yes and no. Periodically, each government sends inspectors to calculate total reserves that are in the ground and inventories that are in storage. They will visit storage facilities to see if what the company has reported is actually there. Add it all up and you get data from each country that sets the world commodity price. But these inspectors don't personally weigh all the minerals piled up; they rely on checking that the paperwork agrees all the way along the line."

"Can't they just look at the pile of minerals and see that it's way more—or less—than what the paperwork says?"

"Here's a tidbit most people don't know that Sasha told me about. The companies are always notified in advance about these visits. There have been rumours of companies who want to under-report—like Southern, in this case—going into their warehouses, loading a bunch on trucks and just driving around until the inspection is over. Mineral "in transit" doesn't count against the total."

"And while those trucks are clogging the streets of Singapore or wherever, they get to say: "Oh my Christ, lookee here: we got us a shortage! Time to jack prices. Jesus, that's not a thumb on the scale; it's the whole fist. What I don't fully understand is why the rough stuff around here? Things seemed to be going according to plan."

"I've been thinking about this," Alex said. "The only explanation that makes sense is HDW must be in trouble. Big trouble. They've got their own cash and hundreds of millions in loans out on Southern to get the mines really going and to start new ones. Never mind what they owe on the rest of their companies. Their biggest cash cow must have been White Iron with their massive government contracts."

"But, for the moment, all quiet on every front," I said. "You're out of Afghanistan, out of Iraq and other major brawls. No wars mean no major cash flow coming in from White Iron."

"Wagner must've bought into White Iron big time, maybe billions for larger and larger slices. So, there's a lot riding on their rare mineral play. Maybe everything. And they're scared."

Exactly how could we get our arms around the depth and breadth, the sheer size of the scheme that Wagner had hatched, the many moving parts he was orchestrating? Short answer: we couldn't.

My wee brain hurt from looking at all the financial and geological shit going on. Time to have a face-to-face chat with myself.

Mirror, mirror on the bathroom wall, why can't little Jakey just let this all go?

Mirror's got a point, Jake. You can't possibly care about the accuracy or fairness of the world's fucking neodymium supply.

Oh, yes, I can, Jake, you goddamned moron. Two good people are dead and another one is seriously injured who otherwise wouldn't be if Wagner hadn't put his money-grubbing wheels in motion. And now, thanks to him, you and Alex might just have to keep looking over your shoulder forever.

We'd come this far, way past the point of no return. Cut and run now, with all the shit that had gone on was impossible. As impossible as being able to do anything about it.

I was encouraged, however, by one simple fact that had been confirmed to me over the last several years during my escapades on both sides of the US-Canada border. The authorities—local, state, or provincial police, and national law enforcement agencies—are overwhelmingly staffed by honest and amazingly dedicated men and women who want bad people caught and their crimes punished so the rest of us can safely get on with the job (and joy) of being human beings.

Right then, Alex and I needed those kinds of people and all the power they could bring to bear.

And, finally, we had a coherent story to tell them.

CHAPTER TWENTY-FIVE

F igured the place to start was by calling Oklahoma. Stay with me, folks.

Tulsa was the heartland city that was at the heart of a national extortion plot of tribal casinos. Humbly, I had a hand in uncovering that deadly scheme last winter. That's where I came across FBI Special Agent Tasker who, although he was a dick to me at the outset, turned out to be a stand-up guy. He led the cavalry charge to bust the baddies in a cross-country dragnet, stories of which still sporadically popped up in the news.

As I was dialling the FBI field office, I realized I'd never learned Agent Tasker's first name. For all I knew, it was 'Agent.' I don't know if the receptionist remembered me or recognized my name, but I was put through to Tasker right away.

"Agent Tasker!" I said when he picked up. "Just how the fuck are you?"

He was momentarily taken aback.

"Christ, I hoped to never hear that voice again," he finally said. We shot the shit about last winter's casino debacle. He told me that the arrest phase was pretty much over, and he was happy to report that "we got 'em all." A lot of trials of the low-level guys were also done with a 98% conviction rate. Some bigger murder trials of the more senior criminals were upcoming, and he was confident of 'til death do you part real soon' convictions.

"Wild guess," he said. "You didn't call me just to chat about the cases."

"Sure, I did," I tried to assure him. "And I wanted to see how my Okie buddy was doing. Oh, and I was wondering if you knew a good FBI guy in Tampa."

"Oh, Jake. What kind of shit show are you starring in now?"

I briefly laid out the ugly scenario to date, the murders, the possibility of this thing being far-reaching, and my distrust that this whole affair would be pursued. He thought for a while.

"As a matter of fact, I do know someone," he said. "Special Agent Turner."

"I can trust him?"

"Her. Vanessa Turner. I met her when the Russians were running an undocumented migrant operation through the Port of Tampa. The workers were winding up at meat-packing plants around here, so I worked this end. She's good people."

"I don't imagine she'll talk to me out of the blue."

"Why would anyone? But I'll make the introductions." I thanked him and gave him my burner number.

"I'll also warn her," he added.

"About how nasty these people can be?"

"No. About how nasty you can be."

I got off the telephone smiling. One of the few good things that came out of all the clown jobs I'd been involved in over the last several years—in addition to still being alive against the express wishes and efforts of a lot of people—was the amount of fine people I'd met.

Along with Tasker, there was a family restaurant owner in Eugene Oregon, a genius young hacker now living anonymously somewhere in Southeast Asia, the construction manager of the new, almost-completed casino up the road in nearby Sand Key, a Dominican police inspector who, in addition to saving my Canadian bacon, was classy and incorruptible, the head of security at the

Tulsa Hard Rock, an ex-biker from New Jersey now "retired" in the Caribbean, a former English professor of mine, among many others. We had kept in touch, and they stood out for proving to me just how stupendous humankind can be.

I didn't have long to wait for a call from the FBI field office in Tampa. At noon the next day, my burner rang.

"Mr. Lydon?" said a rich Lauren Bacall-ish voice. "Special Agent Turner."

"Thanks for calling. And it's Jake."

"Tasker said I should talk to you, Jake. That's good enough for me."

"What else did he tell you?"

"Not much. He mentioned some pretty big names He did say you were…what's the word he used?"

"An asshole?" I said, taking a not-so-wild guess.

"Something like that," she said, chuckling.

"That son of a bitch! I mean, he's not wrong, but you should at least have to find that out for yourself."

"Let's set up an appointment."

"Here's the problem: I'm pretty sure I'm being watched, and I know my house and phone are bugged. So, you can't come to my place, and I can't go there."

"Where can we meet?"

Remembering my first encounter with Matt Kilmer, I said: "The beach is probably safest, if that's OK with you."

"That could work. Where?"

"Indian Rocks at, say 18th Street? Sundown."

"Good. Is tomorrow night alright?"

"Yes! How will I recognize you?" I asked.

"I'll find you," she said. "Still have long hair and a Hawaiian shirt? Somewhat older gentleman?"

"Don't know if that sets me apart from the Florida boomer crowd, other than not being a gentleman."

"I'll know you. Right now, I'm looking at your arrest photo from Boston."

"Oh, that. Bastard wouldn't let me brush my hair."

She laughed, probably politely. "See you tomorrow." And she was gone.

Alexandra was pretty excited to learn that we weren't going to be on our lonesome any longer.

The next evening around six, we carried our director's chairs and full solo cups down to the shore, walked a couple of blocks north to the 18th Street ramp, and set up at the back of the beach near the sea oats. The crowd was building.

Just before sunset o'clock, I saw a striking forty-something couple standing at the ramp's end, surveying the audience, ostensibly looking for a place to set up their temporary camp. She was very pretty, her colour and body type reminded me of Serena Williams, while he was much taller, with a lithe swimmer's body and was a Patrick Mahomes lookalike, although he wore the apparently mandatory Tampa Bay Buccaneer jersey. They picked a narrow unoccupied stretch of sand directly in front of us.

I was calculating the extent of their obstruction of our view when he clumsily jostled me as he struggled to unfold his chair. He instantly apologized. Being Canadian, I reflexively said I was sorry too, but for what I didn't know.

Seated, he twisted around and extended a hand. "Devin Turner," he said.

Introductions were made all the way around, followed by brief but pleasant chit-chat about the sun and the crowd around us.

Guys do what guys do when they find a common sports interest: they crap on each other's team loyalties. I started things off by riding his ass about liking the fuckin' Bucs while he shit-talked my Raiders. We laughed like hell, looking for all the world like two couples making friends with each other after accidentally meeting on a beach. It wasn't exactly bullshit either. It was pretty obvious from the jump that they were, in Tulsa Tasker's words, good people.

True, our conversation was stilted—snippets of louder personal conversation interspersed with hushed details of the Byzantine plot I believed we had uncovered—but it somehow worked. My interrupted description wasn't exactly linear or straightforward either; there were too many moving parts. But when we started talking about the hijinks at the mines and the potential billions of dollars on the table, I could see that Agent Turner was putting the pieces together.

"This is big, Vanessa," I said.

"Seems that way. Sounds like New York, St. Petersburg, Atlanta, at a minimum.

"Really, it's international. You can toss in Vietnam and Brazil," I added. "Probably Oslo, Pretoria, and Panama, too if you count a few of Harrison Wagner's other companies that are head-quartered there and that have connections to Southern Cross."

Like any good cop, she wasn't about to simply take everything I said at face value. I wouldn't and I'm me.

"Do you have anything that looks like proof?" she wanted to know.

"Picky, picky, picky," I said. "Beyond two deaths and a shooting that each make absolutely no sense and the shut-down investigations that make even less sense, no, not really."

"There are the bugs they planted," Alex offered. "There were three, but we gave one a bath to let them think that everything else they heard was real talk."

"Smart."

Alex then piped up. "You should come back to our place. I'll show you a bullet hole in our window along with those electronic listening devices."

"That's a great idea!" I said. "New friends who met at the beach having a nightcap? Believable as hell. Especially the nightcap part."

After thinking about it, Vanessa agreed, and we trooped back to the hovel just as soon as the sun went down.

Along the way, Turner wanted to know if we could talk without being heard. I told her we had checked out our patio area pretty thoroughly.

We paused as we walked up the driveway and Alex showed Vanessa the recent small-calibre ventilation that had been added to our side window.

We set up on the patio just as the last shred of daylight died and the solar lights flicked on.

"My name is Todd," I said, "and I'll be your server tonight. Would you folks like to start off with a drink? I have beer, gin, tequila, and a cheeky Pinot Grigio on offer."

Devin took a beer, and on-the-job Agent Turner asked for water and to use the facilities.

"C'mon," Alex said. "I'll show you, give you the 10-cent tour. Please excuse the bug problem."

"That's some pretty fancy high-tech," Vanessa said after they emerged.

"And then there's our kidnapping," I said. "Tell me about that."

I described the late-night abduction—hoods, whacks in the head, and all. Our plane ride, likely to Atlanta and back, after a brief but really shitty meeting with George Keitel.

"And that proof, I mentioned?" Agent Turner persisted.

"You don't believe me?"

"I'm starting to. But you have to understand that I have to get a lot of people at the Bureau on board."

"How about N65180T? That jet had to file flight plans."

"Play along, Jake," Vanessa said. "So, you know a private jet flew from Clearwater to Atlanta—maybe—and back on the night of February 12th. So what? All sorts of websites could've told you that. Everything else—including whether or not you were even on that flight—is easily denied."

"But I'm a witness; I was there too!" Alex said.

"You're a couple, so not really credible on your say-so alone. And still not enough to show objectively that you were actually on board."

"OK, how about this?" I said. "They're gonna have a hard time 'splainin' how both mine and Alex's fingerprints are on two sets of flight stair railings. And a really hard time downplaying my finger-prints on the underside of the first aisle seat on the left of that jet. The same prints they'll find on the bottom of a metal chair in the hangar in Atlanta."

That got everybody's attention right quick.

"You did that?" Turner asked.

"Part of your idle curiosity?" Alex said.

"Well-played, dude," Devin added.

From the look on her face, I had just moved the bar on Vanessa's trust scale.

"Vanessa, I gotta ask you: do you have any idea what's going on with the St. Petersburg Police? They're in your backyard."

"I haven't heard or seen anything bad about them. We work with them all the time. Of course, I heard about the death at Crescent Lake, but it was described by the St. Pete cops as local and gang-related, same with Purdy's supposed home invasion. We wouldn't be involved. And about the hit and run near here. A simple traffic accident. As I would expect, Pinellas County Sheriff didn't even refer it to us, so that's a red herring."

"But there's something else going on. Hale's case got somebody in Washington interested enough to kill any investigation."

"I can't help you there. My best guess: they were too busy, so they let it drop."

"I don't buy it," I said. "This is organized."

Vanessa paused, and her expression got a whole lot more serious.

"There's another possibility. Maybe the St. Pete guy referred it to somebody at the FBI he knew would kill it. These people talk to each other, mostly on chatrooms."

"'These people?'"

Here, Vanessa looked genuinely sad.

"There's an element—a small element—in our police forces, in the FBI, and the military that figure they can write their own rules, decide for themselves what to enforce and on whom because they believe that everything's broken. When you think that way, you have to use your own hammer because, after all, you're the folks in charge. You have to maintain if not law, then order. But it's their idea of order. They forget the law they swore to uphold. As far as I'm concerned, they're terrorists, pure and simple. And I can't begin to tell you how much that pisses me off."

"I bet it does, but this is not that. This has fuck-all to do with ideology or politics or some fucked-up view of patriotism. It's about money. That's it, that's all."

"For everybody that's involved?"

"Yup. For the few at the top—Wagner, Keitel—massive amounts of money, we're talking hundreds of millions of dollars in profit, maybe more. For everyone else—and it's really not that many—they're paid to follow their leaders' orders, so yeah, in a way, it's money for them too because they get to keep their jobs."

"You understand this will take weeks, maybe months to put together."

"Months?!"

"Think about it. We need DOJ involved, probable cause, judges, warrants, wiretaps, foreign agencies, folks on the ground."

"I have to get back to Canada by the end of April," I said. "Otherwise, I lose healthcare for at least three months, and have to re-start all the bullshit paperwork to prove I live there."

"We'll fix that."

"In the meantime, what do you want us to do?" Alex asked.

"Absolutely nothing."

"Perfect! I happen to be an expert at that," I said.

"But you have to be available. There's bound to be questions about how you learned what you did."

"Alex here has some paperwork that might help. She can retrieve it from the cloud."

"Already did," Alex, the smarty pants, said.

"Good." Vanessa said. "Devin, don't you have to use the little boys' room?" she asked, indicating his waist band.

"As a matter of fact," he said. "I'll show him," Alex volunteered.

"Aren't we fucking clever?" I observed as we waited.

"Don't get so smug yet," Vanessa said. "There's a lot of work ahead of us. And a lot of ways it could leak out."

When they came back out, Devin was making a faint sound, the sound of paper rustling in his waistband.

"Let's get back to talking about what's going on inside the St. Petersburg Police Department."

"In some ways, it doesn't even look like they're related," Vanessa said.

"But they obviously are. Two murders, starting with Bob Hale

and his connection to Southern Cross, then Matt Kilmer, my original source, then Quentin Purdy, Kilmer's original source, gets shot
up. All three investigations cut short, two of them we know were
spiked by one guy. And the same guy leans on Forensics to force
Purdy out and then probably organized the attempted hit on him
when Purdy squawked. What's that tell you?"

"Frankly?"

"Well, of course."

"You folks might be next."

CHAPTER TWENTY-SIX

A lex and I looked at each other.

"I don't think they'll risk it," I declared.

"Again frankly, Jake...you're full of shit."

"That's not the first time, he's heard that," Alex offered. "Maybe that was true at one point, no, I'm sure it was true,"

Agent Turner pressed on. "But they might be desperate right now, and, as you folks just convinced me, there are billions of reasons why they would take the risk."

"What's it mean?"

"It means you can't stay here. I'm sorry, but we have to move you to a safe house. We need you alive."

"What, like leave with you now?" Vanessa was thinking on her feet.

"No. Not yet. I didn't see any suspicious bodies at the beach or here, but that doesn't mean they aren't around. If you disappeared with two people you supposedly just met, that would tip our hand. Wait a few days, tell people you're going back north, pack up the place, load the car, and say your goodbyes."

Alex and I looked at each other. We were at the point that we had a pretty good handle on what the other was thinking and feeling without a whole lot yakking.

"We'll talk about it," Alex said.

"You people aware of a material witness arrest?" Vanessa asked.

"Yes, ma'am," I said. "We'll talk about it."

"Talk now."

Alex and I went around the house to our reading patio. There in the dark, we held a short conversation.

"They can't force us," I began.

"Well, they can. But Vanessa won't arrest and hold us," Alex said. "If she did that—if we just disappear—they'll know and that'll blow up her investigation before it even starts."

"I honestly don't think Keitel or Wagner are that worried about us. So far, we've proved to them that we've thrown in the towel."

"We've been careful. We'll just keep being careful."

We emerged from the darkness and informed Vanessa of our decision to stay put. She was pissed, but seemed less so after we explained our logic. Better to hide in plain sight and continue to not be a problem for Keitel et al.

"You sure?"

"Pretty sure, is the best we can do."

"I'll do some digging. That Henderson you mentioned. I know him, but not that well."

"His was the loudest voice in cancelling the investigations. Not their police chief, not the PR folks, and not, I'm sure, the other detectives."

"Meaning?"

"Let's look at the overall picture. First choice: Goal2Go or, more likely, White Iron has their fingers in all sorts of official pies and have had those tentacles out for years. Second: assume Henderson's part of that disaffected group of cops you described. Maybe, he already knew of a sympathetic guy at the FBI that he met in one of those chatrooms who he could refer the case to, sure that he'd stop the investigation. Or White Iron hooked him up with one."

"Doesn't make a lot of sense. Why would he take the chance of kicking the case up to the Feds?"

"It was actually pretty smart. He knows a lot of people in his department are pissed that he stopped looking into it. So, he bypasses you folks in Tampa, goes to his connection in Washington who kills the case at their end. Then Henderson can turn around and say to his people: "See, the FBI doesn't think there's anything there either."

"Just as easily, they could've sent it to us."

"Henderson would've had to have done that. He didn't. He knew who to call. Down here, the murder was news; up there, it's just a statistic. One more body in what? Twenty thousand gun murders a year."

"Closer to twenty-five."

The Turners then left, and we straightened up the patio.

Alex was disturbed and disgusted by the fact that ex-soldiers would actually do the dirty work involved in executing Hale, smashing into Kilmer, kidnapping us and who the fuck knows what else. I wasn't.

Do your job. You hear that all the time in football. The players have their separate assignments and, the idea is, if every one of them doesn't think about anything else going on, if they just carry out their assignment, then you win as a unit. Even though it's all based on the shaky premise that thems that are paying you know what the fuck they're doing with their game planning. And that what they're doing is right or good.

In Robert Hale's case, they were ordered to do it, and, like good soldiers, they obeyed the order. Let's bet, for maximum deniability, it was some non-specific direction like "Hale needs to be silenced" or "Hale has to stop being a problem. Just handle it. Oh, and spare us the details." Sort of like the way England's Henry II mused aloud: "Will no one rid me of this troublesome priest?" and then four of ol' Hank's soldiers, chock full of initiative and bucking for promotion, took it upon themselves to murder Thomas Becket, the frigging Archbishop of Canterbury and in his workplace.

And then came Matt Kilmer, a dying old guy who wouldn't let it go. The order would have come down to whomever whacked Bob Hale: "Clean up your mess."

Even the fact that our kidnapper was called "Major Keitel" by his droogs when he's a weekend warrior in the reserves speaks volume to a chain of command he and his hired thugs were used to. How often have we heard the catch-all excuse for any shitty act: I was only following orders.

So, we waited. And waited. Alex and I pinballed between growing comfortable with nothing apparently happening and antsy because nothing was. Meanwhile, we hoped the police operation was being set in motion. At times, we took our frustrated impatience out on each other which wasn't fair to either of us.

Working on the book proved impossible. I couldn't focus and you gotta focus. Other than fucking around with grammar and phrasing on the parts I had already written, I still had no idea about the book's middle part or end part (which, I astutely guessed, the book should have). And I couldn't concentrate enough to figure out what those might be while we waited for a centipede's worth of shoes to drop.

So instead, I pissed away time on the Internet where I officially became the last person on earth to discover TikTok—and then fervently wished to undiscover it.

This alleged phenomenon is just an endless compiling of the inane, mundane, and insane captured or staged for a camera, all of them with hundreds of thousands of "followers," serving only to prove we're all incredibly fucking bored and that there's a lot of people out there who have a highly inflated view of themselves as being even remotely interesting and who are really bad at lip-syncing and "dancing."

Alex and I would distract ourselves by discussing and arguing "big" issues. She's smart and feisty; I'm feisty.

Free speech? Sure. That and really good cable television separate us from the plentiful dictatorships in the world. But 'flooding the zone' with engineered campaigns, fake headlines, manipulated photos and videos? Am I supposed to defend your right to say stuff like that? I can't do it, if you deliberately make shit up to cause confusion, alter reality, create fake photos, libel a rival, or evade the law. Alex wanted to somehow outright ban that crap; I would let it exist but spend more effort disproving the bullshit.

We both allowed that the scary part is fewer and fewer people actually care whether what they're watching or reading is true or not, as long as it contributes to what they already believe in their hearts, not brains. Then, presto, it becomes truth. For all time, because it'd be unimaginable to admit ever that you might have been mistaken, no matter what evidence you're shown.

Alex surprised me with her semi-staunch support of the 2nd Amendment while I, a foreigner, was more in the camp of "What the fuck are you people thinking in your defence of a poorly worded 250-year-old sentence?"

Somehow, we both knew that these debates, while lively, entertaining, and somewhat revealing, were really just a way to pass time.

So, we drank instead. And waited.

CHAPTER TWENTY-SEVEN

To be fair—something I'm not famous for—Agent Turner was good about updating us as much as she could.

It was always me calling her for news until one morning I answered the burner.

"Jake, it's Vanessa. I debated telling you this but thought you should know. Henderson, the St. Pete cop, may think something's up."

"How?"

"He got wind that we were asking around. One of our agents said that Henderson called him about questions he'd been putting to one of his homicide detectives. Our guy told him that it was just routine, that we often conduct scans like this on people we work with. But he's not sure Henderson bought it."

"And what am I supposed to do with this happy news?"

"I urge you to take us up on the offer of a safe house."

"Pass."

"Suit yourself. But be careful." And she was gone.

I told Alex about this new wrinkle, mostly because I didn't want to get shit from her for withholding upsetting info. We agreed that we wouldn't go into hiding out, but that we should be more vigilant than we'd been recently.

Two nights later, after we'd gone to bed, there was a loud knocking on the kitchen door. In our forerunner of the tiny house trend, it sounded close enough to have been coming from our bedroom door. I roused myself, stumbled down the hallway and across the kitchen. The stove clock said 1:48. I grabbed the largest knife I could find from the drawer and opened the door a crack, bracing it with my shoulder in case someone heaved from the other side.

"Get a beer!" Jack roared.

"What the fuck are you doing here?" I asked.

"I'm thirsty."

I wasn't about to turn him away and, now that he had mentioned it, I had become powerful thirsty myself.

"Gimme a second," I said. "Meet you on the patio and, for Christ's sake, keep your voice down."

Alex was standing by the fridge as I made my way towards a beer. In her shortish Patriots jersey, she always looked mighty fine— except, tonight, when the angry/disgusted expression on her face marred the picture.

"You really need to find another class of friends," she said, opening the fridge door.

"One beer and he's outta here," I promised, knowing it was a lie. This was Jack after all; one drink was not part of our track record. "Go back to bed, babe. We'll keep it down."

Jack, with a cigarette between his teeth, was in the act of pouring a stiff one into the glass he'd brought when I came out to the darkened patio. We sat in silence for a bit. For all I knew, he was enjoying the dark and stillness with the slight streetlight highlighting the palm leaves. No breeze, plenty of warmth.

He chugged his drink, poured another full glass from his omnipresent Jack Daniels bottle and sparked another Camel.

"What's up, Jack," I asked.

"Nuthin,' goddamnit. Just looking for a friendly face."

He drained his drink and was pouring another when I crept

back into the house and quietly retrieved two beer. Keeping pace is a little rule I have, a rule I could see that was about to be sorely tested.

I tried, gawd how I tried to keep up, but he was on a jag, as we shot the shit about...not much, really. But something wasn't right.

He wasn't his usual jovial self; he was drinking almost, I don't know, desperately.

In the midst of our inconsequential chatting and consequential drinking, Jack asked me out of the blue if I had learned anything new.

No way was I going to tell him—or anyone else—about the involvement of the feds in kicking the investigation up many, many notches.

"I've got jack-shit, Jack. I'm out. Let somebody else sort it out. Or not."

"You sure?" he wanted to know.

It dawned on me. Even though Jack was pounding 'em at his usual prodigious rate, his hand was rock-steady when he poured. There were no slurred words and he seemed completely clear- eyed and -headed as he stared at me.

"Mind if I have a shot of Jack, Jack?" I asked. "I may be over-beered."

"Sorry, bud. Just enough for me tonight." That did it. Jack was nothing if not generous.

"Jack, you have to tell me: have you been ratting me out from the start or did that come later?"

"What the hell are you talking about?"

"Oh, come on; you're not playing with kids here. I'm betting you're drinking cold tea right now."

I pointed at his glass. He looked at it, I swear, as though he was surprised to find that he wasn't drinking booze. Then he looked at me.

There is that moment—there is always that moment—when the bullshit ends and there a clarity, an absolute knowledge that the lying is known. It's in the eyes. As it has been since the day Thog told Gort that the lopsided stone wheel he sold him was the latest transportation improvement.

"You ever been caught and can't get out of it?" Jack asked quietly.

"Yeah, years ago," I said, remembering back to when I was notionally employable and had an actual job as a PR and Investor Relations guy for a big computer services company. But that, I reminded myself, was a case of self-blackmail. I never quit or tried to change my insane hours because I was also making an insane amount of money for an English lit grad. I made the trade and, for better or worse, lived with it. Until I couldn't.

"So, they bought you," I concluded.

"They don't think you're telling the truth about backing off."

"But I am."

"I don't think so either."

That's when the gun came out. An ugly little black thing that he pulled from his cargo pants.

"After years of heartache and goddamned sweat, I've got nothing. Not a goddamned thing," he said, as if it was a perfectly legitimate explanation for the weapon's sudden appearance.

It's almost funny—weird, for sure—but there was a sort of calmness that swept over me after I'd judged there was no superstar action move I could make on him. I wouldn't get halfway across the table before I had a new hole or two in me.

Over the last several years, I've had guns pointed at me way more often than I'd ever imagined possible. It's always the same. I get in a zone of some kind where I know that the words I use would —or wouldn't—save my Canadian bacon. So far, three for three at the plate by going on offence rather than just blubbering for mercy.

"You don't have anything?" I said, eyeing the deadly little accessory he had just produced. "Gimme a fucking break! You had a good friend."

"I had nothing to do with that! They came to me later. In fact, just after you visited my goddamned apartment. That same night, they were hiding in the bedroom when you came back from seeing Borje."

"But you knew what they had done!"

"And that night they reminded me of it. So, I had a pretty good goddamned idea of what they were capable of."

"So, you faked getting loaded, just like you're doing now. That little planned fishing trip of ours the next day. Any chance you were told to push me overboard about twenty miles out?"

"Not told. It was implied," he admitted. "How do you imply homicide?"

"What they said was: 'We don't think Lydon's letting this go. Find out what he's up to, what he knows and what he's guessing at.'"

"Am I missing something? Nowhere did I just hear "'Kill the bastard!'"

"One guy made it sound like he was thinking out loud. He said: 'You know the easiest thing would be if Lydon just disappears. Why don't you take him out fishing? You'd be well out to sea, wouldn't you?' What's that sound like to you?"

"Let me get this straight: I got to not drown that day only because the seas were too rough!"

"The water wasn't that rough."

That stopped me, told me something about the man with the gun across from me.

"Thanks, I guess, for not murdering me at sea that day. But still, you went along."

"When I was in Colombia in the late '90s digging for emeralds, I think—"

"Spare me one of your fucking shaggy dog stories, will you?"

"There was an expression there," he said, ploughing on. "I guess Escobar used to say it all the time when he was leaning on someone. He'd ask: Plato o plomo?"

"Silver or lead."

"So, yeah, I goddamned well went along. And they said they would take care of Bob's widow. My other choice was dying, for Christ's sake!"

"That fishing trip was months ago. Why are you here now? They know I'm out of it."

"There's a guy in Washington who picked up word that you were just bullshitting them. Like you're doing to me right now...Lawrence."

"Now what?" I asked. "Another fishing trip or are you just going to shoot me here, and claim—what? —self-defence, stand your ground or some other such bullshit in my own backyard? And then, what's the next step? Go inside and murder Alexandra in her sleep?"

"I don't know...I don't," he said. Pretty clearly, here was a take-charge kinda guy now reduced to desperation, a guy who hadn't begun to think the whole thing out.

We looked at each other. Those eyes I just mentioned were saying something else. He was helpless, and he wasn't used to that. That made him unpredictable. Careful now, Jake.

"Look, Jack—and trust me when I tell you that I've never said this to anyone aiming a gun at me—you're a pretty good guy. There has to be another way out of this."

Jack put the gun down on the glass tabletop, its barrel mercifully pointing away from me. Jack looked almost relieved as I must have; it's what he wanted to do in the first place. C'mon, Jake. Time to put the think-think-thinking gear into overdrive.

"You haven't committed any crimes that I can see," I said.

"Threatening to kill you might qualify."

"This? Never happened. You were just showing me your new toy."

"But I knew about Bob, about all the goddamned trickery at the mines," he pointed out.

"You found out well after the fact; then your silence about it was coerced. And the mines, you didn't know for sure. You had your suspicions, but how could you really know? They had benched you. Remember? You knew fuck-all about what was going on overseas."

Jack was doing some of his own think-think-thinking when I asked him if he was sick of drinking tea yet. He smiled and I slid a Yuengling over to him.

"We're going to get these fuckers," I said. "All of them." We clinked bottle necks.

I didn't have much choice but to tell Jack about the FBI operation.

"What happens to me after?"

"I can't imagine anything less than full immunity if you play ball. And after that, I gotta believe things'll turn out alright for you."

"How do you figure?"

"You still own 60% of the mines, don't you?

"We do—Borje, Mick, me and, I guess, Bob's estate," Jack answered, brightening up a bit.

"HDW is a criminal enterprise so, sad to say, you likely won't get to keep your share. They can't hang onto their ill-gotten gains including the increased value of Southern with all its claims and inventory."

I suggested the hard truth that his baby would probably be sold off to pay the fines and lawsuits that were sure to arise.

"But look at the bright side," I said. "If this goes according to plan, HDW is fucked, Goal2Go is fucked. White Iron might be fucked, although they'll claim rogue employees went moonlighting as mercenaries for Keitel, their former boss, on his little assassination fever dream. Keitel might decide to flip on his former boss, so he doesn't go down alone. The guys running Pretoria and Olrud and Darien are in for some hurt for faking up their paper- work. I can't imagine Mick skates; the bullshit documents began at the mines. He must've known about it."

"So, what you're saying is, after all that is: I'm shit out of luck again."

"It'll take a while, but, when the dust settles, there should be millions left over. In the meantime, you might want to look into that Walmart job."

"So, what do we do?"

"First off, who came to you?"

"That night? A couple of army-looking guys, but they weren't. I was supposed to report anything to a Mr. White; they gave me a phone number. I called after our little boat cruise, told him that you didn't know anything about anything."

"404 Area code?"

Jack nodded.

"That's Keitel in Atlanta. You call him again. Tell him that I'm still just thrashing around here, that I thought something was going on at the mines, but I didn't know what, so I quit looking. Tell him that I also started out fixated on the St. Petersburg police but got nowhere with that too."

"OK, then what?"

"Fuck all. Except you have to talk to the FBI, tell them everything. I'll set it up."

"And then?"

"Then nothing. We wait and hope like hell that Keitel buys your reporting. And you have to try your fucking hardest to act normal while I do the same."

"Somehow, I think my normal and yours is a bit different."

A COUPLE OF DAYS LATER, I got a surprise call from Jeanine Purdy. Quentin had been released from hospital and was back at home, bedridden and still under a lot of heavy medication. Despite that, he, in her words: "was being a royal pain in the ass, like he always is."

"Sounds like he's getting better," I said.

"Thank the Lord, he is. But that's not the real reason I called— he told me to."

"What's up?"

"A beautiful flower arrangement was delivered to the house this morning. There was a card with it. I read it to him. It might've been the drugs, but he got tears in his eyes. All he said was 'Tell Jake.'"

"Mind reading it to me?"

"Quentin," she began. "I am so sorry it came to this. I never meant for this to happen. Goodbye. Leo."

"Who's Leo?"

"That's the name they call Lionel Henderson at work."

I called Vanessa to let her know that I had just had the St. Petersburg Chief of Homicide Detectives' suicide note read to me over the phone.

CHAPTER TWENTY-EIGHT

T he punctuation to the cryptic florist's card came the next day in the form of a front-page news story about the discovery of Lionel Henderson's body just west of the Sunshine Skyway, the giant bridge crossing over Tampa Bay from St. Petersburg to Bradenton. His corpse was found washed up on one of the pilings supporting the Skyway after boaters reported an abandoned vessel drifting in the Gulf of Mexico a half-mile from the bridge.

Foul play was not suspected. An autopsy was pending.

Of course, some media decided it was murder, as they linked Henderson's death to Quentin's shooting and an unsolved gun death of a beat cop three years earlier to speculate there just had be a pattern. One headline blared: *Who's Killing St. Pete's Cops?*

Vanessa Turner had an entirely different take, based on something known as facts. She told me that when the FBI searched Henderson's apartment, they found a journal he'd kept for years. She described it as a series of unofficial notes he'd made on homicide cases he worked including the Crescent Park shooting of Robert Hale.

Apparently, within hours of the murder, he'd decided—along with everyone else involved—that there was no way in hell a stray bullet had killed Hale. That afternoon—at 2:13, as he noted—he took a call from Washington from a Special Agent Glenn Putnam of the FBI's Criminal Investigative Division. Henderson was to meet him the following morning at a private hanger at the St. Peter-Clearwater airport on a matter of utmost importance.

He was instructed to say nothing about the meeting to anyone. Repeat: anyone.

"Does Putnam even exist?" I asked.

"Yes, he does. Bear with me."

At the meeting, Putnam introduced himself as working for their Counterterrorism unit within CID. He had badges and business cards and general paperwork proving his identity. He had Henderson sign a secrecy oath which promised severe penalties for disclosing anything he was about to hear to colleagues, the press, his own goddamn family.

Then Putnam laid out the bare bones of what Hale had allegedly been doing for thirty years as an illegal weapons dealer, arming various rebel and terrorist organizations in places unfriendly to American interests. Putnam had a passport transcript of all the foreign places Hale had visited under the perfect guise of an international mining executive. And he had a fake record of hefty financial transactions Hale had made on an offshore account in the Caymans. But Hale, the story went, had recently kicked up his criminal activity a big notch when he played a major role in a plot by foreign terrorists to stage a 9/11-type event in Miami. A decision was reached that Hale had to be eliminated. Not arrested but eliminated to stop his crucial connection without jeopardizing the efforts to round up the major players posing an imminent and colossal danger.

"And a seasoned cop bought the whole bullshit fairy tale?" I asked.

"Pretty much," Turner said. "In the margin beside the plot description, he wrote: "Sounds far-fetched but what do I know?" He had misgivings that he wrote down in his notes, chiefly about how Hale was able to supposedly get away with decades of deception and why there hadn't been a less lethal way to handle him. Obviously, Putnam had anticipated the questions and invoked both the Patriot Act and security clearances several times while vaguely talking about the joint operation of the FBI, CIA, Homeland Security and USOCOMM at MacDill reaching their decision to take Hale out using a private contractor. Henderson recorded a quote of Putnam's: "You aren't supposed to hear about the bad actors we stop or how we stop them; you only hear about the ones we miss." As well, he noted the phrase Putnam had used: Terminate ex-judiciously.

"And all Henderson had to do," I said, "was wait a couple of weeks, shut down the investigation, and take most of the heat while passing some onto Putnam."

"That was the idea. But in another note, Henderson wrote about us asking around about him. He admitted to tipping off Putnam to his fear that everything might be unravelling. I guess Putnam went apeshit. Said he'd have to handle it."

"So, Putnam figures that maybe it might fall apart. And if it was, Alexandra and I must have been the catalyst. We're the key witnesses. He panics, calls Keitel who advises him to play it safe and not to get his foursome of soldiers involved because, for sure, they would bring heat. Instead, he enlists Jack because he could get close to me without suspicion."

"I'm pretty sure that's how it played."

"However improbable, that covers off Hale's death," Vanessa said.

"Did Henderson talk about Quentin Purdy?"

"He did. That's what broke him."

Vanessa went on to describe how it unfolded, with the caveat that her narrative was only based exclusively on what Henderson had written. When Henderson ended the Hale case, Purdy was incensed. He told the forensics head that if he didn't call in the FBI in Tampa, Purdy would. Instead, Purdy's boss told Henderson who duly reported it to Putnam. Putnam went bullshit, ranted about endangering the whole operation, along with thousands of lives, and demanded that Henderson do something, otherwise Putnam had a way to deal with Quentin. Henderson begged for Quentin's life and proposed he'd retire Purdy and threaten the fuck out of him.

"The sad thing," Vanessa said, "Among many sad things, is that Henderson's plan was working. It would appear that Putnam became convinced that Purdy wouldn't stay shut up, and the rest… well, you know what happened."

Vanessa then summarized Henderson's last entry in his notes where he apologized for everything to everybody—his cover up of Hale's murder, his likely indirect role in Matt Kilmer's hit and run, his informing on Purdy's dissension that led to his near-death and his giant stupidity in being sucked into the scheme. "'I am a fucking idiot who caused a lot of people a lot of pain because I thought I was helping'—were his last words in his notes."

There was a long pause on Henderson's final sentence when Vanessa finished.

"Any chance Henderson made the whole story up and wrote it down after the fact to cover his tracks?" I finally asked.

"No. We found his fingerprints inside the same hangar where we found yours. CCTV footage has him at the airport at the time he indicated."

"Poor bastard. He wasn't guilty of anything," I said. "Except trying to do the right thing."

I imagined the torment he'd suffered, knowing that.

And surprise, surprise, Keitel had lied to me about not being involved in the botched attempt on Quentin Purdy.

EVERY YEAR, I'm a serious contender for Most Impatient Man on the Planet sweepstakes. I'm pretty sure I've had at least three Top Ten finishes. I wanted to get gone. Back to the northern hovel and as far away as I could from the convoluted mess that had fucked up most of our winter. We had virtually stopped talking to anybody, found it harder and harder to pretend to be normal. And you can only get so much excitement in feeding lettuce to a turtle. Even Carl, my ever-wise northern neighbour, mentioned my skittishness when he called to see why our return to the lake had been delayed.

"It's still fucking cold up there, right?" I said. "We're having a great time down here."

"Then how come, I wonder, do you sound like you're in a dentist's office waiting on a root canal?"

I discarded the notion of making a drive-all-night run for the border. It wasn't just the thought of becoming wanted in two countries as a fugitive material witness. The trip would've crippled me.

Think harder, Jake.

As it sometimes does, a plan emerged. I discussed it with Alex who thought it might work. Then I called Agent Turner.

"So, Vanessa," I said. "How's tricks?"

She was pleased with her interview with Jack Duffy; he couldn't corroborate a bunch of our allegations, but he filled in some blanks about how HDW operated and how things ran at the mines. And about Keitel conscripting him to get at me. He was promised immunity—as he should've been.

"Anything else, Jake? I'm kinda busy, thanks to you."

"Sorry for your troubles, but I'd like a favour."

I took her impatient sigh as permission to proceed with my pitch.

"We want to blow this pop stand. You really just need us around for the kidnapping, right?"

"I suppose. But it's not 'just'. We found the hard evidence that'll bring a minimum 20-year stretch in a federal prison for Keitel. It may be the easiest and strongest case we have right now. We prove the rest of it, and he gets consecutive sentences. He's gone for a couple of centuries."

"It'd be kinda cool if he wound up in a prison that Goal2Go provides security for. But seriously, you've got plenty of time to actually charge him with kidnapping. Years, I bet."

"What are you suggesting?"

"Just delay it a bit. We go home, you bust him, identify us only as an unnamed foreign national and an American citizen. Then we swear we'll be back here for any deposition and the trial."

"I'll try, but it's really out of my hands. It's a lot easier if you stick around and let it play out. It's going to go down soon. I promise." Her definition of soon and mine turned out to be quite different. Weeks passed. Aside from the occasional question from Agent Turner, we perfected our ability to bide time.

But as we blew through the two-month mark since we'd contacted the FBI, I sensed that the pace was quickening. Although she wouldn't or couldn't confirm the timing, Vanessa's conversations were more hurried, her voice more insistent.

Until one morning, I got a call from her.

All she said was: "Watch the news, starting at two o'clock."

CHAPTER TWENTY-NINE

S imultaneous police raids are an awesome thing. Especially when they play out in real time on television.

Alex and I were parked in front of the TV at the appointed hour.

I had to give the FBI props for their media awareness. It was no mistake that the proverbial gaggle of reporters just happened to be at the sites of these raids as they were unfolding. Live footage and on-the-spot reporting were only possible if they had been tipped off. People don't tend to notice these massive coincidences of, say, a camera crew one evening just happening to be at the home of Olrud's CEO a few minutes after the Oslo police teams moved in or at the Panamanian polo field when Patel was hustled out. Just a couple of calls in every targeted location: Show up at this address at such and such a time.

The biggest public stink was in the States. Nationally, there was a helluva brouhaha over the arrests of Harrison Wagner, George Keitel, and White Iron's Trevor Symes. A very few people have any practice at perp walks, but I'll give two of them credit. Wagner and Keitel were properly silent, walking statues, their fixed expressions grim, their eyes downcast as they were led through the media gauntlet. Symes, on the other hand, did not go quietly into that good afternoon. His eyes blazing, he pumped his fist in the air and yelled such things as "Witch hunt!" and "Hoax!" Not a good look for him.

Several large news organizations pieced it all together in a couple of hours because that's what they do. Centrally, CNN, the *New York Times* and Reuters had bolted together reports from their bureaus and stringers in Oslo, Pretoria, Panama City, Hanoi, and Rio de Janeiro to determine that what their audiences were seeing or reading about was a co-ordinated global law enforcement operation.

More kudos to the FBI PR department for having sent every involved law enforcement group the same talking points (that they all used): If I were writing them, here's the statement: "The police action today was carried out to target a complex, illegal international plan devised and executed by a number of companies and persons within different governments. We expect the charges against them to include murder, attempted murder, conspiracy to commit murder, kidnapping, bribery, extortion, falsifying business records, tax evasion, and financial fraud, among others."

But I wouldn't have promised a press conference at 9 PM (EST time), because that's where the PR folks fumbled at the five-yard line, as it were. The media gathering we watched did not furnish much more detail beyond what we'd already heard, but rather featured the standard line-up of different agencies congratulating the fuck out of each other on their "outstanding co-operation."

The sole highlight for me was the FBI Deputy Director noting that their Tampa field office did an excellent job leading the operation. She also gave thanks to two unnamed former public servants whose "courage and perseverance had triggered the entire investigation."

But all the shouted questions to them either went unanswered or were met by vagaries.

So, when the talking police heads clammed up, the talking news heads took over, dropping their speculation engine into overdrive.

In a matter of hours, certainly over the next couple of days, more concrete stories started coming out. What I love about the media is their innate ability to whip itself into a frenzy—sort of like giving a dozing police bloodhound the scent of a kidnap victim's clothing. When it was established that the mining industry lay at the core, off they charged, triangulating with the recent unsolved murders in St. Petersburg to the name Bob Hale which begat Southern Cross which begat the world market for neodymium which begat the location of the mines which begat a connection to Mick Rogers, the Australian pleading with his government to get out of a Vietnamese jail and on and on.

Amid all this begatting, every named company and embroiled country rushed to contain the damage, swiftly proclaiming that they and the international commodity trading system were chock full of integrity.

At that point, all I could think about was that Alex and I were unscathed and anonymous. I wanted us to heave a massive collective sigh of relief. But I couldn't. I'm the kind of person who doesn't just wait for the big-boned lady to sing. I wait until the concert's over, she does her mic drop, goes to the dressing room, changes into street clothes and is signing autographs in the lobby of the theatre before I can declare an episode over.

CHAPTER THIRTY

One afternoon as I returned from a shopping expedition, I discovered a bicycle I didn't recognize leaning against the wall.

It was a real sleek sporty jobbie, an Orbea Orca, a brand I didn't know—although, after my childhood Schwinn, I knew shit about any bikes. It had a very high seat and drop-down handlebars and I lifted it easily with a forefinger. Unless Alex was angling for a spot on the Tour de France, we had a visitor.

I opened the kitchen door to see that it was Borje Hallstrom who'd come calling.

Passing strange was the fact that he and Alexandra were sitting side by side on the couch. That's when I saw the panicked look on Alex's face, then her hands bound at the wrist and resting on her lap, then the knife he held in his lap poised over her rib cage. Elapsed time: 1.5 seconds.

Gone was his habit of nervous eye wandering, replaced by an icy blue Nordic glare.

"What the fuck?" was my idea of a conversation-starter.

"I must settle this business with you," he said.

"Too late, bud. You gotta know, it's all over."

"Yes. That is why I am here."

"Help my little pea brain understand."

"You cost me tens of millions of dollars."

"Gosh, genius, your five million bonus ain't close to tens of...."

His stare said it all.

Oh, fuck, oh, fuck, I thought. He had to have been in on the deal with HDW.

Now, at that moment, I would've loved the leisure time to figure out how he was connected to Wagner's scheme, but there were more pressing matters at hand. I immediately slipped into my in-your-face smartass persona—although that wasn't much of a stretch—to, once again, test its success in life-or-death situations. "Look, Sven," I said. "Let me make it up to you. Wait, I'm a little short this week. Will you take a cheque?"

"You are not as amusing as you think you are."

"I see, Mats, this judgment based on that long line of famous Swedish stand-up comedians."

"Again, you are not funny."

"Tell you what, seriously this time, Nils, how about you logically direct your illogical thirst for revenge at me? She has nothing to do with any of this. She's just a girl."

"Yes, but she is also a witness."

"Torvald, Torvald, Torvald, you fake Viking pansy, come through me first. Deal with her later."

I don't know—or care—what got to him: My misnaming or insulting his heritage or questioning his manhood or if he really was just a sexist. Whatever it was, he was pissed. He roughly pushed Alexandra away, got up and circled the coffee table to face me in the space between the TV on one wall and the couch on the other.

A word about our fight arena: small. You could remove every stick of furniture, every cupboard and appliance, knock down all the interior walls in the Hovel, and you'd still have an area smaller than a standard professional boxing ring.

I didn't think Borje had made it common practice to engage in hand-to-hand combat, but, on the other hand, he was in a helluva lot better shape, and he had at least a five-inch reach advantage over me. Oh, and he had a big, nasty knife that extended his reach by another foot.

He tried a few tentative pokes at me. I danced out of way. He took a wide backhanded slash that missed but followed it up with a lunge that found my side. Fuck, that was an owie.

Momentarily, he paused, maybe because he'd surprised himself by inflicting the knife wound. From my slightly bent position, I launched a helluva shot to his mid-section below his breastbone that hurt him. He dropped the knife as he clutched his bruised guts.

Everybody has a rough idea of a boxing stance. But not everybody has the capacity to leave that pose and punch another human being as hard as they can in the face. Despite years of regularly getting the shit beat out of me, my amateur boxing had granted me that ability. I used it after Borje swung wildly, awkwardly. I moved in under his missed blows and caught him with a solid uppercut to the chin. To my utter dismay, it only staggered him, didn't take him down. He regrouped and we faced each other.

Without a trained referee, most fistfights degenerate into grappling and thrashing around. And with no soundtrack, all you hear is a lot of grunting. So, we did some of that as we struggled with each other to reach the knife that had skidded under the TV stand. Unless you've been involved in one of these wrasslin' free-for-alls, you can't possibly imagine how exhausting it is. In under a minute, with muscles straining and adrenaline rushing, I was bagged. That's when the momentum of the scrap changed. I don't know about you, but I can't stand movie fights with the mandatory damsel doing fuck-all except looking distressed and acting useless. Not Alexandra. Just as Borje retrieved the knife and was straightening up, she threw herself off the couch and onto his back, drawing her bound hands over his head and around his neck.

Together, they madly staggered and whirled around, crashing into the TV, bringing down the pole lamp, smashing assorted bric-a-brac. He managed to reach across his chest and over his shoulder to draw the knife deeply into Alex's triceps. She screamed in pain as he twisted around and reached under her armpits. He straightened up and heaved her over the coffee table, back onto the couch.

The pain in my side disappeared and I went insane. I bull-rushed into him, the force ramming him into the wall by the front door. Pinning his knife wielding right arm against the door with my left, I summoned up all my strength and unleashed a furious right into his startled face.

Not-so-fun fact: When your head is tight against a hard surface —say, the cinderblock wall of an old Florida hovel—it's got nowhere to recoil and help absorb a blow.

By the loud crack, I knew I had done damage. Broke his nose for sure, but just as likely broke his jaw too. Blood was gushing from his mouth and flattened nostrils, but he didn't make a sound. He was out cold. I let him slide down the wall into a crumpled sitting position and more or less collapsed on top of his inert body.

I turned to see Alex struggling towards me, but she slipped in the blood on the floor. Could've been mine, could've been hers. Or maybe both. There was a lot of it. We sat side by side. She clutched her arm, I held onto my side, our foreheads touching.

"Just a girl, huh?" she said.

"He didn't let me finish the sentence. 'Just a girl…who's going to kick your Swedish ass and save the fucking idiot she idolizes.'"

Then, improbably perhaps, we laughed. Deep laughs, true laughs.

Now, it finally felt like all the shit was over.

CHAPTER THIRTY-ONE

The paramedics replaced my half-assed belt tourniquet around Alex's arm with a pro version and put a thick gauze dressing on my puncture, wrapping a girdle of about eighty-five yards of tape around my body to hold the dressing in place. Alex decided it was quite slimming. The witch.

We travelled together to the nearest hospital in the same ambulance while Borje got his own chauffeur-driven vehicle, what with him lying inert on a gurney with all sorts of stuff hooked up to him. They did cut away the zip ties he had thoughtfully brought with him that I'd used to truss up his motionless self after I called 9-1-1.

The EMT riding with Alex and me tried to get us to be quiet. He knew the shock was wearing off and the pain was setting in. But I wanted to chat.

"I'm a complete fucking moron," I observed.

"Like I need more proof," Alex said.

"It was right there in front of us."

"What was?"

"When Alice Hale told you that her husband was surprised that' Scandinavians could be so deceptive,' Bob didn't mean one of Borje or Olrud Shipping; he meant both of them."

Despite the red liquid evidence, neither injury turned out to be that serious. My stabbing injury was, more or less, just an aeration of my fat. Alex's cut on the arm took a bunch of stitches to sew up but would heal completely. We both rejected the idea of hanging around to be observed. We promised to watch each other like a pair of wounded hawks.

I did hear that Borje's condition was a helluva lot worse than ours with his split lip, loosened teeth, and broken nose being the least of his concerns. He'd sustained both a severe concussion and a ruptured spleen that required emergency surgery to staunch the internal bleeding. He wouldn't be involved in a police interrogation any time soon as his broken jaw was wired shut.

Our police interview would've taken longer if I hadn't stretched the truth a bit by claiming we were under an FBI gag order and all questions were to be directed to Special Agent Vanessa Turner in the Tampa Field Office.

A cop took us home where we found Stan and Laura. Once again, the police and EMT presence at the Hovel had brought them over. But they weren't just hanging around on the patio waiting for our return to see how we were. They were inside, just finishing the blood-mopping and as much straightening up of our trashed living room as they could do, to the point where the room appeared to be only semi-trashed.

They were alarmed to see Alex's arm heavily bandaged arm in a sling and a big bandage spot-welded to my side.

"You should see the other guy," I said.

"Drinks all round!" Alex announced. "Sorry, hon, I can't help." And she held up her arm.

Personally, I couldn't think of a better time for margaritas. I fired up the blender, watching through the kitchen window as our friends and my lady yukked it up. I joined them with the drinks, and we laughed until…well, my side ached.

CHAPTER THIRTY-TWO

I was surprised—and shouldn't have been—to get this e-mail from my friend Steve Golding a day after the mass arrests:

So, old buddy, old pal, I was watching the news of that dragnet unfolding around the world. I couldn't help but notice that it was centred in Tampa. You're somewhere around there, aren't you? History teaches us that you have a knack for creating shitstorms wherever you go. My question to you: Any chance you might be involved somehow? Warning: I was speaking to Halley about something else and she mentioned that there was a murder case you were sticking your huge nose into.

I wrote back:

That is a fucking lie! My nose isn't that big.

I had already made my mind up that Steve—or anybody else— would never hear the full details about this case from me. Even though we have a six-months-a-year sort of friendship, Steve meant a lot to me. I had lied to him about another of my fiascos; I wouldn't do it again. So, I sent another note:

> *To answer your original question: yes. To answer your inevitable follow-up*
> *question: No, I'm not going to talk about it. To answer your obvious follow-up*
> *to the follow-up: Because it's none of your fucking business.*

That wouldn't end his snooping, but it would give me the chance to get home and tell him to his face to fuck off and that I was tired of supporting his writing career.

One evening in the second week of May, there was a knock at the door. There stood Vanessa and Devin Turner, each clutching a bottle of wine.

"Wanna see a sunset?" she asked.

I walked to the end of the driveway and stared down 16th at the western sky above the ocean.

"Fuck that," I said. "No clouds; it'll be boring as hell."

We set up on the back patio. The mood was a whole lot different than the previous time we'd been in the same position. Oh, let's call it celebratory. Vanessa was pounding the wine while Devin settled for two beer and a bunch of Pepsis. She had earned the kick-back time. Selfish prick that I am, I hadn't really considered how much work she must've put into this investigation, or for that matter, the pressure she would've been under, with her career in the balance, if our allegations had proved to be bullshit.

"You done good, kid," I said.

"We done good," she replied.

"I would've loved to have seen the look on Wagner's and Keitel's faces the second when you busted in."

"Don't forget Symes. Hey, did you know we always wear body cams to prove that our searches and arrests were by the book?"

"Think we could get a peek?"

"I suppose I could do a little editing then arrange a showing."

"I'll make the popcorn," Alex offered.

I asked Agent Turner why I hadn't heard of any arrests in Washington. That killed the joviality right quick as she turned serious.

"They did grab up Putnam with his one-way ticket to Mexico City. The Agency's positive that he had acted alone, under White

Iron's direction. He couldn't really explain why he'd spiked the investigation into Hale's murder. Nor could he defend all the e-mails and phone calls to White Iron and to Keitel's private accounts over some years or his flight to St. Petersburg the day after the hit."

"So, he was the inside man and they got him dead to rights."

"What happened?"

"The Agency decided it would shake public confidence if they publicly arrested him. They did arrest him and are holding him while they decide what to do. On one hand, he can be charged with a whack of crimes up to and including treason but, on the other, I've heard talk of just firing him, taking away his pension and promising that if he said one damn word, he'd be prosecuted forever and could face a death sentence. Pissed me off, because I want to see his ass nailed in public, but I'm expecting to be overruled."

"Such a shame. If you folks in Tampa had been into it at the jump, the whole case would've turned out differently," I said, indulging in a rare and pointless would've/could've/should've speculation.

"Let's talk about Borje Hallstrom, shall we?" Vanessa suggested.

"Don't tell me, don't tell me! Lemme guess," I insisted.

"Guess away."

"He was first in on Wagner's scheme. Before they even invested in Southern."

"He was."

"Wagner did his research and realized that Borje was the golden goose, an extraordinary talent. In order to keep him, he promised a whole lot more than five million."

"He did. In fact, he'd already paid him more than five mill. He also guaranteed a percentage of the returns from the two working mines and anything in the future."

"But," I said. "When Robert Hale started nosing around about mine yields, Borje got jumpy."

"He did. Hallstrom let Wagner know."

"And the Bob Hale problem was removed. You guys figured all this out on your own?"

"Not exactly. He sang like a little Swedish birdy when I promised I'd do what I could to protect him."

"That tip of his led to Bob Hale's murder! Tell me that mother-fucker isn't getting immunity!"

"He isn't. My bad. Turns out I couldn't do much," she said with a smile.

"For all his smarts, he was a pretty dumb shit. All he had to do was wait for the dust to settle and pick up a big chunk from the sale of Southern."

"I actually called him a dumb shit for that exact reason. He said, and I'm quoting here: 'No, either the FBI or Jake Lydon would find me.'"

"He's not wrong. My money's on me, by the way. No offense."

"None taken."

"So, he was going to kill me—us—then fuck off to Paraguay or someplace else with no extradition."

"You are hot tonight, mister. He already had tickets for Asuncion for the day after he came to see you."

Mercifully, that was it for discussion about the case that had consumed all of us for months. Hugs all 'round when the couples broke off.

"Can we go home now?" I asked, as we stood by their car.

"Yeah, but we'll be in touch."

We finished packing and loading that night then spent the next day saying our goodbyes. At the other end of my migration circuit, there was always a tinge of sadness when I leave the lake hovel and Carl, my neighbour and friend. Now, quitting Indian Rocks, I had the same feeling. A bunch of shitty things had happened over the last six months but, in something of a balancing act, we had befriended some mighty fine people. I was going to miss them. Me, the anti-social recluse.

We first drove to St. Petersburg to see Quentin who'd been home from the hospital for a month. He was up and around but moving slowly, every once in a while, wincing in pain. He saw me wince when he did.

"Isn't any worse than how I felt every Saturday night in college after a game," he said. "Listen: If you ever need a freelance ballistics guy, I'm your man. Reasonable rates."

"What do you charge for absorbing them before you analyze them?"

Jeanine told me that they were planning to make the trip back to Columbus for the 100th Anniversary of Ohio State's stadium in August. I was happy for them.

As we drove away, I felt lucky to have made another connection to a delightful and solid (in every way) human being. Two of them.

We drove to Southern Cross's office on the way home. No pleasant Marjorie, no nuthin.' The door was locked. I peered through the glass sidelight to see the place abandoned. Filing cabinets gone, the lobby sign ripped down, papers scattered everywhere. I had to smile at the handwritten sign on the door. It read: Gone Fishin.'

Back in IRB, I strolled over to the bench on Gulf Boulevard where I knew I would find its namesake.

"Bob, I expect to see you right here on this spot this coming winter," I told him.

"Ah, expectations," he replied. "They have never been friends of mine. We shall see."

I left one final half-smoked cigarette on the bench beside him. It was kinda touching when Bob offered me his hand when I stood to go. He had a surprisingly firm handshake for such an apparently frail man.

We then said our farewell to Don and Ellen, as part of a return engagement with Stan and Laura via a late afternoon margfest. But we didn't go all crazy because we had a 6:00 am rendezvous with the 275 heading across the causeway to Tampa and points way beyond.

After all the goodbyes were said, I did my usual painstaking route planning, suggesting that we could change it up to miss Washington altogether by crossing over to Delaware at Norfolk, then really missing New York to head to Connecticut and up the New England coast with maybe a lazy side trip to Martha's Vineyard.

"I'm sure that's not the fastest way to get to the lake," she said.

"What?! You want to open up the northern hovel with me?"

She nodded, with a smile only slightly smaller than mine.

"Yippee! But I should warn you; it's pioneering at its finest."

"Yeah, well, how about I be the new school marm," she ominously said.

"Fine, but forget any notion of turning it into a luxury lakeside retreat or some other hoity-toity bullshit. It's the fucking hovel."

I had re-hired Michael to watch over the house and yard, we closed and locked up the joint in the early morning darkness, but not before one last hugely satisfying act.

In the driveway, I took a hammer to my burner cell phone, that rectangle of monstrous tech-evil. Shards of it sprayed all over the concrete. Alex was horrified; I was elated, as I sang (badly) Richie Haven's *Freedom*.

I charted the new route, even though she'd already programmed it into the Garmin. Alex got to pick (and pay for) the hotels we stayed at. The Google told us we'd add a half hour by skirting Richmond, thereby avoiding Washington altogether. That's the route we chose. We cut west, running up the Blue Ridge Mountains to the 81 and then north through the Shenandoah Valley.

Our timing was perfect; the valley was in the mood to show off. Apple and cherry trees were laden with pink or white blooms, dotting the rolling green lawns. Trees were fully leafed in that fresh, vibrant green that deepens and dulls over the summer. Horse farms sprawled all over the gentle hills, their lush meadows marked off by white wooden fences. Oh, and there were lots of irritating billboards. But relatively few New Jersey drivers.

We took our time, four days in all, visiting a cavern (I'm still unclear on this whole stalagmites and stalactites thing) and going to the Gettysburg Civil War battle site which was solemn as hell as we stood beside a cannon staring at the verdant valley and imagined the slaughter of tens of thousands of young men.

But in general, for the first time in a long while, we laughed and had fun, although things got a little rocky when Alexandra nixed my desired pilgrimage to the Yuengling Brewery in Pottsville, PA. With her driving and me pretending to be asleep, we breezed through Canadian customs, although I did hear the border guard ask her if I was dead.

"I'm not sure. Maybe," Alex had replied. "But at least he's quiet."

EPILOGUE

There's an incredible amount of wreckage around the unravelling of such a widespread scheme. I know up close and personal that that's the case. After the cameras pack up and the keyboards stop clicking away, the clean-up and tidying goes on. It would be months later when most but not all of the shit was erased.

During that time, a bunch of lawyers would get wealthier. On the day Wagner, Keitel and Symes were arrested, their lawyers were all interviewed and every one of them sang from the same hymn book. To summarize: "We look forward to vigorously defending my client [insert name here] over this egregious [pick one: "miscarriage of justice," "politicization of the justice system" or "baseless accusations"].

Turned out, they didn't have a lot to look forward to. Despite their best legal maneuvers, all three of their clients were tried and convicted of a laundry list of crimes.

Then came the promised investigations into the systemic breakdowns that allowed the criminal trio to operate. Followed by investigations into the investigations.

And, of course, the requisite slew of conspiracy theories about the original, very real conspiracy came next. If I hear the phrase "false flag operation" one more time, I'm gonna fucking snap.

They eventually tracked down and arrested three of the four quasi-soldiers who had kidnapped us, threatened Jack Duffy, killed Robert Hale and Matt Kilmer, and shot Quinten Purdy. That last gang of four member was apparently identified as the sniper by his mates who, facing domestic terrorism charges, turned into a singing trio. They also insisted that this missing guy was the driver of the SUV that had ploughed into Matt Kilmer. The cops did find his Dragunov rifle Kilmer had been right about the weaponry used— but not him. He was in the wind, presumably eluding arrest by fucking off to parts unknown just before the international shit hit the fan.

In the end, a total of just twenty-four people were arrested in various countries that first day, five more afterwards, but only nine- teen charged.

I want to believe that everybody gets caught at everything these days. Cops are smarter, forensics better, closed-circuit cameras and cell phones are everywhere, while crooks seem dumber, and teenagers are still as clueless as I was when I was one. Instantly captured on video are the attempted thefts by porch pirates, drunken driving, random assaults on the street, beer driven brawls at football games. Even politicians, bureaucrats, and cops are busted for being dicks.

But there's one area where only occasionally do you hear about its members being nabbed and jailed: the corporate world. Yet deliberate acts like hiding or delaying safety reports or stealing people's lifesavings are every bit as devastating as they are for victims of a violent mugging.

Nobody senior from either Olrud or Pretoria went to jail. Their CEOs were able to prove they had no knowledge of the bribery going on and were fully co-operating with police. The head of forensics in St. Pete also walked; he had no connection to the scheme beyond doing his buddy, Henderson, a favour by leaning hard on Quentin.

Oddly, there was quite the kerfuffle in Panama over Patel being arrested even though he had had a minor role in the whole affair. He had leaned on a pal at the Canal to ensure that the documents from Olrud's ships passing through the canal agreed with the rest of the paper trail about their cargos. Looked like the local media turned on their bad boy creation and tore him to shreds. And had a lot of fun doing it.

There would be no news—that I could ever find—about what happened to the unmasked government officials in Viet-Nam and Brazil who had ginned the weigh scale results. Maybe they were tried and convicted, maybe they were just convicted and sent to a shitty prison for a long time. Or maybe they were promoted by their governments to avoid admitting some their employees had engaged in "egregious malfeasance" which was just the neutered version of "doing bad shit."

I felt a little badly about Mick Rogers and his fate, even though he must've ratted me out to Wagner after I left Amsterdam. He wouldn't be building his dream house outside of Perth until he finished his lengthy stretch as a guest of the Vietnamese government which, with solid historical precedent, took foreign interference very seriously.

There was a fire sale of HDW's assets. Its interests in a slew of companies brought out a raft of tire kickers and bargain hunters as they picked over the empire's carcass like a school of piranhas feasting on a water buffalo. I mean, who doesn't like a sale? Formerly itty-bitty Southern Cross Mining, however, went for a premium at the auction they held. "What am I bid for Southern Cross...eighteen billion?...Eighteen. I've got eighteen....Can I hear twenty? Thank you, ma'am. I've got twenty...twenty. C'mon, folks, those leases, that inventory...Who'll make it twenty-five?" and so on until the gavel came down on $36.4 billion to "the weird-looking guy with the bow tie and bad teeth." (OK, I made that last part up).

No way could I figure out if Jack got a decent share of what was left after the fines and lawsuits, but I reckoned he would do OK. Same with Bob Hale's widow, Alice, which made Alexandra really happy. Borje and Mick would be shit out of luck, the price for furthering this scheme. No money, lots of jail time.

For White Iron, it was pretty much business as usual. They wound up with a new CEO, a temporarily chastised Board of Directors, new investors, and hopefully, a little less influence on the gears of government, as they returned to the same old business of war.

In mid-August, Vanessa Turner called and asked me if I wanted some good news.

"You'll probably hear about it tomorrow," she said. "But authorities picked up that fourth mercenary, the shooter, in—"

"—Don't tell me, don't tell me!" I said, cutting her off. "They found him in Mombassa in a barroom drinking gin."

"What are you talking about?"

"Oh, you kids! Warren Zevon would be so disappointed."

"He was in Belize," she said, pretending—as many people do when I'm around—not to hear me. "No resistance, should be no problem extraditing him."

"That is great news."

"Now, how about some bad news?"

"Maybe some other time."

"Your deposition," she continued, "with Keitel's lawyers on the kidnapping charge is scheduled for November 22nd. And the Pinellas DA has to talk to you first ahead of the grand jury. Like next week. Unfortunately, the judge assigned to the case has just ruled that you and Alexandra can't stay anonymous."

"Well, shit! Listen: are we safe?"

"I think so."

"You think?!"

"HDW is kaput. Goal2Go is gone—fell apart in the scandal— and Keitel was denied bail. You got Borje; Mick's in prison forever. There's a new crew at White Iron that's recovering and moving on. Why would anybody attempt anything?"

"I don't know. I've heard that revenge can be a motive."

"Oh, sure. I bet there's a shipping agent in Oslo plotting against you right now."

I don't much care what the situation may be, I'm always a big fan of a good piece of sarcasm. And that was.

"Jake," she added seriously, "there's nobody to play the avenger. It's over. We won. The good guys won."

ACKNOWLEDGMENTS

Out of my preternatural laziness, I was tempted to ask readers simply to refer to my last book (or the one before) for a list of the people who made this effort possible. It's the same stalwart

band that I've come to know and love. On keyboards (and mouse), Glenn Torresan for design, layout, and another really swell cover. Playing the editor's red e-pen: "Colorado" JoDee Costello. Back-up vocals: JoDee's husband, Lou, who either likes the books or is excessively polite. Cheerleading Chorus: Steve McGill, Nadine Buckley, Brother Martin, "Gringo" Dave Villeneuve Head Cheerleader: The ever-wonderful, ever-lovin,' ever ass-kicking Maggie Harvey.

Produced by: Ramblin' Ron Corbett, Ottawa Press and Publishing magnate, swell writer, (and inveterate cigarette thief).

I hereby also gratefully acknowledge everybody who, because they enjoy the Jake Lydon mysteries or because they feel socially obligated, shelled out their money for a copy. Thank you! As always and about everything, I assume no responsibility whatsoever for anything wrong in this book.

ABOUT THE AUTHOR

As he approaches his dotage, John Owens has written six Jake Lydon Mysteries, as well as two works of historical fiction, *On the Rails* and *The Sixth String*. He divides his time between Morrisburg, Ontario and places with palm trees and tiki bars. You can reach him via his website: johnowensauthor.com or on social media.

ALSO BY JOHN OWENS

HISTORICAL FICTION

On the Rails

The Sixth String

JAKE LYDON MYSTERY SERIES

Connecdead

Machete

Bushwhacked

Jackpot

Copycat